A Marked Woman

Jeremy Leland was brought up in Egypt and subsequently went to Wellington College and to St Martins and the Slade Art Schools. He returned to Ireland to the ramshackle family estate near Drogheda, Co. Louth, where he farmed for ten years. He also exhibited in Irish shows including The Living Art and The Oireachtus.

He has published five previous novels: *A River Decrees, The Jonah, The Tower, Lirri* and *Bluff,* and a collection of short stories, *The Last Sandcastle.* His stories have appeared in *Argosy, The Irish Press, She, Transatlantic Review, Mademoiselle (USA)* and *The Fiction Network, New York.*

Jeremy Leland now lives in Norfolk.

A Marked Woman

Jeremy Leland

RAMPANT HORSE

First published in Great Britain in 1994
by Rampant Horse Limited
140 Whitehall Road Norwich Norfolk NR2 3EW

Set in 11 pt Times Roman
Cover concept: Tim Bartlett/The Advertising Works
Cover illustration: Dorothy Ransome

A CIP catalogue record for this book is available from the British Library
ISBN 1-898839-51-4 hard cover
1-898839-01-8 soft cover

Printed and Bound by Bookcraft Ltd, Midsomer Norton, Avon.

Crown Court Probation Service
Family Division

M M Clement, Esq.
St Giles Clinic

Dear Mark,

Another assessment for you – a Mrs Kathleen September. I fixed up a preliminary appointment with your secretary. There are funds for about five consultations and we've three weeks till the hearing date.

It's a residence case. Her husband is contesting, claims she has a drink problem. There are three children, a boy of nine with the father and two girls, six and three, with the mother. Either she has a fantastic imagination or her husband is an outrageous psychopath. I'm inclined her way, but the law so far seems to favour the husband. He comes across very well in court. I've enclosed a photocopy of my notes to date. I should be very interested to see what you think.

Sincerely,

Greg Fulcher

SOME people hum when they are distracted, others dance. Mark shifted from foot to foot. Then he stood still, stooping a little to peer at the television.

It was nine-thirty in the evening. Kathleen was leaning back on the sofa watching a David Attenborough documentary. The children were in bed, the washing-up done, and tomorrow's school-clothes sorted out. She thought Mark must be waiting for a phonecall.

Although he moved surreptitiously, turning his back to mask what he was doing, she suddenly realised he had picked up her handbag and was furtively rummaging inside it.

'What are you doing?' she exclaimed.

There was the click of a purse. 'Put it back,' she cried, jumping up and trying to wrest it from him.

He fended her off. 'There's only twenty quid here. Where's the rest?'

'That's all there is. It's the housekeeping.'

He twisted away, keeping his back to her. 'You should have about £90.'

'You know perfectly well I don't have that sort of money.'

He tossed the bag to her, the money still in the purse. 'Keep your hair on. You're the one who's always going on about waking the children.'

She returned to the sofa, clutching her bag, watching him suspiciously.

His eyes seemed to cloud, their gaze sliding round the room. 'Shall we take the kids and go to the May Fair at the weekend? Give them an outing. They'd enjoy it. All those horses, and the camel races, and the go-karts and the fair with the roundabouts and the bumper-cars. They'd love it, wouldn't they? And I know you dote on those stalls that sell brooches made of sea shells, and the home-knit sweaters and the herb teas and the people who sell wind-generators and books on organic farming.'

'D'you really mean it?' she asked, surprised. 'Is that why you wanted the money?'

‘That’s settled then.’ He went out of the room.

Still hugging her handbag she sank down into the cushions of the sofa, drawn back into the nature film. A Bengali tiger was hiding in the reeds on the edge of a lake, mouth agape as he stalked a group of Sambar deer who were wading through the water munching water-lilies. The next moment he could contain his hunger no longer and bounded forward. As he raced through spumes of spray and the deer dashed through the lilies, she felt a sharp pain in her neck.

‘Where is it?’ a voice hissed in her ear.

An arm had crept round her to clamp her shoulders against the cushions. Tilting her eyes down in alarm, she glimpsed a kitchen-knife against her throat.

‘Where’s the money?’

Speechless with fear she tried to shake her head pleadingly. The knife pricked. ‘I know you’ve got it,’ Mark insisted, tightening his grip till she could scarcely breathe. ‘There’s no point in trying to pretend you haven’t.’

She gurgled in terror. ‘There’s only about £60. I’ll show you.’

He released her. Trembling, she got up and went to the mantelpiece. It seemed so easy to open the back of the long-dead black marble clock she had bought in a jumble sale, take out the bundle of notes and toss them to him. ‘That’s all there is to pay the electricity and gas.’

He pocketed the money with a smile of satisfaction. ‘Good girl. There’s no point in making a fuss. Husband and wife should share everything between them.’

She heard the front door shut. Still trembling, she pressed her throat where he had held the knife, found blood on her fingers. She went to look in the mirror. There was a small nick in her skin.

She stood frozen. He terrified her when he became ruthless like that. She had nothing in her repertoire for handling such situations, and each experience paralysed her, left her dismayed at her own ineffectiveness. Tears leaked out along her eyelids, clogging her vision. How would she pay the bills now?

The stillness of the room seemed to deny that anything out of the ordinary had occurred. From the ceiling a Chinese paper lampshade floated serenely as a full moon. Over the fireplace was a large

Rauschenberg print in an aluminium frame. On the floor a Turkey patterned carpet, wrinkled and threadbare, indicated their meagre resources.

Kathleen did not care for the Rauschenberg. It was Mark's, a relic of his advertising days. She had bought three stained hunting prints from a junk-shop, flying horses with their legs outstretched like tuning-forks, and a pair of much-glued-together china statuettes in eighteenth-century costume. Something to resurrect memories of her childhood and match her old family photographs in their ebony frames.

The largest of these photographs hung behind the sofa: a sepia of young women in bustles about to ascend into a gig outside a porticoed mansion, with a whiskered gentleman in tight check trousers and tiny bowler hat helping them, while another sat waiting on a tall hunter. Two of them were her great-grandparents. Mark had no family pictures. Whenever he mentioned his family, which was rare, it was in terms of derision.

She heard the sound of crying upstairs. Holding a tissue to her throat she went up, and found Sarah, aged two and a half, sitting up in bed. 'Nasty dream,' she wailed.

Kathleen sat on the bed to hold her and soothe her. She stayed rocking her till they fell asleep together.

When she woke at seven the next morning and went into the bedroom to change, there lay Mark asleep. She had not heard him come in. How innocent he looked, she thought, beautiful as the television tiger.

'I'm not taking the car this morning,' he said after breakfast, tossing the keys onto the hall table. 'Chap from work's picking me up on the corner. See you later, darling.'

Darling? How was it that his endearments always made her uneasy?

Later, after David and Vicky had left for school and she had washed up, she was upstairs making the beds when she happened to glance out of the window. Down in the street two men were walking round the car, a green Fiesta. One had a notepad in his hand, the other was looking up at the houses. The first man took out a ring of keys, selected one and opened the door. They both got in.

She flew down the stairs. By the time she reached the pavement the car was at the far end of the street, turning into the main road. She ran back inside to phone the police.

'No, I don't know the registration,' she explained. 'Wait a minute, the keys are here, it may be written on them.' She read out the number.

I hope Mark won't blame me, she thought agitatedly.

She was returning with some shopping in Sarah's multi-wheeled buggy, the child running on ahead, when she saw the police car in the street. A young policeman followed her up the red tiles to the front door. 'Mrs September? It's about the car you reported stolen.'

Although the policeman was awkward and slight of stature, his dark uniform gave him an ominous presence as he stood in the front room. 'Where does your husband work? Why didn't he take the car into work today? What time will he be back tonight?'

At first she chatted the questions away without thinking. Then she became aware he wore an expression like a teacher at school holding his breath as he glanced at a page of her work.

'Is there something wrong?'

'Those men you saw this morning taking the car weren't thieves, Mrs September. They were repossessing it for the car-hire firm that owned it.'

'There must be some mistake,' she cried. 'That can't be right.' But even as she spoke the doubts were running through her head. She saw the men again, the one with his notepad checking the car, the other looking at the house numbers. That they appeared so businesslike had puzzled her at the time. They had not looked like thieves. O my God, she thought, Mark will be angry. I shouldn't have rung the police.

All that evening, dealing with the children, putting them to bed, she grew anxious that he had not returned, that he had not rung her, afraid he might have been arrested, not sure what to do.

She was so relieved as he came through the door, she thought for a moment that he was smiling and she needn't have worried. Then she saw the line of his mouth was sharp as the blade of an axe. 'You stupid bitch.' He came straight across to her. She put up her hands to protect herself and the blow drove her own fist into her mouth. It knocked her backwards across a chair so that she fell into a heap on the floor. He stood over her. 'Why did you call the police?'

'I didn't know,' she shouted. 'I thought it was our car.'

He kicked her. 'You bring nothing but trouble.' And he kicked her again.

'Please.' She began to cry.

He had already turned away in disgust, and threw himself into a chair, his face creasing like thin leather. He stared moodily across the room as if he had already dismissed her from his thoughts.

She could feel that her lower lip was split and crawled across to get a tissue to dab her mouth.

'I told the police I was looking after it for a friend who'd gone to do a job in Australia,' he said, staring up at the ceiling. 'How was I to know it wasn't his? Ignorance may be no defence, but why should I have suspected anything was wrong? They asked me what his name was. Baverstock, I told them. But the car was hired under the name of Downing, they snapped back, thinking they'd caught me out. So I made the point that if he'd meant to hang onto the car, presumably he would hardly have used his own name. That had their logical minds fooled. They believed me.'

She could see him crowding them with his persuasiveness, oiling them with charm.

'Good job they didn't know I'd been sacked this afternoon after the assistant manager found out.'

'Why don't you ever tell me anything?' She couldn't stop crying.

She wanted only to communicate with him, to get him to realise how much she regretted being the involuntary cause, that it wasn't her fault. If only he would take her in his arms and ask her forgiveness for striking her. But the only way she could express anything was to dissolve into a weak and tearful mess, knowing that would annoy him even more and would almost certainly drive him away.

The front door slammed.

The next morning she was woken by him standing beside the bed in his underpants, holding out a cup of tea. He fluffed the pillows up behind her so that she could sit up. 'How would you like it if we were independent, had our own business out in the country, perfect for the kids, lots of fresh air and freedom to run about, a chance to make some real money? It's an idea I've been working on with a bloke I know, and now the opportunity's come up. I'm fed up with living in the stuffiness of the city and I know you love being out in the country. Shall we give it a try?'

'What would we do?'

He sat on the bed beside her. 'It's a boating business on the Broads, it's all there, waiting...' He described the new life, painting the scene, embellishing it, weaving patterns of plausible possibility.

The thought of the fresh air, the river and the lakes appealed to Kathleen.

It had never occurred to her that their new home would be a large fibreglass cruiser. At first the novelty obliterated any other concern. The children were delighted, especially to be delivered to school at Horning in their home. But she did find it unnerving having to show so many people over the boat. They always behaved as if they expected to be taking it over later in the day. Mark said it was the demonstrator, but she couldn't help noticing that he always moved the boat off somewhere else immediately after anyone looked over it.

She believed the bookings she took were for other boats, presuming them to be out on hire at the time, that he went off to arrange all this. She could not be certain when she first realised that the only boat they had to hire was the one they were living in, that the people who were shown over it or sent their deposit by post to an address in Wroxham, would find when they came to take up their booking that there was no boat. By the time the whole subterfuge dawned on her, she was appalled to think she had been an unwitting accomplice all along.

When she tried to remonstrate, Mark laughed. 'I don't do anything. When they say we want to hire a boat, I reply, fifty pounds deposit. I don't specify the deposit's for the boat-hire. I don't make any contract. It's they who make all the assumptions. People are so stupid.'

'We're never going to get away with it,' she cried. 'It's conning people, we'll end up in prison.'

Mark dismissed her fears contemptuously. 'You never try to understand. The law doesn't protect fools. I'm doing all this for you, for all of us. Don't worry about it. I know what I'm doing.'

'So whose boat is it?'

'It belongs to a friend.'

She bit her fingernails, riven with anxiety but afraid of arguing further. She was torn between what she felt she ought to do, to take the children and leave there and then, or to do what she wanted more than anything, to dissuade him from the folly of it all.

Events moved faster. Despite painting alternative name plaques to screw on, changing the registration numbers, and using rolls of coloured sellotape to add flashes round the hull, his efforts at disguising the boat failed in the end. Early one morning three men who said they represented the owners, a hire-company, caught up with them near St Benet's Abbey. Hirers had been getting a bad name, business had been falling off. They beat Mark up, threw him and all their possessions into the river, hustled Kathleen and the children onto the bank and took the boat away.

Kathleen jumped in fully-clothed to pull Mark from the water. She rescued whatever bits and pieces she could and assembled her half-conscious husband and the tearful children on the bank. It was an isolated spot, surrounded by marshes and grazing land. She waved frantically and called out to every boat that passed. Those aboard could see quite clearly the bedraggled young woman, the prostrate man and the crying children grouped on the bank. But though they stared, none of them stopped.

She had lost count by the time a boat slowed, seemed to reverse grudgingly, pulled into the bank. It might have been the eighth or ninth. The irony was not lost on her as she found herself fabricating a story. She was so beside herself with anxiety about Mark's condition that it was not difficult to sound convincing. 'We were robbed, our boat and most of our things taken. They beat up my husband. We must get him to hospital.'

The couple on the boat offered to take them to Horning, the nearest point to telephone the emergency services. While the man steered the boat, his wife helped Kathleen make the semi-conscious Mark comfortable on a bunk. He groaned when they took off his wet clothes. Kathleen had managed to fill a suitcase before they were thrown off, but mostly with children's clothes. They wrapped him in a jumper and blanket. There was one dry skirt for herself.

The woman was nervous, looking up and down the river apprehensively. 'We must get onto the police at once. It's dreadful to think decent people aren't safe on the Broads. Nobody warned us of this sort of thing.'

'It's piracy,' said her husband, a flabby, pot-bellied man, putting his shoulders back and sticking out his chin. 'It's criminal. They'd better not try anything on us.' But Kathleen could see that he too was nervous.

The children, dazed by what had happened, clung to her. David tugged at her arm. 'But why did those men say the boat was theirs?'

'They meant it's theirs now,' said Kathleen quickly. 'Look at the heron,' she added, pointing at a bird standing on the wooden piling before a thatched house. 'He's got a fish in his beak.'

'How can you tell it's not a she?' asked the pragmatic Vicky.

At Horning, Kathleen ran to find a phonebox to call an ambulance. She lied to their Samaritans that she would contact the police. Then she propped Mark on a bench, thanked them effusively and persuaded them that she could manage now and they should continue their holiday.

Mark was several days in hospital. He suffered concussion and three broken ribs. Luckily he had neglected to inform the council they were vacating the house, so the tenancy remained intact, despite the backlog of rent demands on the mat. Kathleen and the children were able to move back in. She felt miserably guilty at paying off the debts with the sodden wad she had found in Mark's jeans. She presumed it was all that remained of the ill-gotten boat-hire deposits.

WHEN the young woman first entered his room at the clinic, the therapist thought her face resembled a piece of crumpled fabric that had been washed, wrung-out and dried a hundred times; her dark-ringed eyes regarding all around her without expectation. It was not unusual in his experience.

She had brought a six-year-old girl who refused to be separated from her, and he pulled another chair over so that they could sit close.

He checked her name, then smiled encouragingly at her.

'I don't know what I'm supposed to say,' she said.

The child wriggled on her chair as if to embed herself into the seat, never taking her eyes off his face.

'Try to think of me being here to help you,' said the therapist.

'Why me?' The woman frowned as if this was not the response she had expected.

He did not recognise her accent. It was as if each vowel was endowed with a small soft underbelly. He sat opposite her, looked again at the notepad on his knee. Mrs Kathleen September. He wrote down so many names in a year he forgot most of them. If the stars were supposed to affect personality, why shouldn't a name, he thought, half-hearing the Forest duet from Lakhme in the back of his head.

Mrs Kathleen September, 19 Partridge Rise.

Married, or in that limbo between the state and its final disintegration. Three children.

'Tell me the worst thing that's affecting you?'

She pushed a lock of brown hair back from a cheek. 'There are so many.'

Delaying tactics, he thought. To repel the overcrowding anxiety. A mess of debts, heartless employers, crazy neighbours, crafty landlords... But he had his brief with this case; straightforward assessment. A matter of residence, with a divorce in the offing.

'Pick one to start with,' he suggested.

A subliminal shadow of animation flitted across her features, an attempt at a smile too scared to display itself. He had the impression of a part of his consciousness being snagged by a tiny hook.

'I need somewhere to hide,' she said.

'Hide?' he repeated, not sure he had heard correctly.

'It's all right where I am for the moment,' she added. 'But it's bound to be found out soon. Then I'll have to look for somewhere else.'

'I like it where we are now, Mummy,' said the little girl, turning anxiously to her. The woman slipped a hand round the child's shoulders and hugged her protectively.

'It must be very stressful to have to keep moving,' he murmured.

Mrs September's face quivered. 'Nobody understands. I can't make other people realise how difficult it is. Not even my solicitor. Perhaps he feels he has already done all he can.'

The therapist, though steeled by years of listening to calamities, could never curb himself from being drawn wide-eared to the edge of each new misfortune. 'What happens each time you are discovered?'

'I'm harassed, intimidated, attacked.'

'And the law cannot protect you?'

Her eyes stared blackly. Sick wild animals may appear to gaze upon human interference with stoical indifference, he thought. But if he was the instrument of any hope, she was looking right through him and far beyond the other side.

'The law? The law's useless. It doesn't even believe me.'

He could tell it was about to come, the tremor through the body, the flickering in the eyes, telltale to earthquake-watchers that the building is about to rend. It needed but one touch.

'Tell me about your husband?'

'At one house we lived in, he found out the address by taking a forged residence order for Vicky here to every primary school in the city.'

As the words began to pour, tears leaked down her cheeks, trickled over her lips. The child leaned close to her.

'Now I'm in trouble with the local education authorities because I keep her back from school in case he tries to take her. Social Services are threatening to take her into care, even though I school her every day. He wants to get custody of her, and Sarah as well, she's nearly three, I've left her with a friend today. He knows that will finish me, that he's won everything, I'll have nothing left. He's already got David. He's nine. Mark made the most outrageous promises to him to make him tell the social worker he'd rather live with his father.'

The therapist felt a qualm of uneasiness at the name Mark. It was the same as his own.

She pulled up her sleeve and presented her left forearm to him. 'Feel the bone there. Though you can probably see the bump and the misalignment,' she added, as if thinking he might be embarrassed to touch her. 'He pulled me through a doorway and slammed the door on my arm.' She lifted a handful of her brown hair away from her neck, twisting her head to reveal a hairpin scar beneath her ear. 'That was when he hit me with a plate.'

She sat back, breathing hard. 'When he's angry I'm a straw before the wind. My solicitor got an injunction from the court to keep him out of the house, but it was as much use as the piece of paper it's written on. He tricks his way round everything. You see, when he finds me, he doesn't arrive like some raving maniac, threatening to beat me senseless. He's all solicitous and charming, enquires how we all are, brings us presents, and acts hurt when I tell him to go away. He never shows any hatred or violence if there's anyone else near or anyone might be listening. It makes me go cold all over when I hear his voice now.'

Her anguish was such that Vicky had slipped off her chair and inserted herself within her mother's arms, clinging tightly to her. The therapist felt alarmed that the small girl should be listening to such tales, however much of it she might have witnessed at first hand. He could see from her white face how the telling drained and exhausted her as much as it did her mother. He made a note to suggest it might be better to leave her behind for the next session.

'He's managed to convince everybody that I'm a drunkard. The social worker and the court probation officer, they all believe him, he fills the bin with empty bottles, no use me telling them I don't drink. That's why they never lifted a finger when he took David from me. He was so smart, so persuasive, and he told so many lies, even David believed him. Of course he doesn't look after David at all. He put him with his sister's family. Mark could charm a firing-squad to hand over their rifles. I may be able to talk with someone like you in a quiet room like this, but he makes me go to pieces. It's like being locked in a room with a giant scorpion.'

She paused, shivering. The therapist, shaking his head in sympathy, kept breaking the eye contact, like an engineer who modulates valves to maintain the balance.

'I can't go abroad to get away from him, I haven't any money. I did have a little in the beginning, but when I became pregnant with David, Mark persuaded me we should use it as a down payment on a house. While I was working I gave him money towards the mortgage. Then a year after David was born we were evicted. He had never paid a penny into the building society. It came as a terrible shock. "It's all right," he said, "the council'll have to rehouse us with the baby, it's much cheaper living in a council house and they do all the repairs."'

She shook her head as if still amazed that it had happened.

'Now I can't use council accommodation any more, because I have to keep moving to get away from him. But how can I find places in private houses with two small children and landlords always wanting deposits and rent in advance? So far I've been helped by friends. But each time I move I have to notify the DSS, and they stop the giro while I reapply, and that can mean weeks without any money. My whole life is spent watching over my shoulder, planning the next move, going down to the benefit office or the City Hall to try and persuade them to give me something. It's unbelievably exhausting. We're reduced to living out of a few suitcases so that we can travel light, make a midnight flit. It means we have few clothes, few possessions, it's very insecure for the children. All the time the social worker and the probation officer come after me for moving, for not sending Vicky to school, for not telling them where I am. There are court hearings that keep getting postponed because Mark never turns up, or his solicitor obtains another adjournment. He's trying to prevent a divorce. He won't let me go.'

'Why do you think he keeps persecuting you like this?'

She shook her head, her lank hair becoming disarrayed. She pushed strands away from her face. 'Sometimes I think it's his pride at me rejecting him. My friends think he's not right in the head.'

The telephone on the table buzzed. He lifted the receiver. 'Yes?' He glanced at his watch. 'Right. Thanks.'

'I've taken up too much of your time,' said Kathleen September, stirring herself, picking up her handbag. 'I expect you think I'm exaggerating.'

The therapist could see her expression walling-up against the moment of dismissal, her eyes glazing as if certain the interview was one more waste of time.

He handed her a card. 'I don't think we should let the grass grow on this business. I take cases at this address this evening. I'm free about six-thirty?'

The small hook of a smile appeared, as if grateful for anything. 'Thank you. If I can arrange a baby-sitter.'

AFTER Kathleen September had gone, the therapist sat for a moment like someone caught unprepared by a thunderstorm, awash with the sense of his powerlessness in the face of events outside his control; the notes on his pad the stains of nature passing.

Clients could weave fantasies of persecution that would convince the steeliest sceptic. But even if what she said was true, it would be difficult to intervene at this stage without further investigation. He had to be like the farmer viewing the black clouds looming over his harvest, and trust in providence.

Meanwhile others were waiting outside.

His next case was an adopted girl of sixteen, who had found out the whereabouts of her real mother, but lacked the nerve to make the contact. The difficulty in reassuring her was the possibility that her mother might not want to see her.

Then he had an emergency case of a young man who, the previous evening, had caught his wife in bed with another man. He was still swollen with outrage like a bull elephant. After thirty minutes listening the therapist suggested the man might consider reasons that his wife was seeking love elsewhere. Perhaps because she was not getting it from him? Under normal circumstances it would have been too soon for such confrontation. But under these conditions he didn't have much time. Also he knew the suggestion had been coloured by his own experience, an emotional infiltration he disliked. Instead of the angry response he half-expected, the man slumped in his chair and nodded in agreement, the rage drained from him. Inwardly the therapist wiped his brow with relief.

It was five-thirty when he arrived home.

His house was part of a modern complex beside the river, close to the city centre. Young trees rustling with full heads of late-summer leaves stood among flagstones, pleats of concrete steps unfolded to the dark river below the brick bulwarks of tall four-storey terraces; each with velux windows like sunglasses on their foreheads, which gave spectacular views over the city.

It was more spacious than he needed now his family had grown up. Occasionally they came for a weekend, usually after a break with their most recent partner: Angela, a middle-school teacher in Colchester, Marianne who worked for a London publisher, and Nicole, still at Cambridge, doing languages. He had once regretted having no son to carry on the name of Clement, but it no longer bothered him.

The interior was in complete contrast to the neat exterior and architecturally smug surroundings. In an ordinary interior each room is easily identified for its purpose, dining-room, bedroom, sitting-room, kitchen, etc, but here it was unclear which was which. At first sight the rooms might have been ransacked, papers and books strewn everywhere, across the floors, over the chairs. At second sight the piles of books had simply slumped sideways, countless papers had been put down, lay where they had been forgotten. Paths had been forged like an ice-breaker pushing through the floes of newspapers and journals. The third sight might include a tall fridge-freezer sharing an alcove with an eighteenth-century longcase clock, or a television completely buried beneath papers; or a concert grand piano and a double bed sharing a room little bigger than themselves. In the largest room an old kettledrum stood in the centre, bearing a potted fern and a lamp set to shine down on an enormous sofa of chafed and stained leather, most of it buried in sheets of music. The room that might have been the kitchen seemed more like a china store, every inch of surface stacked with quantities both clean and unwashed. The only recognisable room was the bathroom. Despite overflowing with clothing, a row of wrinkled clean hanging over the bath, unwashed strewn on the floor, the porcelain of ablution at least gave the impression of normal, damp use.

If his neighbours knew little about him, the one common factor they would have agreed upon was that he played the piano. Often loudly. Opinion was divided as to how badly. Not many pianists can make the Moonlight Sonata sound as though it was written by John Cage; though still recognisably the Moonlight Sonata. The unkindest suggestion was that he played it with his feet. But he did try not to disturb. The piano shared his bedroom because it was the only room that did not directly abut another in the next-door house. Which was also the reason he slept there.

He saw his playing as a relief to come home to, to wash away the strains of the day, as others might eagerly plunge into a gin and tonic or a can of lager. Once his hands spread across the keys he could forget the abysses he had all but precipitated into, the embarrassing failures to comprehend, the insensitive gaffes, the inept advice. He could carry himself away on a whirling thermal of emotional escapism, sometimes even trying to reproduce full orchestral forte in thunderstorms of crashing chords.

He was self-taught, had learned to read music but relied generally upon ear, though most of his neighbours would never have anyone believe other than that he was deaf. But he was able to think music, and did so much of the time, so that he might cross a street, his head quite empty of thought but flowing with notes to the extent that a warning motor horn became part of the orchestration, as much as the screech of tyres, and chance alone had so far kept him intact. Then why the lack of communication between mind and fingers, his critics might have asked.

He had bought the piano with a legacy. The great ebony ship of humming wires had required a window removed and a crane to get it into the house.

'For God's sake, Dad,' Marianne had said to him. 'You don't have to use the loud pedal all the time. It doesn't hide the mistakes one bit.' 'Why shouldn't he?' demanded Nicole. 'It makes it all sound smoother.' 'You always stick up for him,' sneered Marianne. 'Sucking up so you can be his favourite.' 'I do happen to have views of my own,' retorted Nicole. 'Funny how they always happen to coincide with his,' cried Marianne triumphantly. 'Children,' he exclaimed. 'Children.' And the chord rang through the empty house. It was disappointing that after all the years of conscientious parenthood they should still fight each other for the flimsiest reason.

That evening his mood turned him towards Petrushka. The piece was filled with the phantoms of childhood dreams, volatile, dramatic music racing with pursuit. He could always manage to transpose the orchestral gist, the mood, the excitement, the intensity. His detractors could never forgive the cacophonic froth of his mistakes, but he did have one or two devotees. They saw his playing as colourful, the equivalent of fauvism.

After half an hour's work-out he went into the kitchen and poured himself a glass of sherry and made a salad niçoise.

Cases were often disturbing. Strange coincidence that the date that day should be the first of September. Could be a pseudonym of course, chosen from calendar or even a song. But what had sharpened the interview so uncomfortably was her husband's name. Each time she had mentioned it in connection with the man's behaviour, he had felt guilty by association.

Perhaps he would mention it to Madeleine. Discussing cases outside the clinic might be unprofessional, but there were occasions when he needed a ladder of common-sense to escape from the incestuous mole-runs of cognitive behaviour and Gestalt. When he could distract her from her coital hunger.

Sometimes he felt Madeleine was too big for him, both in physique and in personality, but too generous with her feelings to escape from. She was a notable in the community, local councillor, solicitor, mother of four grown-up children, on innumerable committees and fund-raising groups, her name always in the paper, a forceful and articulate woman. But once the front door had shut the world out, she was a melting overweight heap of insecurity whose emotional need was identified in intense sexual gratification. Though he suspected his interpretation was an excuse for his own inability to ever quite assimilate her.

There were occasions when he found himself half-drowning in the tidal wave of her lustful desires, and become an unwilling partner dragged along in the undertow, just as at times he felt squeamish at her steam-rolling political expediency. He had known her for many years, since long before her husband died. He suspected his resistance to any inclination they might marry was really her own, but clung to his own reluctance however much he suspected he might agree should she suggest it.

Tonight she was chairing a public meeting examining proposals for a sports centre. They had made no arrangement to meet later. But should the need take her...

He set off for his evening stint at the Aid Centre. The room he used there was much like the one at the clinic. A box containing three assorted armchairs assembled from earlier times, a table bearing an ashtray and a box of tissues, on the walls a calendar and a poster of the cathedral for the music festival, and a window that peered through the leaves of an architectural birch at the postmodern rooftops beyond. As at the clinic he had provided his own addition to the room: a coffee machine perched like a piece of sculpture on a filing cabinet in the corner.

His first client was a girl of sixteen who had left home to share a flat with a girlfriend, and whose parents were threatening to seek a court order for her return. Since the overbearing restrictions of her parents had triggered her decision to leave, and she seemed adult for her age, he enjoyed playing devil's advocate, encouraging her in her independence and how she might best maintain it, while thinking how he might have felt if she had been one of his own daughters at that age.

He had not been certain that Kathleen September would come.

'I found a baby-sitter,' she said, a little breathless. 'My landlady actually. She knows about everything. She's very sympathetic. Her husband gave her a hard time too.'

He turned a chair for her to sit on, bringing his own a little closer. She was wearing the nondescript brown skirt and beige blouse of the morning, but he noticed she had washed her hair and there was a touch of lipstick on that brief hooked smile.

His anxiety over the names was spurred again as he addressed her as Kathleen, least she should quite reasonably request to use his own first name.

'Talking is dry work,' he said, going over to the cabinet to activate the coffee machine. It was already primed with water and ground coffee. There was a tray with clean mugs and bowls filled with packets of sugar and small plastic cartons of long-life milk. He was never entirely happy about the centre secretary's motives in treating him so considerately; a little too close to mothering him.

'You never considered leaving your husband at this stage?'

She stared at him anxiously. 'But I had nowhere to go. How could I leave with three small children?'

'So you were going to stand by him, whatever he did?'

'I know what you're saying,' she said, drawing in her breath and looking away. 'It makes me shiver whenever I think back. I've often asked myself since, why did I hang on so long? But he was my life, he was my husband, father of my children. That bound us together, whatever was happening, however wrong, however unkind he was. I kept making excuses to myself for everything, you see, hoping that one day things would get better. I don't know if you can understand.'

He handed her a mug of coffee, offered her milk and sugar. 'You could imagine no other alternative, you felt bound together in your daily struggle for survival, caught in what seemed like an awful, inevitable process..?'

Her eyes were wide with apprehension as if visualising how easily her viability could be washed away. 'You do believe me, don't you?'

'What reason have I to disbelieve you?'

'You mightn't believe me if you heard his version.'

He sipped his coffee. 'Why don't we leave him for the moment? Tell me something of your childhood.'

'**EVERYONE** used to say Collon was unusual for an Irish village because it contained so many fine Georgian houses. It was at a cross roads on the side of a hill and had been gently decaying for a generation. In a wood at the top of the hill was hidden a mansion which had been built by the last speaker of the Irish parliament before the Act of Union. In my childhood monks inhabited it. A penniless Russian princess used to live in the old court house, and her husband grew mushrooms. In my grandfather's time there had been a popular tennis club, and in the winter everyone who had a horse went out with the Louth Hunt. My father had land and business interests, shares in a bakery in a nearby town, in an oil distributor, and he had brood mares.

We lived in a house so packed with furniture it was more of a repository, room after room of woodwormy Sheraton and Hicks furniture, mildewed chesterfields, display cabinets packed with dusty Belleek and Rockingham delft and Waterford glass, and oil paintings on the walls dark as if they'd been done with creosote, and every window had great shutters which were cranked shut every night. Out at the back there was a stone coach-house crammed with decaying pony-traps and dusty old motor cars, some there since the Troubles, and rows of stables round a yard, and sheds of hay that smelled like tea and piles of steaming horse dung. It wasn't till I came to England that I realised you get the same smell off a barrowload of fresh horse manure as you do off the blue water in public swimming-baths.

My mother was beautiful but she had a bad skin and was always coating it with creams and lotions so that kissing her cheek was like pressing my lips against a cold pancake. She was always going off to her dressmaker in Ardee, or to play bridge, or arranging dinner-parties, and in the winter she went hunting three or four days a week. Her skin was better in the winter. She used to talk down the back of her nose, sounding like a kazoo. My father teased her sometimes about her County Kildare accent. They were all supposed to be snobs down there. If ever she mentioned the forty bedrooms they had in her family home, my father would remind her of the grass growing through the flagstones in the hall and the marble staircase shored up with tree-trunks.

She was always trying to organise me to go to pony club or have dancing lessons or practise the piano. But I wasn't at all sociable. She wanted a daughter with style she could show off instead of the scruffy let-down in jeans who wandered about the fields or lay on her bed reading all day. I went through school with my head stuck in books. I could never get enough of them. Private, portable worlds that go on inside your head and you can hide away in the attic or the hayloft to read. Much better than the television that sat there in public in a little sitting-room. If they found me watching it my father would complain about my sprawling about wasting electricity and useless as a cat, and my mother said I made the place look untidy.

On one corner of the village cross-roads were the grounds of a ruined house which had been burned to a shell and never rebuilt. It stood back from the road among overgrown trees, enclosed behind high railings and walls, a lost wilderness. But once inside you could still see the shape the gardens had been, walk down the overgrown paths, under the wild laurel arbours, crawl beneath trellises that had collapsed under the weight of clematis and American Pillar roses. The vines had burst through the roof of the vinery, a maple had fallen across the ornamental pond, and one of the village boys had sprayed metallic paint onto a statue of a nymph, and then ivy had coiled itself round her so she looked like a girl in a torn green dress wearing iridescent stockings. I could be alone with my daydreams in that garden, and nobody would bother me.

My best friend was a girl called Carmel Clinton. Her father had a big store in Dunleer. We used to go out riding together, take sandwiches in an old khaki haversack. D'Arcy, the groom, said it was a World War I gas-mask container that had belonged to my grandfather. Carmel was a dreamer too, but mostly about boys. She never stopped talking about them, the ones she fancied, always trying to engineer meetings, plan the clothes she'd wear, what she'd say. But nothing ever came of her plans because she always chickened out at the last minute. I haven't seen her in ages.

Then when I was fourteen my parents were killed in a car crash on the Dublin-Naas road. So I came to England to live with my mother's sister near Basingstoke.

It was so different over here, a kind of enforced liberation. My aunt and uncle had four children of their own, and I had to share a bedroom with Aileen, who was so brainy I didn't dare speak for months for fear of my mistakes being paraded for everyone else to laugh at. My aunt was very kind, she made a big effort to make me feel at home. But she was always apologising for me, poor Kathleen, you know, she's lost her parents, poor Kathleen, she had to leave her lovely home, poor child, it's not easy for her. My father's affairs turned out to be in chaos, and to pay off all the debts everything had to be sold. So then it was poor Kathleen, all her family money gone. For God's sake woman, my uncle would growl, that's all in the past. Kathleen has us now, doesn't she?

He was kind too, though he had a terrible temper. He threw a book at Aileen once and it missed her and broke my nose instead. When he collected me from the hospital he took me straight off to buy an expensive leather coat he knew I coveted. I still have it. Once we saw a man come out of a house to get into his car and there was a cat asleep on the bonnet. He hurled it off into the road and it was crushed by a passing van. My uncle rushed across and knocked the man down. The case for assault was thrown out by the judge who said cruelty to dumb animals was a despicable crime. I was ever so impressed by English justice. More fool me.

He was a real hard-line Tory though, always going on about the unions ruining the country. Aileen was the radical in the family. You're all bloody wets and liberals and muddy-minded socialists, he shouted at her one evening. You think money grows on trees, that there's a God-given right to work. Greed, that's your working class, out for anything they can grab. No thought for tomorrow, don't care if they strike and the firm goes under and the country sinks.

What about the greed of the employers? Aileen came back quick as a needle. Exploiting the workers, paying them chicken-feed to enable themselves to live in luxury? You'd argue green was red, he shouted at her. Then he turned on me. What do you think, Kathleen? I don't know, I replied feebly. Of course you do, he exclaimed, and he leaned across and nipped my earlobe between finger and thumb. There, he shouted, do you have an opinion about that? The tactics of the bully, said Aileen. You're the living example that England could produce as good extermination camp monsters as Nazi Germany. I thought he'd kill her, but my aunt dragged us off to do the washing-up. She was quick at defusing rows. I felt desperately inadequate. I longed to manufacture smart responses that would impress my uncle.

After we'd gone to bed I heard Aileen sobbing in the dark. What's the matter? I whispered. I hate him, she said. But I hate myself worse. He goads me into losing my temper so that I'm just as bad as him. I got into her bed to comfort her. Kathleen, she said, what are we going to do about you? The world's full of people like him. How're you going to manage if you don't learn some confidence in yourself? She forgot all about the row with her father and sat there lecturing me on having opinions, about social injustice, racism, nuclear energy, pollution. Now you've got something to say to my father, she said. But I'd hate to disappoint him, I replied. You don't mind disappointing me? she cried. But he's a man, I said. Men are bigger and more important than us. She became really annoyed then, so I got a full lecture on feminism as well. By the time she finished the dawn was coming up. But it's hard to change instincts you've grown up with.

We became like sisters after that. Maybe we complemented each other. I was the introvert, lived my life through the people in books and plays, whereas she was the extrovert, always going to meetings and parties, determined to forge a path of her own.

It seemed like no time at all before we were going off to different colleges.

College was another enforced liberation, only this time I went in over my head. There was so much energy and so many people from so many different backgrounds. Suddenly I was free to drink myself stupid, dance myself wild, and stay up all night, listening to the starry-eyed struggling up the peaks of philosophy by candlelight. At last I was a sociable animal, but when I look back I see it most of all as a giant game of snakes and ladders, with the ladders for rushing into love and the snakes for being rejected. Each time I threw a six and thought, great, here's the man of my life, I'd fall straight down the longest snake, right back to the beginning. I never seemed able to judge a man, when to say no, this isn't for me. You think you know the creeps, that they're easy to recognise. But it's those who share the same interests, the same values, they're the ones who trap you, especially the ones who listen, who seem to treat you as an equal. They turn out to be tape-recordings, they've learned how to play a particular tune of reasonableness that makes you happy to be screwed by them, and then you find out that screwing's all they ever wanted. At least there were women friends, sharing the pain and the post-mortems, laughing it away. And the next week we'd be screwing some bastard like he was our only salvation.

After my degree I got a job in an advertising agency, and that was where I met Mark. He was a copywriter. I don't think he was very good. But he had the trick of sounding as though he had but to curl his tongue round a concept and it would bend the country's ears inside out.'

SHE paused, frowning as if she found the recollection disagreeable. She picked up her mug, found she had drunk it dry. Mark Clement rose to fill it for her. 'Is this really helping?' she asked.

He regarded her with a quizzical lift of his eyebrows as if she ought to have known the answer. There was often a misty lack of focus in her dark-rimmed grey-green eyes that he found oddly appealing, like a curious little phrase of music that he would keep repeating over and over again.

'It's odd to think that now you know so much about me, but I know nothing about you,' she said.

Few clients ever surface from their self-obsession to remark on that, he thought, agreeably surprised. 'It all helps. But it's going to take a bit of time yet.'

'You've been very generous with your time,' she added. 'Very patient with me.'

He thought it noticeable that her face, which in the beginning had resembled little more than a lump of clay, was beginning to take shape as if invisible fingers were forming its features. By talking she was reaffirming herself. It was another indication of progress.

In the days after Mark's return from hospital he sat about the house, snappy as a caged crocodile. Rows were frequent. Money was short again. There was only a little Income Support while the Department of Employment investigated why he had been sacked from the job with the Press.

One evening a friend came round and took him out for a drink. Steve was the sort of successful grafter Mark envied, a sharp-eyed, buy-cheap-and-sell-dear man. He was short and balding, with fingers like courgettes, and drove a large Granada. He had found Mark work before, though Mark had tried to cheat him the last time, so Kathleen was surprised to see him again.

It was a relief to have Mark out of the house. It made her feel as if she'd just stepped from a skirt two sizes too small. She was in bed and asleep long before he returned.

The next morning he was down at eight with the children, dressed in a clean shirt, shaved smooth as a teacup and with dark rings under his eyes.

Kathleen raised an eyebrow. 'Where're you off to?'

The children regarded their spruce father with interest, especially when he clutched his head in anguish at the clatter as their mother knocked a spoon into the sink in her haste to reach toast smouldering under the grill. 'Have we any Alka-Seltzer?' he moaned.

She fetched him two aspirin which he gulped down with mouthfuls of hot tea. She was about to cook him some breakfast, but he glanced up at the wall-clock. 'I must go,' he exclaimed, kicking his chair back.

'Where to?' she asked.

'I'll tell you when I get back.'

'Give us a clue?'

'Kitchens,' he said, slipping through the door.

David rescued the next pieces of toast. 'He's not going to be a cook, is he?' He frowned doubtfully. They knew Mark found it difficult to remember it was necessary to fill a kettle with water before switching it on.

When he returned that evening he had an armful of presents. Kathleen's finances had reached such a low point that their evening meal was faggots, potatoes and carrots. 'Look what your clever Daddy's brought you,' Mark announced to the children. 'Your favourite sweets. Red roses for my lovely wife, and a bottle of wine to celebrate my appointment.'

'Appointment?' echoed Kathleen.

'Can we have wine too?' asked Vicky.

'A sip,' he replied, ruffling her hair, so pleased with himself he couldn't stop prancing about the room like a racehorse.

'Can anyone guess what I'm going to do?' he asked as they all settled round the table, the bottle uncorked, the hot faggots aromatic in their sauce, the steaming potatoes speckled with parsley and pepper like large white marbles.

'David thought you might be a cook,' said Kathleen ladling out carrots freckled with basil.

Mark laughed. 'Can you see me stirring saucepans?'

'Washing-up?' she suggested.

'Such a high opinion of my abilities,' he scowled.

'Don't keep us in suspense,' she said hastily.

He took a deep breath, looking round at each in turn. 'You don't realise how lucky you are to have a father like me, always able to find a job like a conjurer pulling rabbits out of a hat. Where would you all be without me?'

They looked at him in bewilderment, as if to be without him had never occurred to any of them. 'What you need is friends. Nobody can manage on their own. It pays to make friends, they always come in useful.'

'But what is it?' asked Kathleen impatiently.

'Steve knows a man who has bought a warehouse full of kitchen units, really classy stuff from Germany and Denmark, top-quality craftsmanship, lovely teak and oak panels. And this chap, whose name is Micklewright, wanted someone to get the stuff moving.'

'Are you going to fit them yourself?' asked Kathleen.

He scowled. 'Of course not. I'm going to be the manager. In charge of selling and organisation. There'll be teams of fitters to install them.' His good mood returned. 'We're going to be rich. We'll go on holidays, David'll have a new bicycle, Vicky can have ballet lessons, Sarah a kitten and you, Kath, all the new clothes you've ever dreamed of. We'll put a kitchen in here that'll dazzle the neighbours, built-in oven, fridge-freezer, the lot. This is our lucky day.'

Kathleen raised her glass. 'To success. Let's all drink to the new job.' But inside she was uneasy; there had been these euphorias before.

'Can I have some more wine?' asked Vicky holding out her emptied glass.

'A budding lush like her mother,' said Mark, dolloping a splash into her glass.

Kathleen coloured. She only had to have one glass and he would immediately start casting aspersions, as if he had some inbuilt phobia about drunken women. She knew his mother had fallen to her death from a window clutching a bottle of gin when he was in his teens.

He held out the bottle. 'What about you, David?'

David wrinkled his nose. 'I don't like it.'

'Come on. You've got to be big, learn to take your drink like a man.'

Kathleen felt her skin prickling. The conflicting messages he dished out so breezily were alarming. She bit her lip to refrain from comment.

After the children were all in bed and she was doing the washing-up, he came up behind and slid his arms round her waist. He stripped her of her apron and led her to the sofa in the sitting-room. While he rolled on top of her, nuzzling her and sliding her skirt up, caterpillar-coloured footballers darted about the bright green television screen to a rowdy invisible chorus.

It could not be said that he made love to her, but his sudden overpowering lust impaled her with a desire that had no time to be fulfilled, for all too soon he faded away. The silent horde despatched inside her, she thought sadly. A swimming race without a prize.

She noticed the next day that he was collected and returned in a large white van with KITCHFIT in red letters on its side. Then a few days later he had the use of a smaller van for himself which he kept outside. But he would not talk any more about the job, except to say that everything was going fine.

'Men never do,' said Linda, a blonde from five doors down who blithely squeezed her ample figure into size 14s.

Three of them were sitting round the table drinking coffee together, the third an old college friend of Kathleen's called Clare, with straight hair fringing her round face, who lived a few miles outside the city. From the kitchen came the din of small children playing with saucepans and baking dishes.

'Harry could spend every day skiving off work for all I'd know,' said Linda. 'When he comes home he shuts it out, won't tell me a thing about what he does.'

'Bill's the opposite,' said Clare. 'He comes home and acts out the entire day in the kitchen while I'm making supper. He plays every part with total recall. We don't need television, Bill does it all, a mini Grange Hill, takes off all the staff and every little horror. Trouble is he does a couple of hours marking after supper as well, then just goes to sleep. Our sex life is down to the odd chance I roll against him in the bed and find it all lovely and hard, quick, stuff it in before it goes soft again. I had this wonderful dream, he says at breakfast, a fantastically sexy woman came into my bed and raped me. Me, you oaf, I say to him. Randy little sod, he gasps, all shocked. He thinks women should wait till they're asked.'

Kathleen sighed. 'I envy you two. At least you can plan your lives knowing tomorrow's going to carry on like yesterday.'

'I wouldn't mind a bit of variety.' Linda tossed her dyed blonde locks. 'Life's so bloody boring there are times I could explode.'

The noise from the kitchen became louder, shrieks of laughter that suddenly turned to tears. Clare went to investigate. 'What a lovely mess,' the others could hear her say.

'Mummy, Tessa hit me.'

'It was an accident,' protested Tessa.

'Accidents will happen. You look all right to me.' Clare returned and sat down. 'We'll have to give your kitchen a good clean before we go, Kath.'

'Wouldn't it be great to be a kid again,' lamented Linda. 'Messing about all day.' She turned to Kathleen. 'What exactly is Mark's new job, then?'

Kathleen shrugged uneasily. 'All I know is what I told you,

selling fitted kitchens.'

'But what does he know about kitchens?'

Kathleen felt ambivalent discussing Mark. In her mind he contrasted bleakly with the reliability of her friends' husbands and part of her would have preferred to draw a discreet blind over him. Yet although she felt loyal and protective she longed to air her fears, seek reassurance.

Clare knew this of old. 'Maybe it'll work out this time, Kath. He's got to stick some time. I always thought he'd make a great salesman.'

'Yeah,' agreed Linda. 'Sell you the carpet off your own floor, sell you a holiday in your own back garden. Harry's a rice pudding compared to Mark. Maybe we should have an exchange system. When you're crying for a bit of security I'll lend you Harry, and when I'm dying for a bit of danger you can lend me Mark.'

There came a clang from the kitchen, then a wailing began. Above it rose the voice of Clare's four-year old son John. 'Accidents will happen.'

'What have you done?' demanded Clare, as Kathleen scooped up the sobbing Sarah.

'Her head hit the saucepan,' he claimed, frowning as if even he was puzzled by his explanation.

Tessa was lying under a pile of baking tins, conpletely soaked, smiling beatifically.

That weekend Mark took his family to Great Yarmouth in the Kitchfit van. Whatever they drove in now Kathleen was nervous that they might be stopped by the owners come to repossess it, but otherwise her pleasure was unmarred. It was the sort of day that made adults children, and children open-mouthed with incredulity and pleasure. The beach itself was windswept and uninviting, the sea rumbling and bending like warm lead, but they ate hot dogs and ice-creams in a carriage drawn by a shambling horse along the sea front. They hired a circular boat that revolved helplessly about a boating-lake, then spent hours in a giant funfair sampling merry-go-rounds, ghost-rides, giant Ferris wheels and the roller-coaster, with more ice-creams and bags of crisps, till sleepy with so much ozone and exhilaration, they drove home.

'That was marvellous,' said Kathleen later that evening after the children were all in bed. 'I haven't enjoyed myself so much in years. Thank you, darling.' They were stretched out on the sofa before the television, allowing Dynasty to perform upon their retinas. She leaned close and kissed him, feeling benign with sentiment.

'You thought it was great, did you?' he muttered, staring rigidly before him, unmoved by her attentions. 'Trust you to be satisfied by trash.'

Her moment of contentment chilled. 'What do you mean?'

'It was junk,' he snarled. 'A place for riff-raff, boneheads, peasants to enjoy themselves on stupid, simple-minded idiocies. Most of the world are cretins of one kind or another and that sort of place is designed for their piddling amusement.' He turned on her, his fingers sinking into her arm like pliers.

'How can you honestly admit to enjoying it? You know it was crap.' He all but spat. She dared not demur for fear of igniting him further. 'I want better things for my children. Not cheap nonsense. Can't you understand? What good is rubbish for them? It used to be keeping up with the Joneses, now it's keeping down with them. You let me down all the time. It was your bloody idea going there.'

She couldn't bring herself to point it out that it wasn't true, or that he had enjoyed it at the time. 'Where would you have preferred to have gone?'

To her relief he released her and twisted away. He stretched out rigid as a baulk of timber. 'Somewhere to elevate their minds, educate them, broaden their vision, a theme park or a heritage centre.'

The figures on the small screen were performing their predictable Dallas roles, glittering with wealth, the life styles that she knew Mark aspired to, the weapons he needed to acquire to penetrate the indifference he dreaded.

'I don't want them to have my childhood, hanging around waiting for nothing to happen. It was like being locked in a cupboard for sixteen years. I didn't matter, nobody listened to me, they paid as much attention to me as they did to the dog. I never knew I could have ambition, that I could have choices. They cheated me. I want my children to have standards to look up to. I'm going to see to it from now on.'

Whenever Mark launched into such idealised abstractions, stamping about like a hearthrug general, she knew they were a diversion from some scheme he was hatching. In the ensuing silence came her opportunity. 'How's the job going?'

'Micklewright's a fool,' he said, so quickly he might have been waiting for the question. 'I could make him millions out of that stuff. The fashion for fitted kitchens is a bottomless gold-mine. There may be plenty at it, but there are thousands of potential customers riddled with vanity, longing to outshine their neighbours. He's like a bloody tortoise scared of coming out of his shell. If he doesn't, I will.'

It was too alarming to contemplate how. She sat turning sentences over in her head, afraid not to speak.

Suddenly he leaned forward and turned the television off. When he turned back his eyes were half-open cockles, the leer of his mouth a split pod full of peas. The change was almost frightening. How quickly he can switch his mood, she thought.

He pressed his body along hers, running his hands about her. 'You're the best-looking girl I know, Kath. Every time I look at you, all those little American, Russian and Scandinavian judges lift up their cards with tens on them. You've still got the same sexy figure you had when I first met you.' His hands, seeking their own pleasures, touched the vital elements of her sensory responses, but tonight they felt damp and doused. 'I want you,' he whispered. She lay in the limp but correct posture of expectation as he pulled her clothes off. 'Nobody else is as important to me as you are,' he said, and the little voice within her saying, how can you let him con you like this, faded away.

A FEW days later the phonecalls began.

'I'm ringing about the advertisement.'

'It's about the bargain fitted kitchens.'

'Can you send me a brochure?'

'I should like someone to come round and give me a quotation.'

Mark had left a note by the phone. *If anyone rings about kitchens, take their names and telephone numbers.* Tell them I'll be in touch to make an appointment. From then on the phone never seemed to stop ringing, the enquiries came flooding, and she filled sheets with lists of names.

Mark came home in a large, very new, blue van. 'What's going on?' she asked.

'I've got an option on Micklewright's stuff,' he replied, his eyes bright as he scanned the lists. 'I'm on my own now. The cheapest kitchens in the city, that'll bring them in. I'd better start calling some of these numbers back. Make us a sandwich, love.'

The enquiries continued to pour in over the next few weeks, the hall table and the dresser piling up with lists. Mark was out all hours measuring kitchens, coming home to list specifications, draw up estimates, making rough sketches on scaled grid paper. Deposits were already cascading through the letterbox. He took a fat wad of cheques to the bank.

'But the city's full of places that do fitted kitchens,' she said to him, puzzled. 'Why's everyone rushing to buy these?'

'Never bother your pretty little head,' he replied, patting her on it as he headed for the door. Then he turned back, as if he couldn't help himself. 'I put in two tiny ads,' he boasted. 'Only cost a couple of quid each. *Warehouse full of luxury top class fitted kitchens, export order cancelled due to change in exchange rates, give-away prices, free fitting.* People can't bear to miss a bargain.'

The complaints began as an inconspicuous trickle. Promises had been made, nothing had happened, no signs of delivery. Kathleen did not find it easy trying to soothe disappointed customers down the phone. She pleaded with Mark to deal with them, but he seemed oblivious of problems and spoke down the phone as if everything was under perfect control, charming them with persuasive explanations. He had taken on an elderly redundant carpenter and a YTS trainee as an assistant. It looked to Kathleen as though they were making a great show of activity and willing, appearing all over the city, putting in a couple of hours at each house then hurrying off to another, like Beau Geste in a Foreign Legion desert fort filling the crenellations with the dead then running round behind firing their rifles to fool the Tuareg into thinking there was a full garrison to overcome. At times she felt she alone was holding the fort, the telephone in her hands hot as the breech of a rifle.

She was not sure at this stage whether things appeared to be getting out of hand because Mark hadn't taken into account the potential, the sheer flood of orders, or had miscalculated the number of fitters he would need, or hadn't booked sufficient materials; or whether he had deliberately set up the operation with no intention of fulfilling any of the orders. Was he putting on an appearance of running a business simply to acquire the deposits? Yet that would be crazy, she argued with herself, he'd be found out in no time. Though that hadn't deterred him with the boat-hire business, she remembered. But he was so frenetically active, so convincing on the phone that even she found herself believing every word he said and felt he was merely over-reaching himself.

Although he had bought toys for the children, given her money for clothes, his only extravagance was a smart grey suit for himself and a second-hand white Sierra car.

But the strain began to tell on her. The pace was getting out of hand. Now she found herself having to make promises on her own account, over-anxious to appease irate customers, sending messages to the fitters.

In the middle of one morning he rushed into the house, shouting at her. 'You stupid bitch, you had £800's worth of materials delivered to 81 Chester Street. I'll have to get it picked up again.'

'But it's part of their order.'

'I can't afford to let them have it yet. Bloody well leave that sort of decision to me. D'you want to wreck everything?'

The colour drained from her face. 'Have you any intention of finishing these jobs?'

'Don't be stupid. It's because we've more orders than we can manage, and I'm having to juggle everything.'

'Then why haven't you taken on more fitters?'

'Every new business has its growing pains,' he shouted.

'But I don't want you to cheat people,' she cried.

He caught her by the wrists.

'I'm doing all this for you,' he snarled, rising over her in a sudden paroxysm of rage. 'You don't understand how things are done.'

The very act of her cowering away seemed to goad him to start slapping her about her head, swinging his arms freely. She tried to duck and raised her forearms to protect herself from the blows, but only when she fell over a chair in her efforts to break away, and lay huddled sobbing on the floor did he step back, rubbing the palms of his hands over his shirt, breathing hard. 'It's your own bloody fault.'

After he had slammed the door and left, Sarah came and crouched beside her. 'Were you naughty, Mummy?'

Kathleen reached out a hand to her. But the child drew away, alarmed by the weeping shivering mass of her mother. Kathleen did not move. Her head rang, her ears and cheeks smarted and burned, her arms ached. After a while she crawled onto the sofa. 'I'll be all right in a minute, darling,' she mumbled to Sarah, who sat beside her sucking her thumb.

Then the phone rang. She dragged herself over to answer it.

'This is Mrs Parker,' said a deep contralto. 'You promised you'd be starting last Wednesday. A whole week has gone by. We're living out of packing cases. It can't go on like this. We've paid you £500.'

'I'll make a note of it, Mrs Parker,' she said huskily, putting the phone down to avoid further argument.

She made a cup of tea and drank it through lips swollen like orange segments, her ears clicking painfully when she swallowed. The bastard, she kept thinking. But it was her own fault. She knew the risk. She should have kept quiet.

There were more phonecalls. She felt heavy and chilled as if she had the flu, and wished only to crouch down in her chair. Most of the calls were new enquiries. It never ceased to amaze her that they showed no sign of abating. Only a few were complaints, wanting to know when work was to start or when it would be completed.

It was more of a reflex action than a positive decision to start responding differently to the phonecalls.

'I'm sorry but our order books are full for the time being. Please call back in a few weeks' time.' The more often she said it, the more she realised it wasn't altruism to save potential customers losing their money, or even revenge, but her own rejection surfacing at last. She grew stronger in her conviction, becoming disgusted with herself for ever having been party to any deception. But she remained unable to go beyond allowing herself this one demonstration, because she was also afraid.

She went upstairs to bathe her face in cold water, anxious that Vicky and David should not notice her pink swollen face when they came in from school, even though it would not be something unusual in their experience. It was a struggle to keep going that evening, to organise the preparation of the meal, restrain the children, remain affable.

When Mark came home he was whistling and exuberant, as if completely oblivious of what had happened earlier. He behaved towards Kathleen like an ever-loving husband, pecking her on the cheek, whirling round the kitchen. 'Hallo darling, hallo kids, how've you been, how was school, what were you doing today, how's my little Sarah?' He opened a paper bag he was carrying and produced a box of chocolates. 'Look what Daddy's brought you for afters.'

Perhaps children imagine all parents behave like this, she thought, dimly aware that her numbness seemed to be suppressing all indications of resentment as she struggled to concentrate on the cooking.

'We went to a museum today,' said Vicky, always prepared to engage her father seriously. 'We saw guns that had really really killed people.'

This piece of painful child perception went unnoticed. 'Great,' he said. He turned to Kathleen, for once vocal about the business. 'It's piling in like an avalanche. I got an order today to supply and fit a new housing estate. Forty-six houses. It's a killing.' His glee knew no bounds.

After the children were in bed and she had washed up, summoning up her last resources of energy, she hung onto the doorknob of the sitting-room, looking in on Mark sprawled before the television. 'I'm going to bed.'

'But it's only half-past nine.'

'I'm absolutely shattered.'

'So what have you been doing?' he asked, eyebrows raised disparagingly. 'I've been hard at it all day, organising the business, running from one job to the other, keeping the clients happy. You can't be that tired. Come and sit here and give us a cuddle.'

'You know perfectly well why I'm tired.'

'I don't know what you're talking about,' he retorted easily.

She had no intention of arguing and turned to drag herself upstairs. She surmised rightly that he would not stop her.

'You don't know what it's like to do a hard day's work,' he shouted after her.

She fell into bed and did not wake till the alarm rang at seven thirty.

Mark insisted she remain in the house to man the phone all day. He was not in the least concerned about the number of complaints. She did not demur, her resolution undermined by her depression. But she rang Linda.

Linda came round at once. As she listened, her lower lip dropped and her eyes widened. 'You know my feeling about the matter, Kath. If Harry so much as laid a finger on me, he wouldn't see me for skid marks. No man should treat a woman like that. If he's really conning all these poor bastards, we ought to go to the police.'

'We can't do that, Linda, please,' pleaded Kathleen. 'He's still my husband. I don't want him to end up in prison. There's got to be some other way.'

Linda shook her head. 'You can't go on like this. He treats you like dirt. You should get out before he does you a real injury.'

'Where would I go? How would I live, I haven't any money?'

'What about all his loot? There must be some lying around?'

'I wouldn't touch it if there was,' said Kathleen. 'It should be given back.'

'What are you paying at the supermarket with now?' cried

Linda. 'You know perfectly well none of this is going to go back unless you send it personally. You've got to have something. You can't go on like this.' She turned her head to listen. 'It's gone very quiet upstairs. What are those two up to?'

'D'you want a chocolate biscuit?' Kathleen called.

The two small girls came eagerly downstairs. For a moment their mothers stared, knowing something was amiss, till they realised the two had exchanged their clothes right down to their shoes, Tessa in Sarah's blouse and dungarees and Sarah in Tessa's dress.

'Who am I supposed to take home with me?' asked Linda as they munched their chocolate biscuits.

'Me,' announced Sarah. 'I'm Tessa.'

This was too much for Tessa. 'No, no,' she wailed, pulling Sarah's clothes off herself. 'Look, Tessa's inside.'

'Listen, Kath,' said Linda later, as she was leaving. 'If things look like getting rough, belt round to mine. If you can't, scream your head off, make sure the windows are open, somebody'll hear. I'll prime Harry. He'll sort Mark out. I know some women stick to a bastard because he's all they've got, and the devil you know's better than nothing, and all that crap. But I don't see how anyone can love a shit who treats them like a toilet roll.'

After they had gone, Kathleen made lunch for Sarah and herself. The idea of leaving Mark stuck in her throat like a fishbone. It was impossible to imagine herself apart from him, visualise life on her own with the children. Yet she felt she was clinging to the notion that the family should stand together as if it was a waterlogged, worm-riddled raft that was about to sink and carry her down into the depths. But she could not rid herself of a kernel of optimism. The devil she knew was merely misguided and needed enlightenment. There must be some way he could be dissuaded from his path.

David came home from school with a wooden box he had made in woodwork. To the expert eye it was clumsy, not even square, but it worked, and she felt proud of his handiwork and praised him. But when his father came home and he showed it to him, Mark grimaced, shook his head. 'You want to do better than that, David. Look how crooked it is, I don't call that very good.'

'Mummy said it was great.'

‘Women don’t know anything about woodwork.’

Kathleen saw she was doubly condemned by the remark; David now resenting her for having falsely raised his pride.

Throughout the evening she steeled herself to approach Mark. She churned over possible gambits in her head all during supper and getting the children to bed. How could she avoid antagonising him with her very first reference? Each time she thought of an opening, she could hear him instantly disparage it. She had never been able to out-argue him.

After the children were in bed and she came down to wash up, she found he had stacked all the dishes at one end of the table to create sufficient space to spread out notebooks and papers. In her head she could hear herself pointing out that he could have carried the dishes out into the kitchen. And his self-righteously indignant response; why didn’t you clear the table yourself before putting them to bed, when you know I’ve got all this work to do?

At least his mind would be on the subject, she thought, trembling as she swallowed a breath.

‘Some of the people on the phone are very rude...’

‘That’s why I’m reorganising everything,’ he said, not lifting his head from a list he was making. ‘So that we can keep them happy.’

She nerved herself to continue. ‘But you’ve taken hundreds of orders, and each one you’ve told you’ll start next week. How can you manage without taking on more fitters?’

‘I’m doing exactly that,’ he said, his lip curling with irritation. ‘I’m taking on two extra fitters, even though it’s an expense I can’t really afford.’

‘I hate having to lie to people.’

‘It’s not lying,’ he snapped. ‘It’s normal business practice. I had to take sufficient orders to make sure I could get the stuff cheap enough.’

‘But what happens if they sue?’

He flung his pen down and sat back. ‘For God’s sake, Kath, what’s wrong with you? We’ve only been at it a few weeks. I’m not properly organised yet.’

She wondered if she had been maligning him with her doubts, that he really intended to straighten out the confusion and fulfil all the orders. ‘It’s just that some of them are getting suspicious.’

‘Just keep telling them it’s the suppliers, that they’re behind with despatching our orders. It’s not our fault.’

‘You do intend to build all the kitchens, then?’

‘What d’you take me for?’ he snarled. Then he lowered his voice to a resigned wheedle. ’Look, stop bothering me, let me get on with this, I’ve masses to do.’

She knew he only used that tone of voice when he was hiding something. ‘Think of the risks,’ she said anxiously. ‘Think of the children.’

‘For God’s sake.’ His voice began to rise again. ‘I know what I’m doing. Can’t you see that I’m doing all this for the children, for all of us? Now leave me alone.’

She carried a trayload of dishes into the kitchen. She’d approached him all wrongly, she thought, crying into the washing-up water. She should have known she wouldn’t be able to get through. How had it got to this state? It hadn’t always been like this. Surely they had been able to communicate on the same level once? So where had it all gone wrong? When he lost his job at the agency, that had been the turning point. She had been pregnant with Vicky and David had been a toddler. There had been security with the advertising agency, a continuity to prop him up. No need for devious scheming. But that wasn’t true either, she thought. It was his scheming that had got him sacked. She wiped her eyes with the back of a wrist. Who wants to admit they’ve been a fool all along? He’d always been like this.

The next day, at about three in the afternoon, Mark came back to make some phonecalls. She was ironing in the kitchen. Sarah was watching a children’s programme. ‘Kath,’ he called, a sharp edge to his voice. He was holding the notepad for the lists kept by the telephone. ‘I don’t understand why there’s not been a single new order. The only ones are those I took. Have you been round with Linda? Wasting hours gossiping when I specially asked you to stay in?’

She shook her head, stiffening. ‘I had to go out shopping, not for long though. You can see I must have been here, to take all the complaints. Maybe... word’s got round.’

‘What do you mean, word’s got round? What about?’

She avoided his eyes. ‘That nothing gets done.’

He seized her by the wrist. 'There must have been more orders. They wouldn't have suddenly stopped. What have you been up to?'

'All I did was tell them the order-books were full. To ring back in a few weeks' time. I did it for your sake.'

'You what?' The words exploded from him.

'It's only until you're better organised.'

'You've done us out of thousands of quid,' he shouted, twisting her arm behind her and pinioning her as she struggled to get away. 'You stupid bitch.'

'Don't hit me,' she cried, as he pushed table and chairs out of the way. 'I did it for the best.'

'I'm going to fix you,' he snapped. He grabbed a kitchen knife and pointed it at her. 'Get upstairs.' As they passed he shut the sitting-room door on Sarah watching television.

'What are you going to do?' she wailed as he thrust her roughly up the stairs.

'I'm going to make sure you don't do any more interfering.'

She shivered. 'You're not going to kill me, are you?'

He pushed her across the landing. 'I'm not that stupid. Get undressed.'

'Why? Are you going to beat me?'

'Clothes off,' he snapped, waving the knife at her.

'I only did it to help,' she whimpered, as she began to undress. 'I don't want you to get into trouble.' Not knowing what else to do with them, she draped her skirt and blouse over the banisters. 'I don't want you to end up in prison.'

'I'm not going to end up in prison,' he snarled.

'Can't I keep my pants and bra on?'

'Get everything off.'

As she took them off, Mark reached up, unhooked the ring-latch of the loft and pulled the ladder down. 'We're going up into the loft.'

'What for?' she cried, paralysed with dread.

'Get up the ladder,' he shouted, waving the knife at her.

As her head rose through the hatch she hesitated. 'What about the light? There isn't a bulb.'

'You won't need it.'

Suddenly it dawned on her what he was going to do, and she

started to back down, ignoring the knife. But he was right behind her, head and shoulders thrusting under her buttocks, heaving her upwards. She fell over on her side onto the loft floor. As she tried to turn to stop him shutting the hatch, the ladder shot upwards, lifting her legs, knocking her aside. The hatch slammed, shutting her into darkness.

FOR A few moments there was silence in the interview room. Kathleen sat staring at Mark Clement like a medium possessed by an out-of-world presence, seeing nothing of what was in front of her.

'I fumbled frantically about in the dark trying to find the catch. But there was no lever on the inside, only the body of the lock, which was old-fashioned and heavy. I beat at it frenziedly, stamping with my feet on the hatch as heavily as I dared, and shrieking, Let me out, let me out. It remained immovable. I shouted and screamed myself hoarse, hysterical with rage and fear.. Why didn't I resist when I had the chance? Maybe he would never have dared use the knife. I threw myself down on the floor to put my eye to the thin chink of light round the edge of the hatch, but was sobbing and shaking so much I could neither see nor hear anything.

When I eventually calmed down enough, Mark's voice was just audible downstairs, talking on the phone.

Not a sound from the street outside penetrated the loft. A previous occupant of the house had been a photographer and had converted it into a dark-room, boarding the floor, and insulating and plastering the roof and sides. No need for a roof light, of course. And the hatch was very solid. So I was sealed off in complete and silent darkness.

I felt about the floor for something to prise at the hatch. But he must have known there was nothing up there except empty suitcases. Inside one case was a plastic coat-hanger. At the first attempt at inserting it near the lock it snapped. I discovered an old square of carpet. It smelled strongly of dust, but I dragged it over to the hatch to lie on. With one eye lined up exactly over the chink I could make out the Spanish tile patterns of the carpet down below on the landing. I heard Sarah's piping voice. It sounded as though she was saying, "Where's Mummy?" I seized the ladder and shook it,. yelling at the top of my voice. Suddenly there was a bang underneath. I stopped, lay flat on my stomach and looked through the crack. There was a dark shape there.

"Don't waste your breath," came Mark's voice just below me.

"In five minutes there'll be nobody here. I've packed the kids' clothes. I'm taking them to Isabel's."

Isabel was his sister.

"I'm sorry," I pleaded. "Please let me out. I won't do it again."

There was no answer, the dark shape had gone. "Please," I screamed. "Let me out. Please." I seized the ladder again, shook and rattled it in the desperate hope of breaking the catch. Then I threw myself down on the piece of carpet and lay sobbing and snivelling.

By the time I stopped, the silence was deathly. Not a sound came up through the chink. I went cold and rigid with fear. What was going to become of me? The blackness pressed tightly round, skinning me, reducing me to an aching bone or two and a tiny frightened mind. It was stuffily warm, but I longed to wrap myself in something for protection, tried the piece of carpet, found it too stiff and clumsy. I crawled round the ladder into a corner, jammed my back against the gritty brickwork of the two meeting walls, hugged my arms round myself. But the hairline of light drew me back to the hatch. I lay on my stomach, fitting my chest and hips onto the square of carpet, listened and watched. A thin draught fanned my eye. The telephone began to ring. Suppose he never came back? O God, I wept. Please make him come back.

Ordinary darkness can be threatening enough, but this was a heavy black space that extended all the way to infinity, pressing down on my back. It seemed filled with invisible, lurking threats. I listened intently, barely breathing, every tiny sound a footstep. Suddenly galvanised with terror, I crawled across the floor, waving my arms as if to fend off whatever it was. I dragged two suitcases into a corner, crashing my ankle painfully on the ladder, made a barricade of the cases and huddled behind them, pressing myself against the walls, staring wide-eyed. The faint glow leaking through the joints of the hatch billowed malignant shapes into the dark. My mind became my vision, inside out, black and smoking. Trying to take hold of it between my eyelids to crush it tight as a flea between thumb and forefinger, it would escape and loom inside me. Stop your nonsense, I shouted at it. The silence became a dense mass of tiny mocking sounds and I sat there petrified, hearing the stealthy rustle of movement, the slithering of a great mass approaching and the deep exhalation of carnivorous breath.'

Kathleen stopped, looked beseechingly at Mark Clement. 'I don't think I can go on any more tonight,' she said, her eyes rimmed with tears.

He looked at his watch. He felt as drained and tense as he could see she was. 'You must go on.'

'Why must I?' She took a tissue from her handbag, dabbed her eyes.

'Because you're still up there in that black hole. I want you to come out of it before you go home or you'll be reliving it over and over again.'

She looked at him, the tissue against her cheek, her lips loose. 'There are people I've told who refused to believe it.'

He shook his head. 'That was their problem.'

She sighed. 'You're right. It was a black hole. I didn't know what to expect. I was terrified his intention was to abandon me and I'd die up there.

'Each time the phone rang it brought a fragment of reality, a tiny bell of hope tinkled. Each time it ceased, the silence plumbed deeper than ever.

Then suddenly there were sounds below. Mark had returned and was talking on the phone. It was enormous relief just to have him in the house. I crawled back to lie on the carpet, an eye to the chink, revelling in every noise. Perhaps he hasn't abandoned me, I kept thinking.

He must have bought himself a takeaway. The smells of chips and fried chicken rose tantalisingly. There was even the coxy tang of the apple he ate afterwards, then the water boiling, the coffee powder he stirred into it, the milk added, I could smell them all. Surely he'll bring me something to eat, I kept thinking. I slavoured up there in the darkness, tortured by the smells.

He was on the phone several times. The television was on as well. Even that was a little reassuring. Then there were footsteps, a shadow passed beneath me, the bathroom door banged shut.

Suddenly there was a loud rasping noise close by in the darkness, like some giant creature clearing its throat, or the rafters rending as if the roof was about to collapse on top of me. It was terrifying before I realised it was only the ballcock releasing water into the tank. It galvanised me into banging on the hatch. "I want to use the lavatory, Mark," I shouted. "Please, please let me out." But there was no response. Pressing my face to the chink, I could hear him on the phone again. I lay there weeping silently, wondering what must he have told the children. They would be bound to be anxious, puzzled, however plausible he made the story.

Hearing him coming upstairs again was like a castaway on a desert island seeing masts appear on the horizon. Then, abruptly, the little reassuring crack of light went black.

I was so paralysed with fear no scream would come. It took some time for reason to point out that it only meant he'd gone to bed. At least he would be asleep just underneath me. I lay listening to the slowly diminishing drip in the water-tank.

It was ironic that in the absolute darkness my fear ceased. It must have been the reassurance of his presence in the house. I felt free to roam the loft, feeling my way about, measuring my domain, fingers creeping over the joints in the gable brickwork, hands sliding over the plaster. I found a solid bench against the far gable. On one end stood the water-tank, at the other end was a sink. When I turned the tap, water flowed. I made a cup with my hands to take a drink, wondering as I did, how long I could last on nothing but water. It gave me hope, that tap, plants lived for months on tap-water. Surely I could survive till somebody noticed my absence?

Then I banged my head on the slope of the ceiling. The stars behind my temples were spectacular, though more like fireworks. Do the blind see stars? But I was blind. And deaf, as far as the outside world was concerned. Only my skin was loud, like scraping sandpaper, limbs rubbing past each other or brushing against the walls, my feet padding on the floor. Together with my anxious voice questioning noisily inside my head.

Touch became like a newly discovered sense. I lay on the floor, half-dozing through the hours, half-forgetting my predicament, and traced out definitions of my body, making a mental silver line round limbs black as charcoal. My sense of scale grew wildly distorted, sometimes my body felt small as a figurine on a mantelpiece in the house in Collon. At other times my fingers went rambling across a whole county of flesh. My ankles had the hardness of a pony's fetlocks, me and D'Arcy in one of the dark stables, checking for swelling. A heel cupped in the hand was round as an apple, a Blenheim from the old orchard, that I craved to sink my teeth into and savour crisp succulent flesh breaking amongst my teeth. A thigh was like the bark of a young ash tree warm with sunshine which I wrapped my juvenile thighs round to climb up to find a nest. My breasts were the muslin bags of cream cheese hung to drain in the dairy, later squeezed to extract the last of the buttermilk. My nipples were black raisins that no amount of contorting could quite bring within reach of my black lips.

Restless, I became a nocturnal creature on the prowl, a crawling spider, arms waving like antennae, feet reaching out tentatively. The dark air brushed my skin like dry fluid. The black confinement made the sophistication of a mind obsolete. In this state all fears and anxieties fell into abeyance, their function redundant.

I found a stack of old newspapers. Shaking them out filled the air with dust. I laid some out in the farthest corner and squatted on them to relieve myself, tearing pieces to clean myself, bundling all the sodden paper into a parcel, trying to obliterate the smell.

I curled up on the carpet and tried to sleep. But it was hard and uncomfortable. The night air was colder, it felt tight round my bare body. I fetched more newspapers, opened them out and covered myself like a tramp on a park bench. The smell of the dust was sickly. Exhaustion brought fitful patches of sleep, interspersed with twisting about to find a comfortable position, and keep the newspapers from sliding off. Sometimes I woke to find myself crying, tears rolling down my cheeks like berries, dropping to become absorbed in the carpet. It might be like this to be dead, I thought. I dreamed in brilliant colour and light, and woke disappointed to find myself still in darkness.

There were tiny sounds from outside which filtered in, faintly recognisable as cars in the street, dogs barking, but scarcely noticeable against the louder noises inside my head. I could make soothing evocations of nostalgia that were endlessly hypnotic. Rubbing an ear created the hissing of waves on shingle, the drenching and the sucking of the tide. Tapping my teeth made the percussive background to old tunes that kept playing in my mind. Scratching my scalp was like the crackling of the hay when I used to climb over the bales to find somewhere quiet to read.

It was the impression of illumination that made me fully awake. However minute the light source, it blazed like fire through the cracks round the hatch. I rolled close to it and peered down, waiting, listening. Then the smells of food rose again, smells of milk and sugar on cornflakes so vivid I could feel them in my throat. The delicious scent of marmalade spread on buttered toast. I went across to the tap for a drink.

Nothing came out. I banged it, kept turning the knob. But there'd be water in the tank. I climbed onto the bench, stood up carefully, reached in. Empty. It didn't make sense. How could there suddenly be no water? How could it have been emptied without my knowing? The bastard, I shouted out. The bloody bastard. He must have turned off the mains and left a tap on to drain the tank during the night. Then real fear returned. The fear that he intended to leave me up here to die. Clinging onto a pipe, I leaned right into the tank, hips pivoting on the rim. There was an inch in the bottom. I brought my face down and sucked at the water. Save it, I thought. Just drink a little at a time. My hair had fallen into the water and wet strands stuck to my shoulders, liquid trickled down my breasts. My hunger was agonising.

When the front door slammed a shudder ran through the whole house. I wept at the sense of abandonment. Sometimes I lay by the crack of light round the hatch, sometimes I prowled about. By now my eyes had adjusted to the tiny amount of light let in round the hatch and could make out the entire shape of the loft. Downstairs the phone kept ringing. There was knocking on the front door. I shouted, but to no avail of course.

Sometimes when the phone rang the voices on the line came clearly into my head, complaining, haranguing. The slightest trifle of sound wove into intricate possibilities, hallucinating people into the loft, irate customers clamouring and urging the calling-in of the fraud squad, Linda and Clare climbing up the ladder to discuss what should be done, even my aunt arriving, with that familiar lilt to her voice which reminded me of my mother as she exclaimed, poor Kathleen, look how thin she's become.

I thought of myself as a vast black body filling the entire space, bulging into every corner of the loft like a trapped balloonic Gulliver. But the hardness of the floor kept insisting that my bones were coming through my flesh. The dryness of my throat and the constriction of my empty stomach contrived to suggest that the decay of death was already taking place. The telephone bell rang with the urgency of the ambulance siren hurrying to take my lifeless corpse in the hope of resuscitation. I grew afraid to touch my body, certain that to grip my breasts would make them stay deflated, that to rest a hand on my hip would make it sink in as if the flesh had no more resilience than damp sand.

I lost all sense of time. Sometimes the cracks of light were there like golden wires, noises rose from below like the pick and shovel of rescuing miners coming closer, phones trilled all round me, ringing up the chimney breasts, hiding in the suitcases, voices hovered in the air, smells rose like pungent gases and swelled into the great abandoned dining-hall of my stomach.

Sometimes when all was black and silent, I lay collapsed like a person so ill that dying has become irrelevant. The feelings that amounted to myself, or the person I was accustomed to being, no longer had any account. I was just a jumble of random thoughts and reactions like a drawerful of odds and ends that ought to be sorted out and most of them discarded. It became impossible to think in sentences. Pictures would no longer remain intact in my imagination, emotions became unfeelable, thoughts were like droves of leaves falling in random swirls, and I was rushing about, gathering them up in armfuls, trying to stick them back on the trees.

All of a sudden this state of disintegration was pierced by a terrible rending noise, as if the house was breaking up. It still took a while for realisation to dawn that it was the tank. Water was hissing and splashing into it again.

Before I could make sense of it, there came scratching noises at the hatch. Then suddenly light burst upwards like a great fountain of white paint splashed over the walls. The ladder creaked noisily as it began to descend. I had to squeeze my eyes shut, the light was so brilliant.

Mark's voice entered the roseate tent of my head. It sounded cold and terribly precise. "You'd better come down."

At first nothing would move, thought and action all stuck fast. I lay like someone paralysed by a stroke, frantic to communicate but bereft of speech. Then I managed to crawl across to the hatch.

The light was searing. My first thoughts were, thank you, Mark, thank you ever so much, thank you for letting me out and saving me from death. There was nothing but gratitude and relief in my mind as I climbed backwards down the ladder. The light was dizzying, loud as a fanfare.

"You're filthy," his voice spoke casually out of the blinding light. "You'd better have a bath. The children'll be back from school in an hour. I told them you'd been in hospital."

I stood swaying in the glaring light, still blinded, head spinning. My throat was so dry I could only croak. "How long have I been up there?"

"I don't know," he replied irritably. I haven't counted. "A few hours maybe."

Bastard, I thought, feeling my way to go downstairs. Rough counting up in the loft suggested several breakfasts and suppers had passed. I gripped the banisters tightly. I felt faint and was still blinded by the light.

"Where are you going?" he called, coming down behind me.

You'd think he'd know, I thought. It must be obvious.

"There's no point in ringing the ..." His voice tailed away as he saw me go into the kitchen.

I opened the fridge and squatted on the floor, selected cheese, cold sausage, a tomato. But I could not cram them in ravenously as I longed to. My mouth seemed to have lost its aperture and most of its function. I could only lick at the flavours, nibble, take small bites, sip milk out of the bottle, stick a tongue in the yoghurt.

Mark came in and threw a dressing-gown over me.

"Where's Sarah?" I asked, a cheese-cracker flaking down my chin.

"I'm going to fetch her now."

The phone rang while he was gone, then suddenly stopped and voices began to float in the air. I realised he'd installed an answerphone. Despite eating so little, my stomach ached as if packed with rubble. When I saw myself in the mirror he was right, I was filthy, grey with dirt. I went upstairs to have a bath and wash my hair. I lay a long while in the water, reflecting on all the little pleasures of bathing, of being suspended and cuddled in the hot liquid, all the trickling and slurping noises echoing inside the enamel walls, the smells of soap and shampoo. It was amazing to be alive.

It felt strange to wear clothes, the fabrics coarse on my skin, waistbands and straps constricting like wires.

"I'm glad you're better, Mummy," said David when they came back.

Vicky hugged me and wouldn't let go. "Were you very ill?"

I held her. "How many days was I away?"

"Four," she replied pityingly, as if appreciating that the sick mightn't notice the passage of time.

It felt like an immeasurable gift to have the children restored. I was still consumed with gratitude at my release. While imprisoned in the loft the future had been an unlikely prospect. But sitting there overwhelmed with the pleasure of my children's company, I felt a change come over me like the passing of a dark cloud. The seeds of resolution had been taking root of their own accord. Whatever the future was, it had to be somewhere away from Mark.

'I'VE never told anyone what it was like in the loft before.' Kathleen rubbed her brow. 'It's been weighing on me like a guilty secret.'

He noted the brief hooked smile again. Sometimes it was like a small throw-away mannerism, a worn keepsake, the jaded hope of the insecure, or the twitch of a stump echoing the gesture of its amputated limb.

All the while she had been recounting her story, melodies from Scheherazade had curled through the back of his mind. Continuing even as one half of him considered her behaviour, gauging the degree of her objectivity, how much she might be exaggerating for effect or from paranoia, while the other half had been shocked and outraged at her treatment.

What kind of bastard would do that to a woman like... he turned back a mental page to regard her physical appearance... what kind of woman was she? Could she have goaded her husband with plodding insensitivity or exasperated him beyond endurance with crass stupidity? But this was no vacuous face, however haggard, there were dimples of sensuality and the leaven of intelligence. It seemed more likely that she had unwittingly tied herself to a psychopath.

He sat back in his chair, reflecting. 'You underestimate yourself. You've shown that you could change. You decided to take positive action, something you hadn't always done before. Isn't that good?'

She frowned. 'It sounds unnatural when you talk about me like that.'

'Then let's not talk about it any more tonight.' He put his notepad on the table, and the gesture of terminating the session made her stand up, gathering her handbag, straightening her clothes.

'I didn't realise it was late,' she exclaimed, looking at her watch. 'I've taken up so much of your time.'

He got up to open the door for her. 'Have you far to go?'

'It's about fifteen minutes' walk,' she replied. She hesitated. 'I didn't give the clinic my real address. I hope you understand?'

'I'm beginning to. I imagine you feel at risk even walking home through the streets. I would have offered you a lift, but I don't own a car.'

She frowned as they went downstairs. 'There aren't many men who don't drive. Were you banned?'

He laughed, turning towards the office door at the foot of the stairs.

She jerked a hand up to her mouth, paling with anxiety. 'That must sound very rude. I'm sorry. I'm so clumsy.'

He turned back. 'I don't find you at all clumsy. I think you're a very attractive person.' He patted her arm in a brief paternal gesture. 'I use a car so rarely living in the centre of the city, I gave mine away to my eldest daughter. I'll see you tomorrow.' He smiled and went into the office.

He thought of those words, an attractive person, as he walked home, not sure if he was embarrassed at their gaucheness or their presumption. It might be fundamental to his work that he try to restore clients' confidence, let them see themselves at least as wholesome, normal, real as anyone else, but sometimes he alarmed himself at the injudicious manner in which his more spontaneous comments emerged. For clients might out of their own necessity read significances in them other than he intended.

There was a refrain that often bothered him: the unloved become unlovable. Love being the elixir of life. The salvation to all their problems was unattainable because their condition of desperation had weakened them to a state of unattractiveness. Where were the princesses to kiss the toads into princes, or vice versa?

It was disturbing sometimes to sit across a room and talk to sad, depressed people, aware of this factor. As if there was an urge in him to lean forwards, take them in his arms, these people misshaped by their isolation and unhappiness, kiss them and whisper the words they longed to hear, when personally they held no attraction. It was like imagining offering to a lonely gay the comfort of his body, no worse than what he allowed doctors to do to it, except that the very thought of intimacy with a man was repugnant. But he knew what this inclination really amounted to. It was to have the power over experience. Like playing God.

The evening was balmy, a light breeze brushing the leaves, the streetlamps like fragments of moon papering the trees. From their raised brick beds cotoneaster and stachia threw dusky sprays, leaves dark as mussel shells. The looming tower of the Catholic Cathedral was lightly hued with the first flushes of its nightly illumination.

He walked home among young bedmates with hands strategically cupped, older-fashioned lovers with their legs in unison, elderly couples trembling with optimism. Traffic rushed over the underpass in a stream of red and white lights.

The music he planned to play was ghosting in his head: Satie's Gymnopédies. The ultimate evocation of nostalgia. He saw the lights on in his house as he crossed the dark sipping river. To find Madeleine there released a twinge of irritation he had no wish to admit to.

Her lips closed over his mouth like the two halves of a ripe peach. 'You're late back, darling,' she said, robust in her black skirt and russet floral blouse, mascaraed eyes hooded with desire.

'I had an interesting case,' he said, speaking eagerly as if hoping they might have a discussion. It was the nearest he could get to suggesting he did not feel like it tonight, since in her state of anticipation refusal would be tantamount to insult.

'I'm not going to tell you about my tribulations with the transport plan,' she murmured, breathing heavily, one hand at his crotch, the other undoing zips and buttons. 'Nor am I going to tell you about the other side scuppering our latest scheme to raise cash for housing development.' Clothing slid from her ample form, fell shrivelled on the floor. 'Neither am I going to tell you about the way the new member for Lakenham ward called me an out-dated maverick.'

The hypocrisy was his, of course, he thought grudgingly at his own rapid arousal. .

When she lay asleep afterwards he eased himself away and stood looking down on her. With her head thrown back, her dark hair tumbled about her forehead, the ample flesh drained off her cheeks and jaw, she seemed refreshed and pretty. Why are we so inured to the importance of youth and beauty, he thought? Soothing ourselves with the symbolic salves of vitality to hide the crumbling ahead. He sat naked at his Steinway.

He felt himself settle into the Gymnopédies as if sinking satisfyingly into a warm bath. Notes struck incorrectly or out of sequence or out of time, which so jarred the perfectionists, never registered with him because in his head he only heard the actual music. Had they known this they might have asked, why bother to play the piano at all? A question which would have completely mystified him, since he wasn't playing it for them. But among the neighbours as a whole, the majority favoured his playing the Satie pieces because they were quiet.

Tears clogged the rims of his eyes, as they were wont with certain music. Later he moved into the Gnossiennes. These were sounds that he wished never to end. He would have carried them far into the night, the nostalgia of long-departed, half-fulfilled promise, had not a tumbler of scotch floated across his vision on the end of a bangled wrist projecting from a white sleeve.

Madeleine was tone-deaf. To her his playing was flamboyant, free-flowing, theatrical. She admired his confidence. She could recognise the shape of the pieces, the emotion therein. She also realised his need to play, that it was his only relaxation.

Her replaced skirt rustled as she sat on the bed. He drank a mouthful of the whisky, played a Reverie and some Pensées. Then he put the lid down, picked up the glass and stood up. Madeleine smiled, shiny white teeth seeming to gleam with the pleasure of having recently sunk into the muscle of his shoulder. 'You still have the body of a young man.'

He thought of replying: "And you have the body of a voluptuous tyrant." But thought better of it. Her sensitivity sometimes lay in wait to be trodden on like a diminutive creature lurking in the carpet pile. He sat beside her on the bed.

She took his face in her hands, arching her body over him, nibbled his nose. 'I'm an idealist too, you know.' Perhaps she had sensed his thoughts. 'It's not my fault that the democratic institution is a hoary old board-game that requires much boring footwork, not to mention sycophancy. I have to win sometimes or there's no point in playing.'

'Is that all it's for?'

'Why do you play the piano?'

He drank off the rest of his whisky. 'I think words are like card-tricks. To fool us. Words make excuses, they cover up feelings and emotions as if they're frightened of them. They beggar them the way accountants destroy our pleasures with their figures. Music is the only uncomplicated and direct way I know of expressing what I feel.'

She laughed. 'Is that why you can't say you love me? And hogwash me with the excuse that men can't manage the same verbal exposure of their feelings as women can? Well, I don't mind if it means that men write such beautiful music. Women don't need to.'

He felt guilty then that he could not say that he loved her. He got up intending to fill his empty glass. 'Love is only a paper word. To decorate the rudimentary. Or to cover up the cracks.' He held out his hand. 'Where's your glass?'

She stood up too. 'I must go, darling.' She put her arms round him. 'I don't mind your cynicism. The odd word would be enough for me.'

'But I'm always trying to speak my feelings. Every trivial little word is recognising us as we stand here, our importance to each other, whatever else may happen, however fate might intervene.'

She frowned. 'This philosophising is too much for me at this hour. Are you trying to tell me something?'

He laughed, surprised himself at his outburst. 'Life isn't exactly permanent, is it?'

She gave him one last hug. 'I don't want to think about that. Don't forget we're going to the theatre the night after tomorrow.'

After she had gone he fetched a dressing-gown from the bathroom and returned to the piano, calling back echoes of the Gymnopédies.

Later he went to refill his glass. He cleared an old Guardian off one end of the sofa and found his tabby cat Mo curled up beneath it. Mo was the only cat he had ever met that answered to her name, responding to no other word. He sat stroking her, browsing through his notes.

Was he taking Kathleen September's case too slowly? Suppose her husband found out where she had moved again? Her practical problems looked to need as much attention as her emotional ones. Now that he was getting the picture, his concern had begun to push aside the main purpose of the assessment.

But there was plenty of time for that. He didn't want to rush her. It was always preferable to allow clients time to develop self-awareness at their own pace, the better to understand what fears were eating them away. So many people with problems simply wanted to be told what course they should take, preferring to rely on the facilitator rather than themselves. As he well knew, counselling itself could create a dependence.

Her eyes were unusual, he thought. That darker rim of olive. Did all the Irish have green eyes? He kept hearing the faint dip in the bellies of her vowels in the back of his mind as they softly enunicated her appalling story.

The phone rang.

It was Nicole. 'Hi, Dad. How are you?' Her voice sounded tired. 'I'm all right,' she continued. 'Working hard. How are you?' She's asked that already, he noted, expectant. 'It's always exhausting living a hectic life,' she added. There were pauses as she circled round the cliches of opening a conversation down the phone.

It crossed his mind that it was probably money. 'Something up?' he joked. 'Don't tell me you're pregnant?'

There was a gasp from the other end, then a choking wail. 'How did you know?'

'Aha,' he exclaimed in mock anger. 'Never darken my door again, the disgrace would be too much.'

There was a silence. 'Are you really angry?'

'You know I'd love to be a grandfather. D'you want to talk about it?'

There was another silence. 'I'm sick as mud about it. The doctor accused me of missing a pill, said it often happens. I all but shrieked at him that I took the bloody things every bedtime, like good little girls kneel to say their prayers lest they're struck dead in the middle of the night. Some all-night party I expect, he said, looking down his three-inch nose at all students. Stupid bastard. Anyway,' she sighed. 'It's too late to start blaming anyone. Terence's predictable response is to marry. But I don't want to get married. I mean Terence is fine, but imagine being tied down for life to a man who sings madrigals every Tuesday and Thursday evening forty-nine weeks a year, and cannot begin the day without eating a kipper. I know it's fashionable for girls to have babies on their own, but it would arrive bang in the run-up to my finals. How can I sit exams with a baby chewing my chest? But I hate the idea of adoption, of someone else having my baby. I mean, it'll be mine. And about an eighth Terence's, in my book. You told me in law a bastard starts off being all its mother's. Then how would I get a job with a small child dogging my heels? And small children need their mothers, don't they? Everyone keeps saying, abortion's easy as picking out a winkle with a pin, and you soon get over it. But when I think of that tiny dependent creature growing inside me, I'd feel like Richard III arranging for the little princes to be strangled in the Tower. And suppose I'd had an abortion or had it adopted, and then later we decided to get married? We'd always be looking back, regretting. But if I did as Terence suggests and married him now, I'd feel my arm was being twisted. I don't know what to do, Dad.' The tears flowed at the other end of the phone.

'You've certainly run rings round the reasons,' he said thoughtfully. 'Shall I play the devil's advocate and suggest other angles? Such as that what you have inside you is no more than a tiny package of genes, in no way a person. It's nothing but a model of a human being in kit-form. But what about priorities? Who comes first in all this? You're the here and now. And remember, it was a mistake. Come and talk. Bring Terence too. I didn't know he sang madrigals. I promise not to try to persuade you in any particular direction. I mean I could hire a housekeeper and the child could live here with me...'

She gave a tearful laugh. 'I couldn't do that to you, Dad. I might come down. I don't mind about particular directions. In fact at the moment I almost need someone to tell me what to do. I'll let you know.'

His mood had changed. The vulnerability of women to their fertility could never go away, contraception no more than a flimsy barricade. Poor Nicole. It was so easy to be an immune male. It was as if one half of society were prone to a dread disease that the other half were safe from. He played the Beethoven Emmanuel Sonata. He felt inspired. Always hearing the pure note before any misaligned finger hit a wrong key insulated him from self-consciousness. Whenever he typed a letter, flourishing all ten fingers up and down the QWERTY board, the result was not unlike Esperanto. Perhaps that should have warned him.

He went blithely to bed.

'IT'S INCREDIBLE.' Linda's cheeks were hollow, her eyes glittering like marbles. 'I can't take it in.'

They were standing in the kitchen. The kettle had already boiled, sat ignored, breathing steam.

'I knocked at the house several times, thought you must be out shopping. When I saw Mark yesterday he said, pi-faced as a politician, Kath's coming home tomorrow, been in hospital for a check-up, kids are over at my sister's. I thought it queer you hadn't told me. But the last thing I dreamed was that you were shut up in the loft all that time. Why didn't you shout and scream for help?'

Kathleen's voice still hadn't returned to normal. 'The loft's soundproof. It's all insulated and lined. He wouldn't have put me up there otherwise.' She switched the kettle on to boil again.

'But to imprison you for four days without any food? What kind of man'd do a thing like that? Your David told my Barry you were in hospital. Course Barry never told me, did he? Or I'd have gone there with a bag of grapes. Except you wouldn't have been there.' Linda ran a hand over her arm. 'My God, I still can't believe it.'

'There's nothing wrong with me, Linda, is there?' Her voice started to rise. 'I'd have told you if I was going to hospital, wouldn't I?'

'But how did he get you into the loft?'

Kathleen chewed her lips as she poured out the coffee. 'He had a knife. I was so frightened and he was slapping me about, I didn't realise what he was up to.'

'To leave you up there in the dark, with no clothes...' Linda lifted her arms in speechless amazement. 'How can you be so calm after what he's done to you? I'd be running round screaming blue murder, I'd call the police, I'd see a solicitor. He's dangerous. He should be locked up. If you don't do something, I will.'

'Don't go on at me, Linda. It was a horrible experience. But where's the proof if I went to the police? They'd believe him rather than me, you know him.'

'But you can't let him get away with it,' cried Linda angrily.

'I know.' Kathleen nodded, her eyes brimming with tears. 'So

I've made up my mind.'

'You have?' exclaimed Linda, clapping her hands. 'You've seen the light at last. Are you ready? Have you packed?'

Kathleen pulled off a piece of kitchen-roll to dab her eyes. 'I can't just leave with three children. I haven't anywhere to go.'

'Stay with us. We'll manage. Harry'll shove a boot through Mark's face if he tries anything.'

Kathleen shook her head. 'Thanks, Linda, but it wouldn't be fair on you. There's barely room for four of you, let alone four of us. And Harry'll be at work much of the time. Mark'd do something, I know he would. I've got to get far away, somewhere he can't find us.'

'You ought to see a solicitor.'

Kathleen stiffened. 'A solicitor?'

'Don't look so worried.' Linda put an arm round her. 'My sister used a good bloke last year for her divorce. I'll ring her up this evening, get his name and we'll fix an appointment. Cheer up. You'll be out of this soon. I'll do everything I can to help, you know that.'

Kathleen sagged against her, tears welling along her eyelids. 'I hate it. It's the end of everything, isn't it? The end of the family, it's all spoiled, all gone wrong.'

'Come on, you're not going back on me, are you?'

Kathleen shook her head. 'When I see him now, a shiver goes up and down my spine as if I'm confronting a cobra.' She brushed dislodged hair out of her eyes.

'He'll end up in jail, that man. He doesn't give a damn for anybody.'

Kathleen's face screwed up, squeezing out the tears. 'That's what's so horrible,' she wailed. 'That anybody could be like that, somebody I loved. I can't believe he was like this all along, but maybe I just refused to face it. I always wanted to believe in him.'

Foosteps were coming down the stairs.

'Mummy,' said Tessa, standing in the doorway wearing some of Sarah's clothes.

'Not again,' groaned Linda.

'My clothes all wet,' Tessa said, writhing at the prospect of further revelations.

‘You didn’t...?’ her mother began.

Sarah appeared behind Tessa, dressed in her own, though different garments. ‘We played washing-machines,’ she announced, a forefinger resting on her lower lip. ‘It’s all right. In the bathroom.’

‘Why?’ Linda raised her eyebrows. ‘On second thoughts, I don’t want to know. It’s time we went home. I’ll bring back Sarah’s things later.’ She gripped Kathleen’s arm, dropping her voice. ‘I’ll see you tomorrow. No weakening, mind. Any trouble, for God’s sake scream and I’ll come round with a poker.’

Kathleen always felt overpowered by Linda’s brand of forcefulness.

Throughout the rest of the morning the phonecalls arrived at regular intervals. Dutifully she logged them. Mark didn’t come back for lunch. The phone rang again while she was giving Sarah her lunch. A piping male voice asked for Mr September. ‘He’s not here at present,’ replied Kathleen. ‘Can I help?’

‘My name is Beales. My kitchen was booked for two weeks ago. Nothing happened. Then I was promised it a week ago, then it was to come yesterday. Nothing came. By coincidence, Mrs September, I met someone else who had paid for one of your husband’s kitchens and not received it. What I’d like to know is, are we ever going to get our kitchens, or is your husband a con merchant?’

For a moment Kathleen clutched the phone frozen with indecision. ‘A con merchant?’ she echoed to give herself more time. ‘What d’you mean?’

‘You know what I mean, Mrs September. In other words, is your husband a crook? He put across a very favourable scheme, prices far cheaper than any others for very high quality. He has a wonderful patter, sounds very convincing and businesslike. Otherwise we wouldn’t have paid up in full. Normally I understand only a deposit is required in these transactions, but he was insistent that we would have our kitchens the next day.’

For a moment she wavered. Then the old instincts pushed in. She could not betray Mark, she could not be the one to undo him.

‘I’m sorry, Mr Beales. We’ve been badly let down by the suppliers. A strike at the factory. I believe it’s has been settled and we should get deliveries early next week. I’ll get my husband to ring you this evening.'

'Mrs September, I'm afraid you have the same silver tongue as your husband. How can we be sure?'

'Mr Beales, I don't think you should say things like that. We'll do our best to speed things up, and I can only say that I'm very sorry for the delay.'

She put the receiver down. There was a clammy sweat over her skin and she was trembling. The sooner she got out the better, she thought. Every moment she remained meant she was further contaminated. Here she was lying just like him. The whole venture was trundling along like a runaway train, gaining speed, impossible to stop now, and she'd be trapped on board if she didn't jump soon. And Mr Beales had revealed something she did not know; that Mark was getting the full price out of people. They were as gullible as he was crooked.

There was another phonecall just as Vicky and David came in from school. The voice was elderly, quavering. 'I want to cancel my order for a fitted kitchen, my name is Horsford.' The children were chattering, dumping their bags, getting themselves drinks, making it difficult to hear. 'I should like my money back please.'

'I shall have to ask my husband about it, Mrs Horsford,' replied Kathleen. 'Did you sign a contract?' She didn't intend the question to sound like a threat, merely asking out of curiosity.

'I didn't understand...' the old lady began. Then a different voice interrupted, male, harsh.

'Listen here, you, my mother's an old woman, a bit foolish, over eighty. This man September pushed his way into her house and persuaded her to have a kitchen she can't afford and doesn't need, and went off with half her savings. So I want her money back, understand? I'll break his bloody neck if I don't get it. She was tricked into signing that contract, she didn't know what she was doing. I'll be round this evening.' He put the phone down.

Kathleen leant against the wall. Her heart was thumping, her head ringing as if she had been punched.

She saw Vicky standing in the doorway with a glass of orange squash in her hand, regarding her. 'Was that Daddy you were talking to?'

'Somebody who wanted to speak to him,' Kathleen replied,

aware of the acutely-developing suspicion in one so young. 'Did you have a good day at school?'

'Me and Carol painted a giant rainbow horse.' Vicky followed her mother into the kitchen, chatting away about school as if anxious to paste over her unease at any further risk to her home security. Kathleen got her to clear the table while she started supper.

When the front-door bell rang Kathleen froze in fright, afraid it might be Mr Horsford. She stood listening, one hand on her chest, as David ran to open the door. But it was a friend of his arriving to show off his new bike. She was even more relieved when Mark came back, however uncomfortable and tense his presence made her feel.

She began to tell him about the complaining phonecalls and Mr Horsford, but he cut her off. 'I've rented an office in the city and I've taken on a secretary. Just refer calls to her. I'll put the number by the phone.'

She couldn't help feeling the stab of rejection, that she'd failed him.

'Your refined little soul won't have to suffer any more stabs of conscience, darling,' he sneered. 'It's going to cost a lot, but since you can't handle a few little problems for me while I'm out working my butt off to make you comfortable, I haven't much choice, have I?'

Cheeks flushed, she continued the preparation of supper. Half of her was trying to continue functioning as if nothing had changed. The other half was burning like a furnace. Why didn't she do as Linda had suggested, leave now? What was the point of hanging on a moment longer?

Mark came over to her, his proximity setting her nerves jangling. 'What are we having?'

'Cauliflower and bacon in cheese sauce, and a gooseberry pie I made this morning.'

'You don't need to keep up this pinching and scraping now we've got money,' he exclaimed. 'Let's go out tonight. We'll go out to Buffalo Bill's and have steaks. What do you say?'

She put aside her annoyance at having spent an hour preparing a meal, as she saw the idea sweep the children into a state of excitement. She covered the food with clingfilm, put it into the fridge, went upstairs to put on a dress and change the children. Was this a spur-of-the-moment ploy to avoid a confrontation with Mr Horsford, she wondered as they drove off in the Sierra with its clinical plastic smell.

The restaurant had been designed on the basis that anything American has to be brash, over-emphasised and loud. In this case it was related to the pioneer days, as if America remained stuck among the Western movie myths. The interior was mock rough-hewn timbers and the waitresses wore stetsons and chaps over bare legs. Coloured lights flickered to square-dance music. The children were enthralled. They were the only children there. 'You'll have to be very grown-up,' Mark said to them.

Tonight, thought Kathleen, surprised herself at how detached she felt, Mark is playing at being father. Cynical recognition of his motivations had suddenly become second-nature. He was creating the reassurance that he was a family man. It was particularly unnerving in the light of her intention to break it all up. It was even worse that he kept trying to catch her eye. The only way she could survive the evening was to drink more than her share of the bottle of wine he ordered. She could see him eyeing her glass disapprovingly.

The children had beefburgers and french fries soused in tomato ketchup. 'Looks like blood,' exclaimed their father as it squirted out from its plastic container.

David laughed. 'Or the paint they put on letterboxes.'

The pragmatic Vicky looked anxious. 'I don't think I want any,' she said.

'Never listen to men, darling,' said her mother, daunted by the size of her steak. 'They're always pulling girls' legs.'

'But what would they do without them?' Mark smiled lasciviously at Kathleen, quite unaware how his flirting made her curdle inside.

'Do without girl's legs?' echoed David, learning how being literal could raise a laugh.

Sarah sat on Kathleen's knee, too over-tired to eat. David and Vicky had milk-shakes in tall glasses, angled straws protruding like feelers. They ate slowly, distracted by the coloured lights flashing over the buffalo horns on the walls and the paintings of cowboys whirling lariats on rearing horses. Waitresses came dimpling with prescient maternity to bring Sarah titbits, scrambled egg and biscuits. Kathleen knew her children were attractive, but it annoyed her to see the waitresses thinking, such a lovely family. If only they knew, she thought, hazy with wine, riddled with guilt, as Mark continued to throw out charm in handfuls, the apparently perfect husband and father.

The children consumed ice-creams that were like confections of tinsel and coloured ribbons, and Kathleen had a brandy. Oh God, she thought when the bill was brought and Mark dealt ten pound notes like cards onto the plate. That's money that belongs to Mrs Horsford and Mr Beale and all the rest. I've eaten it knowingly, allowed my children to, I'm an accessory to the crime. The brandy burned in her throat. She felt tipsy as they drove home.

'Can we go to a restaurant where they set fire to your food next time?' asked David.

'Set fire to the food?' scoffed Vicky. 'Nobody would eat it.'

'We'll have to show her, won't we?' laughed Mark.

When Kathleen came downstairs from reading Vicky and Sarah a story, Mark met her in the hall. 'You're looking delicious tonight, darling,' he said, slipping an arm round her waist. 'Bright-eyed and pink-cheeked, utterly irresistible.'

Flushed with booze more like, she thought, and trembled with ghosts of fear as they ascended the stairs, reminded of the last time, of the condemned mounting the scaffold. But this time he was leading her with flattery and adulation. The prospect filled her with loathing, but she felt too drunk to care. How hollow his words of love sounded as he kissed her and undressed her.

How could she lie passive beneath this man? How could she accept his cock rammed into her guts, syringing her with seeds, this man who thought so little of her that he could inflict pain and terror without a second thought? Why wasn't she kicking him off, screaming at him to get out of her sight? Why wasn't she shouting out that she despised him?

She knew it was fear. She didn't want him to hurt her again. It was easier to acquiesce. Besides, there were still vestiges of the old comfort in his holding and stroking her. But she couldn't help thinking of whores selling the use of their bodies. So tonight she was a whore. The payment was peace. Did whores lie absolutely still, just let the man bounce up and down on them? She could not manage that. It was like someone throwing a ball at her. It was automatic to reach out and catch it. Her hips responded to his thrust, her own cravings rose. She thought of the fear that a woman being raped must feel as her body was invaded. But she wasn't being raped, she had acquiesced. She just didn't care.

Mark lay heavily across her, inert as a corpse. If only he were dead... She caught her breath then at the intensity of the thought, guilt screaming like last-minute brakes. How could she wish anyone dead? But death represented the grant of freedom from persecution. That was all he represented now. Persecution. Inside her an army was invading. At least that was as doomed to failure as Napoleon's troops advancing on Moscow, for she was two days from her period. How lucky men were not to have a complicated body with a monthly circus side-show where if a man knocked down a painted target with his pellet his woman could be rewarded with a teddy bear she didn't want.

She was half-drifting off to sleep when there came a loud knocking on the front door. She turned her head to read the clock as Mark stirred. Somehow she had expected it to be at least midnight, but it was only nine-thirty. 'I'll go down,' she said, as Mark rolled over, grumbling. The knocking persisted as she wrapped her robe round herself. Could it be Linda, she wondered?

A large scowling man stood on the doorstep.

'Where's Mr September?' He wore a black leather jacket. On the end of long arms swung hands red as hams. 'I come round earlier but there was nobody in.'

'He's gone to bed,' she began uncertainly. 'He's had a busy day.'

'I'll bet he has and all,' the man sneered. 'Conning more old biddies out of their savings.' He reached inside his jacket and produced a piece of paper. 'I've come round for my mother's money. Just you go and get him out of bed, then there won't be any trouble.'

'It's late,' she said. 'You should go to the office in the morning. All business is done there. This is our home.'

The man moved forward and Kathleen stepped back as before an advancing steamroller. 'Your husband came into my mother's home to do his business, so I reckon I'm entitled to come into his. Especially as he smooth-talked the stupid old dear into giving him the money she's going to need for her funeral expenses. I'm not going to have anyone of my family put in a pauper's grave. I'm a patient man, missus. I don't want any truck with a member of the fair sex. Be a sensible woman and fetch him.'

As she turned to comply there to her surprise was Mark, coming down the stairs in his dressing-gown. 'What's the trouble?' he asked coldly.

'Here's the trouble,' growled the man, shoving the paper at him. 'You cancel this and give us the money back.'

Mark took it and read it. 'What's your name?'

'Horsford, same as hers.'

'Have you any means of identification?'

The man patted his pockets angrily. 'I don't need identification. There's my mother's name there.'

'That's what you say,' retorted Mark. 'Why should I believe you? You could have stolen this. You expect me to give money to a total stranger? And you're threatening me as well? I think the police would be interested in this.' He turned towards the phone.

'Here you.' Horsford lurched forward, brushing Kathleen aside as if she was no more than a door ajar. He grabbed Mark by the shoulder. 'You lay off, or I'll fix you.'

Mark spun round, knocking his arm away. 'You lay one finger on me,' he hissed, rearing up to the man. 'And I'll have you put inside for assault, trespass and grievous bodily harm. Now get out. Any complaints can be dealt with in normal business hours at my office.'

Horsford scowled, backing away uncertainly.

'And just remember either to bring your mother or some means of identification,' Mark snapped, stepping closer.

'I'll be there, don't you worry,' snarled Horsford, backing out of the door.

Mark slammed it shut. 'Cheeky bastard.'

Kathleen had to admire his performance, his ability to switch any blame away from himself. It had the same clarion conviction that used to blow away her doubts.

'Make us a cup of coffee, love,' he said, picking up his shiny new leather briefcase and taking it into the front-room. 'I think I'll take a look at some figures now I'm awake.'

When she brought in two mugs he cleared a space beside him among the papers he had spread out on the sofa. 'Come and sit here.'

He put a brochure into her lap. It was an estate agent's property details. The photograph on the front was of a brick farmhouse. 'I thought it was about time we moved.'

She peered at the details, her head reeling. This was totally unexpected. 'But it's near Ipswich. That's fifty miles away.'

He put a hand on her knee, pushing the robe open to slide it along bare thigh. 'I've put down a deposit on it. And I'm arranging a mortgage. I've formed a new company down there. New pickings.'

Was this really happening, she wondered? It was all getting out of control.

He picked up the mug of coffee. 'I've taken on two more teams of fitters. Things are really moving. Installations are coming on fine.'

'So why do we have to move?' she asked.

'I'm fed up with this poky house. This narrow little street.' He swallowed his coffee, put the mug down and leaned against her. 'You deserve something better and the children will love it in the country. The house has a big garden, there's a barn and cowsheds. The land's been sold off, just a couple of acres left.'

Oh God, she thought, now what am I going to do?

'THAT was the last time we ever made love,' said Kathleen.

She looks tired, thought Mark Clement. Am I pressing her too hard? Her eyes have luminous centres, but they're fogged round the edges, ringed with anxiety and tinged with exhaustion.

'I shouldn't say "making love",' she said. 'Not when it was only a pretence. I don't want to gild what was happening.'

He looked out through the window at the architect's plane tree. Much of Beethoven's Ninth had going been going through his head. 'Could you use a word like fucked, then?'

'I hate to think of sex as anything so basic,' she said. 'When I look back on it now, love seems like some innocent longing I had nursed since I was a little girl, and still didn't know what it was. Perhaps Mark and I never achieved it. We just made play of the idea between us, fooling ourselves that we had it. Perhaps he still kidded himself it was there, like I used to believe my parents weren't really dead, that one day they'd walk through the door, clasp me in their arms, and say, darling, haven't you grown?'

The problem with the intellectual process of assessment, he thought, is that it is too easily subverted by an instinctive desire to converse.

'What did you expect from marriage?'

She blushed. 'I was so green, so stupid. Marriage was going to be unique, as if it was my divine right. Nothing I had observed warned me, I was sure it was going to be like a fairy story.'

'Even though fairy stories never go beyond the wedding?'

She shook her head. 'I don't understand how I was so blind.'

'Thousands of us have done the same. So how did you feel when things began to go wrong?'

She squeezed her eyes shut for a moment. 'I tried not to think about them.'

'Were you angry?'

'I thought I had only myself to blame.'

'You didn't feel Mark had let you down?'

'I was sure it would get better, that it had simply got off on the wrong foot.'

'Since you had so little experience in love from your parents, how were you to know what to expect?'

'My aunt and uncle were very kind. And I know some of the reason I read so many books was to feast on other people's love.' She sagged back in her seat. 'Perhaps it was all that reading that made me a romantic.'

'I think our tendency to romanticise stems back to infancy,' he said. 'The unconditional love that some of us were lucky enough to get from our mothers in those first few suckling months, you know, our every wish granted, all that singing to us, cuddling, stroking, virtually making love to us. But all too soon limitations started to be imposed, conditions set, and we had to face hard reality. Roman-ticism is a reaction against reality, a reversion to early childhood, wanting the impossible.'

She looked shocked. 'Surely there's more to it than that?'

He smiled. 'You were the one who talked of gilding, of the pretence in the expression "making love".'

'But there is love itself?'

'I'd have thought that concept a bit blighted after what you've been through lately?'

She shook her head. 'That was just a nightmare. One of those where you can never throw off your pursuer, where every haven turns into a trap. But you always keep a crumb of hope that something will turn up in time to save you.'

'What form do you visualise this something?'

She looked at him with her brief hooked smile with its pleasurable stab. 'When at last somebody listens and understands.'

Mark left early the next morning, a piece of toast clamped between his teeth, stuffing papers into his briefcase, driving off in the sleek white Sierra so beautifully cellulosed and shiny. Sarah, wearing an ill-fitting pair of handed-down pants like a mop-haired Gandhi in a dhoti, wandered round the kitchen chewing a cold fish finger as Kathleen gave David and Vicky their cornflakes and boiled eggs.

'I dreamed a whole train was stopped in the street outside,' said Vicky. 'It was full of people in their windows looking down at me. Under the wheels was a black cat sitting there. I was afraid it would be killed when the train moved.'

'I dreamed,' said David with heavy emphasis, as if his dream was of far greater significance, 'Daddy had a black beard and was being attacked by spacemen. He just picked them up and crumpled them like old milk-cartons and stuffed them in the bin. Hundreds of them.'

'Why dreams only come when you sleeping?' asked Sarah.

Kathleen watched David and Vicky head off down the pavement. School was about three streets away, and she often thought she should be laying the responsibility of escorting David on Vicky rather than the other way round. Watching their departure gave her an ache in her chest that was both pleasure and pain.

She went up to dress Sarah and found her in the bathroom, her gums and teeth covered in blood. She stood transfixed with horror, till she saw that the child had been squeezing a tube of tomato paste onto a toothbrush.

'Colour nice.' Sarah wrinkled her nose. 'Tastes horrible.' She beamed at the pink water after she swilled out her mouth. Kathleen picked her up and whirled her round, making her squeal with pleasure.

The phone went several times that morning. Each time she dutifully referred the callers to the number Mark had left. She wondered what his secretary was like, how she would feel being bombarded with complaints. Perhaps he would have an affair with her, captivate her with his charm, entrap her into his ways.

Then came a different call.

'It's Isabel. Are you all right now?'

Kathleen tried to think what she might be referring to. She did not care much for Isabel, who was always giggling in the company of men and was bitchy about every woman she knew.

'I'm fine,' she replied cautiously.

'I thought you might have had the grace to ring up and thank me for looking after the kids,' Isabel went on. 'Especially under the circumstances.'

'Circumstances? What do you mean?'

'Come off it, Kathleen, you know perfectly well what I'm talking about. It's not the first time, is it? This drinking of yours. It's disgusting when you've got small children. Mark said he couldn't bear to let them see you, you were in such a state. That's why he told them you had to go to hospital. You're lucky to have such a considerate husband, Kathleen. You've got to pull yourself together.'

Reeling, she tried to gather her wits. 'Isabel, I don't drink.'

'You're not fooling us, you know, Kathleen. Mark's told me all about it. You're only fooling yourself. You ought to get treatment.'

'Listen, Isabel.' Her voice rose. 'D'you want to know what really happened? Your charming brother locked me in the loft for four whole days with nothing to eat. All because I refused to take on any new business. He's busy conning people out of their money for kitchens he's no intention of supplying.'

'That's nonsense and you know it,' exclaimed Isabel. 'Have you been drinking again? Why are you trying to slander him? He's really doing well at last, with a good well-found business, and all you can do is knock him. If you don't pull yourself together, Kathleen, and kick the drink, you'll end up on your own, without Mark or the children.' She put the phone down.

Kathleen stared at the receiver buzzing in her hand, incredulous. There was no end to Mark's lying.

She ought to make a decision. The empty house was an inviting opportunity. Sarah was at Linda's playing with Tessa, and she was alone preparing lunch. Just go, Linda had said. Put a note on the mantelpiece. But she hadn't anywhere to go to. Anyway she felt running was wrong, she ought to have it out with him. The nearer lunch time came, the less was she able to co-ordinate any intentions, the more she felt inclined to put off tackling him, becoming so nervous she was barely able to finish cooking the meal.

She was weak with dread when she heard the front door bang. Mark came in, glowing with smiles, and bearing a bunch of chrysanthemums and lilies. 'Who are they for?' she asked, as he handed them to her, assuming they must be for someone else and that he wanted her to put them in water.

'You, of course, stupid. And here's something else.' He handed her an envelope.

'Thanks,' she said, so confused she dropped it.

'Open it,' he insisted.

There were ten crisp fifty pound notes inside. She gazed at them in fascinated amazement, absurd thoughts racing through her head. Was this her going-away present, had he guessed her intentions?

'It's time you had some new clothes,' he said, waving an arm in an expansive gesture. 'I won a big contract this morning. Fitting out a hotel. Ten thousand as a down-payment.'

Why didn't she throw the money in his face, she thought? In dull confusion she put the flowers in a vase. This was putting her off her stride. She served up the meal, toad-in-the-hole, potatoes, peas and a jar of French mustard. Maybe that was another mistake, giving him his favourite dish.

'D'you know what I've discovered?' he said, forked morsel of sausage poised. 'If there are people like me who are good at selling, there are also people who are born buyers. People who can't stop themselves. Buying to them is an addiction like gambling. They love transactions. I can recognise them like a fisherman knows a good pool. The project manager of this hotel chain, and the architect, both of them. I sold them a fifty-foot fountain a bloke I know has in his back yard and a herd of forty roe-deer coming up at auction tomorrow.'

Kathleen was tempted to think that he probably didn't have whatever he'd promised for the hotel either.

'I sold a kitchen last week to a farmer. He was a compulsive buyer. He goes to auctions and buys barns, Nissen huts, aircraft hangars. They're stacked all round his farmyard, acres of them, most of them still dismantled waiting for re-erection, weeds growing up through them. I'll deliver a few bits of kitchen for him, and I bet they'll just lie around in one of his barns, with all the rest, forgotten.'

'Did Mr Horsford come?' she asked.

'Horsford?' he echoed.

She reminded him of the angry man of the previous night.

'No idea,' replied Mark, pushing his plate forward for a second helping. 'Angela will have dealt with him. She's marvellous. She used to work for a receiver, knows all the tricks for putting people in their place.'

Kathleen brought a dish of peaches for dessert. 'How did you find her?'

'Tried to sell her a kitchen. She's been divorced twice, has a son at public school, runs a BMW and has a share in a villa in the Algarve. The receiver she worked for retired to Spain. He was only twenty-nine.'

He has a cheerful enthusiastic expression, she thought. One that encourages confidence. One that camouflages the fact that he has a cruel mouth, that his eyes have angled hoods which cover their calculating coldness. Aspects of him she had never fully considered before.

'By the way,' he said, as she brought him a cup of coffee. 'I've decided to make the move down to Ipswich in a few days. The owners of the house have agreed to let us rent it till the transfer is completed.'

Her head reeled. It was all moving so fast. She gripped the edge of the table with both hands. The words came out in a gasp before she could stop them. 'I'm not going to come.'

Oh God, she thought, now I've done it.

'I know it's short notice...' he began, then frowned. 'What do you mean?'

'I don't want to live with you any more.' Tears were already blurring her vision. 'Not after what you did to me. You go if you want to. Leave me and the children here.'

'Don't be stupid,' he said impatiently. 'Everything's going to be better from now on. Forget what happened. This is our big opportunity.'

'But I don't want to be involved with what you're doing. It's criminal.'

He got up from the table and she backed away. 'You've got it all wrong,' he said coldly. 'It's a perfectly above-board and normal business.'

'Then why all the lies and deceit?'

'I'm not letting you go,' he snapped, seizing her by the wrists. 'I want my family with me.'

'Leave me alone,' she cried, trying to pull away. 'You don't want me, you just want to use me.'

'You're coming with me whether you like it or not,' he exclaimed harshly.

'No,' she screamed at him. 'I won't, I won't. I hate you.'

'Hate me?' His face became bony and pale.

She saw the paroxysm of rage ripple across his features, his eyes narrowing like the tips of chisels. 'You stupid bitch,' he shouted. She tried desperately to free herself from his grip, glimpsed his fist draw back and begin to travel towards her, almost in slow motion. She was like someone caught in the middle of the road seeing too late the looming truck. Though she tried to duck, his knuckles caught her full in the face. Her head was filled with flashing lights and excruciating bone-crushing pain exploding in her skull, dispossessing her of all reaction save agony. She no longer heard what he was shouting at her.

'MY MEMORY is hazy about the next few days, Mr Clement,' said Kathleen, her face threadbare. 'It's mostly what other people have told me.' She stared before her as if still transfixed by the sight of her husband's fist travelling towards her.

Her eyes moistened and a sob shook her body. Her hands flew to cover her face and muffled cries reeded through her fingers. For a second he hesitated on the edge of his chair. He always felt a flutter of inadequacy when clients broke down; indecision as to whether he should proffer a comforting arm, or refrain from interfering in a natural process, together with the differing theories of counselling practice and warnings of gestures of familiarity being misinterpreted.

This time pity propelled him to kneel beside her and draw her head onto his shoulders. His fingers filled with her hair. 'Let it all go, Kathleen,' he murmured.

He could feel her chest swell in and out like a bellows, the sobs and groans grating deep inside like metal against rock. Her fingers clamped round his arms, her jaw dug into his clavicle and she shuddered as if her body was being buffeted by waves.

Such an explosion of pent-up emotion, he thought. However detached he tried to keep his sympathy, he could feel her pain being transmitted physically into his own body. It was as if she was having a searingly violent orgasm to which he was haplessly joined.

Slowly the shaking shrank to trembling, the sobbing ebbed to sniffles. 'I'm sorry,' her voice squeaked as he gently disengaged himself to ease his cramped knees. 'I don't know what you must think of me, behaving like that.'

'How do you think you've behaved?' He handed her a clutch of tissues from the box on the table.

'Like a child.' She dabbed her eyes, blew her nose. 'Made an exhibition of myself.'

'What good were those feelings doing bottled up inside you?'

'Aren't you treating me like a child, anyway?' Her smile hooked up momentarily, disappeared apologetically. 'I suppose my father wouldn't be much older than you had he lived.'

He could feel the skin of his face rigid as a mask. He wanted to think his discomfort was because her statement negated the establishment of equality between them. But perhaps she needed the father/child relationship at this stage, and he should not discount it. Any role transference would be benign at this point. Only when she identified anger against Mark for his behaviour, or even her parents for their indifference, so spectacularly demonstrated to the unconscious by getting themselves killed, was there a risk she might turn it onto him. Then he would need to take steps accordingly.

'I DON'T know how long I was on the kitchen floor. I heard the children's voices as they arrived back from school, but could only struggle as far as sitting up, tasting the blood in my mouth, barely able to see. I think Mark must have hit me more than once, because as well as my lips being swollen, my eyes were almost shut. When they found me David kept asking, what's happened, what's happened? And Vicky kept crying. I was this misshapen beast which did not realise it was hideous, and so could not understand why everyone was frightened of it. My swollen, blubbery lips could only mumble. I managed to write on a piece of paper, GET LINDA. I could hear David's feet running down the path.

Linda took one look at me and rang the police. She was so angry, if Mark had walked through the door at that moment I think she'd have grabbed a knife from the kitchen and stuck it into him. She lifted me and took me into the front room, put me on the sofa, sponged the blood off and bathed my face, getting the children to fetch and carry. I could hear by their whining how anxious and afraid they were.

When the police arrived Linda did all the talking. My jaw was too sore to move. I squinted at them through my slits. One of the police was a young woman. She went white and tense. But I didn't feel any anger, I just felt numbed. The two policemen wore that kind of "she probably asked for it" expression which women get used to seeing. But the young policewoman urged us to get to a doctor right away not just for treatment, but to obtain a report on the damage that could be used if seeking an injunction in court. Then I should see a solicitor. They would apply for a warrant for Mark's arrest for GBH. She promised to give me a copy of the police report to show the court. If I wanted, she would arrange to take us all to a refuge till we got a court order.

All I wanted was to be left alone, with a couple of aspirins and a deep bed. Linda arranged everything. I sat and sipped warm tea through a straw till Harry came home, then she took me to hospital. All the doctors and nurses in casualty came to see this prize exhibit of a domestic punch-up. While they checked me over, x-rayed me and looked at my teeth, I was regaled with lurid tales of other unfortunate wives they'd patched up. They took several photographs with a Polaroid held together with sticking plaster and sent me home in a taxi. Linda had organised everything, taken in the kids, made up beds. I was put into her bed, Harry was to sleep on the sofa. Poor long-suffering Harry. What are friends for, Linda kept saying.

Needless to say, Mark did not come home.

In the morning my face was a purple cabbage. I didn't want to get out of bed. I didn't want anybody to see me. I felt Linda was being an interfering busybody and wished she'd leave me alone. All I wanted to do was to curl up and hide. I was ashamed. I was hideous and useless. But finally she bullied me into getting dressed. Then she took me into the city. It was embarrassing being stared at, people doing a double-take, as if they couldn't believe what they first saw.

The solicitor, Mr Onion, was quite young. He had thinning hair, wore a waistcoated grey suit and gold-rimmed spectacles. He went pale and muttered "Fucking Ada" at the sight of me. I felt like a leper. Linda did the talking again. Of course I should have been grateful to her, but I hated every moment. It was so humiliating to hear it all dragged out again.

Mr Onion went to work on the phone and arranged a hearing before a judge for that afternoon.

Out it all came again round a table in the judge's chambers. The judge was a spiky man, surprisingly tense, and with hardly any lips. But why did you want to leave, he asked? I'd have thought any man would have been upset if his wife told him she was leaving him. He kept saying, I can't hear you, speak up. But I could hardly get the words out, my lips and gums were so sore. Can you substantiate such an allegation? the judge asked when I told him about being shut up in the loft for four days without food or water. He appeared reluctant to accept the evidence of my face and the doctor's report. But I got my piece of paper in the end, and the police were informed, and Harry changed the locks. The injunction forbade Mark to come anywhere near the street we lived in. It was for three weeks. Till the next hearing. When Mark was supposed to appear.

Twice I saw him drive past the house. Once I saw him parked outside, as if daring me to call the police. Then he telephoned, warning me that if I said one word against him, he'd kill me. Another night someone came round knocking on all the doors and windows till I phoned the police, by which time, of course, whoever it was had gone. He stopped David and Vicky on the way back from school, asked if they'd like to come and live with him. I should have expected that. Unlike him, he couldn't have been very subtle because they were frightened and ran home.

Money was a problem. I had to go to the DSS to apply for Income Support, and then to City Hall about the rent. I went backwards and forwards like a ball in a pintable. You don't need any money, said the DSS, get maintenance off your husband. Try for reconciliation, said the man in the council housing department, then Mr September could continue paying the rent.

Linda and I nearly fell out because she said I was being too feeble. She didn't realise how the whole thing made me feel ill. However bad, my marriage had been everything to me. Maybe my head knew it was all over, but deep down inside, my heart still yearned for us all to be back together again, for it to be like it was in the early days. Surely I hadn't imagined those early days?

It wasn't easy explaining to the children what had happened. They were all acting strangely. Sarah wet her bed and had nightmares, Vicky was clinging and whiny, and David was plain awkward. He wouldn't do a thing I asked him to. Why the bloody hell won't you do what you're told, I shrieked at him one day. I know I'm small, he shouted back. Funny isn't it, how the child wants to be a man so young? You don't think of these things at the time. He was growing up fast. I know he was angry with his father. He could see that his beating me up was the cause of the break-up. But I think he was equally angry with me for letting it happen in the first place.

Weeks after the swelling and dark bruising had gone, discolouring remained, making me look gaunt and sickly green. Vicky, who'd been developing a fascination for horror stories, said I looked like a ghost.

I was shaking at the prospect of seeing Mark at the next court hearing. But he didn't turn up. His solicitor read out a letter of apology, explaining that he was ill with nervous shock at the break-up of his marriage. It was a different judge, a kindly man who asked how I was managing. He had a carbuncle on the side of his nose that he rocked like an electric light-switch while he listened. You don't meet many men who listen, I find. Except you, of course, Montjoy.

"I'm glad you're recovering from your ordeal, Mrs September," the judge said. "We must give your husband a chance to put his case, though. I'll extend the injunction to the next hearing."

Money was still the main difficulty. I never found the envelope with the money that Mark had given me. He must have taken it while I lay unconscious. There was a few quid saved from the housekeeping as the money came in from the kitchen business. However tainted it was all there was. Although I was on benefit, there always seemed to be more bills than money. When Mr Onion wrote to Mark asking for maintenance, his solicitor replied that his client's business was in difficulties.

"But he's got thousands in the bank," I told Mr Onion. "He's ripping off hundreds of people with his fitted kitchens racket."

"We'll get to the bottom of it when the divorce petition is heard," replied Mr Onion. "He has to produce evidence of his means."

Thank God for the summer or I don't know how I'd have managed the gas and electricity bills.'

IT WAS only on the morning of the third court hearing that Mr Onion received a copy of Mark's affidavit. Although he made formal protest he did not seek a postponement. Linda reckoned it was to obscure the fact that he'd neglected to notice its absence in the first place.

The judge was the same waspish man from the first hearing. Kathleen didn't recognise Mark at first glance. Encased in a new suit, he was so sleekly groomed he was barely distinguishable from the court establishment. He sat beside his solicitor, a plump young man with blond hair called Plover.

Mr Plover rose.

'In the first place, my client, Mr Mark September, the defendant, respectfully wishes to inform the court that he was not responsible for the attack on his wife. To prove this we have affidavits from witnesses to show that he was elsewhere on the afternoon in question. Also there are two factors we wish to put forward that may help to throw light on how a misunderstanding has come about.'

He rustled through the papers in his hand. 'The first of these is that my client wishes the court to appreciate that his wife has a serious drinking problem. There have been many days when she has been too incapacitated to know what she was doing.'

'That's a lie,' shouted Linda. 'She doesn't drink.'

'I must ask you not to interrupt,' commanded the clerk of the court.

The judge eyed Linda thin-lipped.

The doughy cheeks of the plump Mr Plover were lightly buttered with perspiration. 'We can produce a police statement to the fact that when they visited the house two weeks ago there was a binbag outside the backdoor of Mrs September's house full of whisky, sherry and wine bottles. We have an affidavit from a witness who will vouchsafe finding Mrs September the worse for drink on two occasions.'

Mr Onion turned to regard Kathleen anxiously.

'This second factor,' Mr Plover continued, 'concerns a

somewhat violent client who erroneously believed he was owed money by the defendant, and who had threatened to call round in person to claim it. We believe it was this man who came round on the day the plaintiff was attacked. That he was provoked into attacking Mrs September through her befuddled response to his demand to speak to my client. In her state it is probable that Mrs September confused this man for her husband.

'In the light of this evidence we respectfully ask the court to remove the injunction imposed on the defendant so that he can return to his home and his children, and try to help his wife with her drink problem.'

'A pity he didn't deal with the drink problem earlier,' commented the judge. 'It might have saved wasting the time of this court.'

Mr Onion appeared to be gasping for breath. 'I should like to request a few minutes to consult with my client.'

He turned to her, leaning close. 'What does it all mean, Mrs September? How am I to reply?'

Kathleen was speechless with shock, her hands crushing each other in anguish on her lap.

'Kathleen doesn't drink,' hissed Linda, leaning across. 'Mark's a bloody liar. That bag of bottles was planted. He came round banging on windows so that she'd ring the police and they'd come and find the binbag. It's a put-up job, can't you see?'

'That man he mentioned,' added Kathleen, suddenly galvanised. 'He came round the evening before. Mark was there. He got rid of him himself.'

Mr Onion lifted his gold-rimmed spectacles onto his forehead as he slid thumb and forefinger under his eyes in an effort to assimilate the information. He picked up his copy of Mark's affidavit. 'If only we'd got this earlier. I shall have to ask for a postponement.' He turned to make his plea.

'You won't expect me to extend the injunction after such evidence, Mr Onion?' asked the judge. He shuffled the affidavits. 'I cannot see the difficulty. The plaintiff's evidence is entirely at odds with the defendant's, so if she wishes to make explanation or to refute his allegations, then get on with it. Do you want a short adjournment to take further instruction? Or if you would prefer it, I am prepared to conduct the hearing from here and question both parties myself.'

As Mr Onion paused, perhaps considering the relief at having the matter taken out of his hands, the judge took his hesitation as assent.

'Then we'll carry on.' He held up the affidavits. 'I take it as understood, Mrs September, that you stand by what you have said here?'

'I do,' replied Kathleen, biting her lips.

The judge looked round the court. 'If the defendant's account is correct, then the plaintiff's could be said to be in error due to her state of intoxication. Under such circumstances the court would not be likely to censure her too harshly. But on the other hand, if Mr September's affidavit is a fabrication then the defendant has put himself at risk of perjury and the liability to considerable penalties. Indeed, I am bound to consider it unlikely that he would venture the risk. Now, Mr Plover, the evidence of your witnesses. Do you have affidavits or are they here in person?'

'Affidavits, my lord.' The perspiring Mr Plover went up to the judge's table and handed him several sheets of paper, then gave copies to Mr Onion.

'May I ask why these were not sent to me before the hearing, my lord?' asked Mr Onion.

'The witnesses are men with responsible jobs,' explained Mr Plover. 'It has not been easy for them to find time to make these statements.'

The judge lifted his eyebrows. 'Mr Onion has a point. It would be in order for the court to postpone the hearing to a further date. Is that what you wish, Mr Onion?'

The distraught Mr Onion leaned towards Kathleen, his eyebrows jumbled with anxiety.

'All I want is to get it over with,' she whispered.

He shook his head, more to himself than her. 'If you would like to continue, my lord.'

'I shall ask you a few questions, Mrs September.' The judge leafed through the sheaf of papers. 'How do you account for the bag full of empty bottles outside your back-door?'

'It was put there deliberately to incriminate me.'

The judge watched her, eyelids heavy as half-opened walnuts. 'Why do you say that?'

'Because I'm not a drinker. My friend here can bear witness to that. Ask the police who came round that night. They interviewed me, they would have noticed if I was drunk. My friend can also tell you that my husband is a liar, that he hits me and he hates to lose.'

The judge waved a hand as if to brush this aside. 'I would rather you just answered my questions. But since you mention that your husband beats you, I see no record here that you ever complained to the police until this last disputed occasion. The fact that you haven't suggests some exaggeration.' He raised his eyebrows. 'Or that you have accepted the tradition that a husband may try to keep his wife in order?'

'I suffered his attacks,' replied Kathleen wearily. 'Because I didn't want to break up my family. But I can't go on. I'm afraid now that he might kill me.'

The judge sniffed and looked down at the papers. 'Your husband states that he was never there on the afternoon in question. I have here two affidavits from individuals who swear he was down in Ipswich at the time. Could you have been mistaken? Might it have been someone else?'

'Surely I would know my own husband? For a start, he came back for lunch.'

The judge waved the affidavits at her. 'Two independent statements that he was in Ipswich. Think very carefully, Mrs September. I may put you on oath.'

'I swear to Almighty God I was not mistaken.'

'I should like to suggest that it is an established precedent that most such attacks are usually domestic,' interrupted Mr Onion. 'Who else would have beaten her so savagely?'

'Such precedents also allow for lovers,' said the judge, perusing the affidavits again. 'There is the question of this man who supposedly wanted his money back. What was your relationship with him?'

'I only ever met him the once when he came to the door to demand his money. He was very aggressive. My husband was there. He told him to call to his office the next day.'

'Perhaps he took a fancy to you and called back when he knew your husband wouldn't be there?'

'Why won't you believe me?' she cried.

'Why don't you ask Mark September to show you his right knuckle?' shouted Linda.

The judge glared. 'This hearing will be conducted in a seemly fashion. You don't do your friend's case any good by such behaviour, young woman. Any further interruption and I shall have you removed from the court.'

Linda blushed angrily. She leaned across to Mr Onion, gesturing at Mark. The judge had also turned to Mark.

'I shall ask you a few questions, Mr September.'

Mark nodded with the earnest air of one determined to be helpful.

'The plaintiff swears that you are the person who caused her the injuries listed in the medical report. In your affidavit you state that you could not have committed them because you were forty miles away. The distance from here to Ipswich can be driven in less than an hour. You could have hammered the daylights out of your wife and been with these gentlemen as they state one hour later?'

'But why would I do something so brutal to the woman I love?' asked Mark in pained tones. 'I have been extremely distressed by her accusations. She's the last person in the world that I would harm. The man who did that to her was a vicious sadist, and I am very disappointed that the police have made no attempt to catch him. My wife has had breakdowns in the past and she has this drink problem, which unfortunately gets worse because she finds it difficult to face up to. I believe that it's an aspect of people who drink that with all the covering-up they have to do, they become accomplished liars. For the sake of the children, I've turned a blind eye to it. For the sake of family solidarity I am prepared to take her back, forget about the false accusations and trouble she has caused, and try to make a new beginning. I would also like to find out exactly who attacked her. I don't know if the court can help here, my lord? Is it possible to direct the police to make further enquiries, because I suspect that due to my wife's accusations that it was me who attacked her, they have looked no further.'

The judge responded to Mark's appeal as if at last he had found an upright and honest citizen he could communicate with. 'You may rest assured that the court will encourage the police to pursue further investigations. It seems to me that the facts have become confused resulting in misrepresentation. These affidavits create a picture that is entirely at odds with that which the plaintiff would like the court to accept. But I shall suspend final judgement till the court probation officer has initiated further enquiries. Meanwhile I am bound to say that under the circumstances I cannot allow the plaintiff's application for an injunction to continue.'

As the Judge strode rustling from the court, Linda turned to hiss at Mr Onion. 'Why didn't you present me as Kathleen's witness?'

Mr Onion raised his fists, rolling his eyes as if to importune the heavens. 'That damned man,' he exclaimed. 'He's as bigoted as the Spanish Inquisition. He deliberately side-stepped any further representation on our behalf.'

'What's going to happen now?' wailed Kathleen, aghast at the implications. 'I can't go home.'

Even as she spoke, Mark had shaken his solicitor by the hand and was turning in their direction.

'You can't let him back in the house after what he did to her,' Linda exclaimed to Mr Onion.

Mr Onion seemed prepared to tear out what little remained of his hair. 'I wish you hadn't agreed to allow the case to continue, Mrs September. You should have warned me the kind of adversary your husband is. I shall have to make representation about the delayed affidavits. We had no chance to be prepared. The hearing was not carried out properly.'

'Come along, darling,' said Mark, joining them. 'It's time to go home.' He beamed at her with easy assurance. 'It's all over now.'

Kathleen shrank from him. 'I want nothing to do with you,' she cried.

'Don't be silly,' he said calmly. 'It's going to be all right now.'

'Get away from me,' screamed Kathleen, throwing herself at him, arms flailing, kicking out.

Mr Onion and Linda struggled to drag her off him. 'For God's sake, Mark,' exclaimed Linda. 'Can't you see you're not wanted here?'

He stepped back, adjusting his tie with one hand, while he rubbed a leg with the other. 'I'll be home for tea,' he said, unruffled.

'He's a cool one,' said Mr Onion shaking his head as Mark walked off.

'He's a bastard,' shouted Kathleen, chest heaving.

Linda looked at her, eyebrows raised. 'At last you're really angry.'

'What can we do, Mr Onion?' cried Kathleen. 'How can he get away with a pack of lies?'

'Nothing till I can get the hearing reconvened. Or he attacks you again.'

A man with one arm half into his raincoat came up to them. 'Excuse me butting in. Hallo, Graham,' he said to Mr Onion. 'I'm the court probation officer, Mrs September. Greg Fulcher.' He continued settling into his raincoat as he spoke, a middle-aged man with square blue jowls and neat, flat hair. 'I should like to arrange a time to come round to your house and see you. Perhaps tomorrow afternoon after the children get back from school, would that be convenient?'

'I won't be there,' replied Kathleen. 'I'm not staying in the same house with that man. Not for a second.'

'I wouldn't do anything hasty, Mrs September.' The man tried a lean smile. 'With the court hearing adjourned you don't want to prejudice your case.'

'Are you telling me that I've got to sit quietly at home and be battered by my bloody husband just to suit the court?'

The probation officer raised a hand placatingly. 'Consider, is your husband likely to do anything that would upset his chances?'

'But how is it going to help her?' demanded Linda.

'A pause like this can help bring both parties back together,' persisted the probation officer. 'Gives them a breathing space to realise that perhaps with a little effort the marriage could be salvaged.'

'Couldn't you work on a reconciliation?' asked Mr Onion hopefully.

Kathleen turned on him. 'What about your reaction when you first saw my face in your office? Was it the sort of condition anyone would feel like giving a second chance to?'

Mr Onion looked uncomfortable.

'Should I go back to a man who smashes my face in?' she demanded. 'Should I live with a man who locks me in the dark without food for four days? Is that what you do to your wives?'

'I don't think that remark's in very good taste, Mrs September,' replied Mr Onion hastily.

'We're here to help, Mrs September,' said the probation officer. 'There's no point in attacking us.'

Kathleen burst into tears. 'You're going home to your understanding wives whom doubtless you love and cherish, and you're judging every other home in those lights. What I have to go home to is terror. Can't you understand? I'm scared stiff of being alone with him.'

The clerk of the court came over. 'Carry on your conversation outside, please. There's another hearing due to start.'

'Come up to my office,' said Mr Fulcher, leading the way.

'I imagine you weren't too happy with the way the judge handled it, Graham?' he said, shutting the door behind them.

'It was a bloody disgrace,' growled Mr Onion.

'As an outsider I have to say, Mrs September, that your husband made you appear a troublesome lush who'd got herself beaten up and was trying to pin it on him. But I must admit the judge indulged your husband. I've read the medical and police reports and seen the photos. In my book that sort of handiwork usually comes from someone pretty close, not a stranger. That personal animosity you get between man and wife going over the top. Or perhaps a lover?'

'I don't have a lover,' said Kathleen wearily. 'Whatever you may think.'

The probation officer nodded. He flipped a card-index on his desk, wrote down a number on a notepad, tore the sheet off and gave it to her. 'If you don't want to go home, you'd better ring that number. It's the local battered women's refuge. You'll be safe there. Tell them I gave you the number, tell them that you lost your application for an injunction today, tell them what your husband did to you.'

'Thanks,' she said, surprised.

'DO I have to keep calling you Mr Clement?'

The question took him by surprise and he almost blurted out, "Call me Mark."

As he swallowed the sentence back, there rattled another code of his profession: not to compromise any relationship between client and therapist by dishonesty. But what about his second name? It was still his name, after all.

'My name's Montjoy.'

'Montjoy? How unusual.'

'An old family name. Clement is French, you see.'

'So now I know two things about you.'

Curiosity always had to be viewed as a healthy sign, he thought. She was waking from her coma of self-absorption like a butterfly slowly easing from its chrysalis. A basis for successful therapy was to create a good relationship between client and interviewer. Not too close, but remembering Breuer's classic point: if someone is drowning, talking to them may not be pertinent.

She tilted her head to one side. 'So you're like me, not a native of these parts either?'

He laughed. 'I was born in a lavatory at Chantilly race-course. The year the broke out. My father was a vet.'

'You don't sound French.'

'My mother was one of those English girls who couldn't keep away from horses. She worked as a groom, tried to pretend she wasn't having me till the last moment. But he did at least marry her and we lived in Algeria till I was four, then we came back and lived in Beauvais till my father was killed in a riding accicent.'

She pressed a forefinger into her upperlip. 'You're not married, are you?'

He raised his eyebrows. 'Is this assumption because my clothes are rumpled or because I don't have to account for my time?'

She coloured slightly. 'I just thought...'

He smiled. 'The intuitive method has its advantages. It's like sketching a portrait and asking the sitter, is this what you look like? So the sitter thinks about himself, my God, have I really got no chin and eyes as close together as a baboon's?'

Her laughter was unexpected, like the jingle of coins in a pocket thought to be empty. It was the first time he could remember hearing her laugh.

The colour remaind in her cheeks. 'And I suppose diversion must be a trick you learned from clients like me?'

He checked his moment of pleasure at her sally. He was neglecting to pigeon-hole every reaction for the coding of client behaviour. She was probably over-reacting from release of tension.

But it was tempting to pursue the interaction. 'You're right that I have no wife.' It seemed an unnecessary distraction to mention Madeleine. 'I brought up three daughters, though. Not easy being a parent on your own, is it? When they began to grow into young women I felt like Horatio defending the bridge over the Tiber against their combined wills. But however independent they professed themselves, it always surprised me how their susceptibility remained, love still came first. I've never been sure whether parents or genes are responsible for all this dependence and insecurity...'

'So you do believe in love?'

He laughed. 'How is it we always get back on this subject?'

'Didn't your daughters have a mother?' There was a tinge of unease in her banter.

'That's another story.' He got up abruptly and went to his cabinet to switch on the coffee machine. He did not talk about his ex-wife to anybody. He stood listening to the echoes that had been filtering through his head all morning. The Rite of Spring. He longed to be at his piano.

'I'm sorry,' she said. 'I'm being nosy.'

'It's nothing.' He was annoyed with himself for allowing his response to be so emotional.

'You know,' he said, laughing. 'We therapists have to fetch our own skeletons out of the cupboard sometimes, dust them down and take them to other therapists for servicing.'

She stared past him, suddenly far away. 'That's what I'm afraid of. That I'll never be shot of him.'

KATHLEEN and Linda walked home beside the main road, leaf-laden trees leaning high over them out of the gardens of redundant Victorian townhouses converted into offices, dentists' consulting rooms and hotels.

Streams of cars and buses swept past, students on bicycles, young women with pushchairs, dyed-haired lovers on the dole in torn black clothing, old people shrunk inside their bent frames. They were all going to their homes, Kathleen thought, their flats, their bedsits, or leaving them to go shopping, see friends, go to work, fetch their children from school. They all had continuity to hold onto. How she envied them. She could not express her despair to Linda striding beside her.

'I'll never believe in justice again,' Linda was expostulating, still angry. 'How can any legal system be fair with judges like that? I've heard stories before, but never believed I'd actually see it happen. Mark wasn't even being clever, just his bloody-minded lying self. Judges are supposed to be people you look up to, then they turn out to be morons.'

Their heels clicked on the paving-stones, traffic burbled, trees rustled, passers-by chattered. As a family they'd been close to destitution before, thought Kathleen. But the prospect ahead now appalled her. To have to give up her home, all the familiar knick-knacks of her small world, to go into hiding, not knowing what was going to happen next, how she'd manage, how the children would survive it all. She felt abjectly depressed.

'If only it had been the judge you had at the last hearing,' said Linda. 'Justice is nothing but a lottery. That solicitor Onion is as much use as a fish, hooked, knocked on the head and filleted before he knew what day of the week it was. I don't understand how Mark gets away with everything. It's like some bloody conspiracy of men, out to maintain their superiority at all costs. They're always in the right, stick together whatever happens, it makes me sick.'

Kathleen nodded her head numbly. There would be nothing left if she gave in. She might as well kill herself.

'Mark's racket must be raking it in,' Linda continued. 'Never seen him so prosperous, expensive suit, trim as a fountain-pen. Appearances, that's what counts. Like those smarmy lying politicians on TV trying to con us because their hair shines like shoe polish, their jaws are pink and they bought their tie at Harrods for forty quid.'

'I wish we didn't have to leave. I know it's only a crummy old council house, but it is home.'

Linda put an arm round her. 'I know, love, I know, but it's only till we get him sorted out.'

Kathleen looked at her watch. 'God, it's after two, and we haven't collected Sarah yet.'

'Don't panic, you've plenty of time. The refuge is taking you, that's the best news. I'll help you pack. If Harry isn't back we'll get a taxi.'

Once they had fetched Sarah and Tessa from Linda's mother and taken them home Kathleen rushed to pack in frenzied panic, afraid Mark would arrive before they were ready and the children were back from school. She kept dashing to the front windows to look out.

She persuaded Linda to climb the ladder into the loft to fetch down the suitcases. She wasn't going to go back up there. Old acquaintances, she thought with a shiver, as she stuffed clothes into them.

'There's so much. I'll never get it all in.'

'Shove what you don't need like winter clothes into binbags, and I'll keep them at mine,' suggested Linda.

When David and Vicky arrived back from school they were upset and confused at first to find their rooms stripped and flight imminent. 'Why must we leave?' David persisted against all explanations, suddenly a pathetic child again. 'Why did the court refuse to give you an injunction? Why doesn't Daddy love you?'

Vicky on the other hand considered it could be an adventure. 'There might be other children there to play with,' she enthused. To this end she rushed backwards and forwards from her case to the binbags, scattering contents and rescuing toys that she felt would impress new friends and make up games, so that her case overflowed. 'I must take them,' she cried, as her mother had to remove things to get the case to shut. Kathleen weakened and allowed her to fill a carrier-bag. David then demanded equal rights. A small placation, his mother considered, distressed herself that he should be so upset.

'I don't know how you're going to manage to carry all that,' laughed Linda. Then she looked at the row of bulging binbags. 'Any more than I know where I'm going to keep all this stuff.'

Kathleen went to the telephone to ring for a taxi. 'You might as well hang on,' said Linda. 'Harry'll be home soon and you could save yourself a couple of quid.'

'I don't want to risk Mark catching us still here. The sooner we're out the better. Come on, let's get the bags over to your place.'

Her nerves were at screaming pitch as the minutes ticked by, and she ran everywhere, taking bags round to Linda's, stacking cases in the hallway, grabbing coats, gathering all the wash-things and towels into another carrier-bag, tripping over Sarah, pacifying her on the run, thinking in the back of her mind that it would be just her luck if Mark came home now.

The moment the taxi arrived she dragged the heavy cases out, soaked with the sweat of fear and effort. She became frantic with impatience as the driver doggedly tried to fit everything into the boot. 'It doesn't matter,' she exclaimed. 'There's room inside.' She crammed carrier-bags in beside the three children on the back seat. 'I'm anxious to get away.'

'Doing a flit with the old man's savings?' asked the taxi-driver.

'Bye, love,' said Linda, giving her a quick hug. 'I'll see you in a day or so. Ring us tomorrow and I'll let you know what's happening. Bye Vicky, David, Sarah. Wave bye-bye, Tessa, Barry.'

Kathleen had eyes only for the end of the road, twisting her head round, expecting to see the white Sierra turning in at any moment. As the laden taxi drew away from the waving hands of Linda and her children, she sank back into her seat as if to make herself small and invisible from the outside. They were safe now, her mind wanted to insist, but she refused to allow it such optimism. I never thanked Linda for all her help, she thought.

'Going on holiday?' asked the driver.

'Just to stay with friends for a few days,' she replied, thinking how fabrication had become second-nature.

'Right weather for a holiday,' prattled the taxi-driver. 'Looks like the harvest's good, too. The forecast weren't too hot in the spring, so I bought my missus a tumble-dryer but she hasn't hardly used it. We've got three same as you. Don't half make a load of washing, do they?'

She was glad to let him do the talking, one of those people with pencil tongues to whom any listener was a scrap of paper to scribble on. He drove smoothly across the city, the large car possessing the quiet unction of a horizontal lift as it deftly slowed and speeded to the change of traffic lights. Several times she turned to glance through the rear window, imagining a white car pursuing.

They turned off a main road in the east suburbs, and after several turnings entered a wide street where most of the houses were set back and hidden among dense overhanging trees. Kathleen peered round, trying to remember the instructions. 'Just let us off by that pillar-box, please.'

The taxi pulled up. There was nobody in sight, only a few cars parked along the pavements. 'What's the number?' asked the taxi-driver, puzzled.

'This is fine,' said Kathleen. 'Thank you. We're meeting someone here.'

He unloaded the bags and cases, and Kathleen paid him. 'There are some flats over there,' he said, nodding towards the brick and concrete bulwarks of an apartment block just visible behind the trees.

'We'll manage, thanks,' she said. He drove away plainly baffled, if not a little offended that she should be so mysterious with him.

She stood on the pavement, the children clustered round her surrounded by their bags and cases, till the taxi was out of sight. Kathleen looked across the road. 'White gateposts,' she said. 'That must be it.'

There was nothing else visible save some chimneys looming high above a thick mass of foliage.

'Come on,' she said. 'We'd better get all this stuff over the other side.'

They ferried everything across the empty road and piled it inside the gateway. Then Kathleen led them up a short overhung drive that curved round till it came to a huge four-storey Victorian house.

They stood and stared in bewilderment. All its windows were blocked off with sheets of corrugated iron. An elder tree was growing right across the front door.

THERE came the sound of voices. Kathleen turned and saw that the drive continued round through more overgrown shrubbery. A pregnant woman appeared in stately pursuit of a toddling child who wore nothing but a vest. The woman was barefoot herself, dressed in a thin purple shift which accentuated her bulky dimensions.

'Is this the refuge?' asked Kathleen.

The woman's cheekbones were like shiny apples. 'You must be the new family.'

They followed her round the bushes and under a tall brick arch, into an old stable-yard, enclosed on three sides by two-storey buildings, the central one surmounted by a defunct clock-tower.

Kathleen's first impression was of a scrap yard. Piles of rough timber and firewood, old rafters and planks, stacks of old bricks, new concrete blocks, a concrete mixer, a battered cream Mini, a blameless Toyota and a rusty Cortina parked side by side, old prams, heaps of junk and above them all, lines of nappies and colourful bunting of knickers, dresses and shirts. In amongst all this played a number of children.

A woman of about forty came out of a doorway. When she saw them she hurried across to meet them, her legs moving with the snip of scissors. She had heavy-rimmed spectacles and hair drawn tightly back from her forehead, and wore grey slacks and cardigan. 'You've arrived, then? Nobody saw you, did they? You let the taxi go before you entered, didn't you? Good. It's best that we take as many precautions as possible. I have to keep drumming it in. The fewer people who know the better.' Her smile finally reached its full span and she took Kathleen's hand. 'I'm Brenda Reilly. You spoke to me on the phone. Pleased to meet a fellow countrywoman.' Then, taking Kathleen by surprise, she enfolded her in her arms and hugged her.

'You'll find it a little primitive. We all have to muck in together to keep the place going, everyone has to do their bit. The council may have allowed us this old ruin free, but that's the extent of its generosity. Come on now and I'll show you round. Tell us your names,' she said, stooping to greet the children. 'David, Vicky and

Sarah,' she repeated. 'That's grand. Now where's all your stuff? Out by the gate? Heavens, we'd best get it in before someone nicks it.'

'There's eight women here all told,' Brenda said as they fetched the bags and cases on an old rubber-tyred trolley. 'Nine with your coming. And three added to fourteen makes seventeen children.' She led them through a wicket in one of the old coach doors. Inside was an enormous space, the ceiling supported by cast-iron pillars. To the left a partition had been taken down and a motley collection of easy chairs and sofas were grouped round the old harness-room fireplace and a television. On the right stalls and mangers had been pulled out, and a kitchen and eating area created. A large double cooker, several fridges, cupboard units and a twin-sink were set against the walls. Across them were lined three big deal tables, surrounded by a variety of wooden and plastic chairs. Right in the centre where the coaches once stood was the play area, play-pens, rocking-horse and toys scattered everywhere.

'Not much privacy, I'm afraid,' said Brenda. 'One big family for support. And we have volunteers who come in to lend a hand, too. I'll show you upstairs. The entrance is outside. It's the old groom's quarters plus rooms we made out of the haylofts. We're putting you in one of them. We had a welsher in there last week. Went back to her husband.' Brenda shook her head. 'Sad really, when the weaker souls give in.'

At the top of the stairs she pushed open a door. 'Our pride and joy. A proper bathroom. There's a shower and lavatory downstairs, that we put in at the beginning. It's all thanks to Fred. He's the only man you'll see round here.' She laughed. 'Though he's hardly a man, more of a fairy godfather. He retired before most of us were born, used to be a plumber. Never comes empty-handed, cakes his wife makes, toys, bits of furniture, a new door, a bath, a bag of cement.' She pointed out of the window. 'He organised us into converting the loose-boxes into bedrooms. Women have come here barely knowing how to sew on a button and gone away knowing how to lay a damp course, wire a ring-circuit, plumb in a tap, build a brick wall, let alone cook for thirty and grow their own vegetables. Have you any skills you can bring, Kathleen?'

'I hope I won't have to stay here very long.'

Brenda let out a hoot of laughter. 'They all say that as their faces sag into their boots when they realise the place isn't quite four-star. I know it must be a bit of a shock, dear, but don't have too high hopes of getting away yet awhile. The law's a lead tortoise. Wait till you hear how the rest have been buggered about.'

She patted her arm. 'You mustn't lose hope. You just need to realise you're up against a male world. That it doesn't care two tuppences about the likes of us. We show up the side of themselves they'd prefer to forget about.' She let out another hoot of laughter. 'Don't mind me. Come on, I'll show you your room. We had terrible problems with these old lofts at first. First it was the rats. The council got rid of them. Then it was the fleas. People got bitten to pieces, so Fred took up the boards and pumped in insecticide. Then everyone was sick with the fumes for weeks. But it's fine now. Yours has a grand new skylight. I daren't ask where Fred gets these things.'

The room was crammed with four beds, a chest of drawers and a wardrobe. To move about it was necessary to squeeze sideways along the gaps as if negotiating an ankle-width maze. The walls had been papered with single rolls of different patterns. Any areas left uncovered had been used for drawing on with crayons. The children's eyes lit up. But Kathleen's reaction was the dismay of realising what she had come down to. This was home now. This must be how refugees felt. A little different from the last time she was a refugee, arriving at her aunt and uncle's, dazzled by its middle-class luxury. But this was safety, she kept telling herself, however ramshackle a fortress. He couldn't get at her here.

'I'll leave you to sort yourselves out,' said Brenda. 'Come down when you're ready.'

'Are you going to sleep with us, Mummy?' asked Vicky, wide-eyed.

Sarah was bouncing on a bed. 'Want to go to toilet.'

Vicky put out a hand to restrain her. 'It'll come out if you do that.'

For the first time a smile appeared on David's face. 'We won't have to go to school tomorrow, will we?'

They had sorted out which bed each was to sleep in, when there came a knock on the door and a young woman entered. She had red hair, wore a black boiler-suit and green beads.

'Hope I'm not disturbing you,' she said in rich transatlantic tones. 'I'm Maggie, one of the helpers, just looked in to see if there was anything you need. You're Kathleen, aren't you? And these are...? You want to go down and explore?' she asked, after the children introduced themselves. 'Your mum and I'll rest here and have a chat.'

'Take Sarah to the bathroom first,' Kathleen called after them, as they set off, led by the enthusiastic Vicky.

'Guess you'll need some linen,' said Maggie, looking round. 'There should be pillows and blankets in the wardrobe. Sometimes the laundry gets a bit behind. Say, it was great you got away OK. Was it any problem? Men are such shits, the things they do.'

As Kathleen explained, Maggie's mascaraed eyes became almost circular.

'Sounds like you had a real rough time. Those judges are pigs, right out of the dark ages, they'd have been top scorers in the Spanish Inquisition. Sometimes I think the entire male sex are just a bunch of psychopaths.'

Kathleen was not sure how to react to such blanket indictment.

'Sure, some are OK,' continued Maggie. 'The guy I live with is a musician, we have that in common, I teach the violin, you know, peripatetic. I mean there's a few here think I'm a traitor, the real misandrists. They'd put the boy babies out on the mountainside. They see this place as their cause célèbre, and they're out to convert. Real hotstuff feminists, I'm warning you. But maybe you feel the same about men, right now? I wouldn't blame you.'

Kathleen shrugged. 'I hadn't really thought...' Her eyes began to mist.

Seeing her tears, Maggie slid across a bed to put her arms round her. 'God, you've sure had it rough. I think you're really brave, honest. You just let it all out.'

Kathleen blinked her tears back, alarmed at the hunger of Maggie's concern. At that moment the door opened and Sarah slipped through, crawled across the bed to climb onto her mother's lap.

'She's sweet, isn't she? So quiet and good. Some of the kids that come here are really unsettled, they cry all the time and their mothers shout at them, and it all gets a little stressful.' She smiled quickly to paper over this admission. 'But we handle it, we're one big family.' Sarah watched her, a thumb in her mouth. 'Have you met the others yet? No? They'll be cooking tea right soon. Don't mind them, some are kind of withdrawn, a bit inadequate, we get a fair mixture. I guess you'll see for yourself. I'll talk to you again soon.' She patted Sarah's cheek and got up. 'Bye for now.'

'Lady gave me chocolate,' said Sarah. 'We go home now?'

Kathleen drew her close and in utter exhaustion lay down on the bed. Sleep enfolded them together.

It was half past six when David and Vicky came to collect them for tea. Rubbing her eyes, she went down with them, Sarah on her hip.

On any other occasion she might have felt threatened by such junk shop interiors and the clamorous confusion of people she did not know. But at that moment to be cut off from the tiger of Mark was a heady relief. As she stood in the doorway, her children clustered round her, she felt she was in a dream.

Women were cooking, setting tables, feeding babies, birding, laughing. As she stood there, uncertain, Brenda came up behind her. 'A quick word in my office before supper, Kathleen. Just to get a few details. Could you spare a minute, Polly?' she called. 'Polly's one of our volunteers. She's a graduate on the dole, a marvel with kids.' A tall girl with long oaten hair and a spatter of acne came over, wiping her hands on her jeans. Brenda introduced them. 'What does Sarah like to eat, Kathleen? Is she fussy about her food? Would you like to go with Polly, darling, and see what there is for tea? It's like a party over there, so many children together.'

Sarah clung to her mother for a moment, then decided Polly was safe enough. 'You two go with Polly as well,' said Brenda to Vicky and David. 'Mummy and I are just going to my office for a chat. We'll only be five minutes.'

'Is it about Daddy?' asked David suspiciously.

'They're so sharp, the young,' said Brenda as they crossed the yard to her office, negotiating stacks of bricks and timber. The office itself was like an adjunct of the yard, except that it was full of paper. Its shelves bowed with the weight of files, pamphlets and trays of loose paperwork, overflowing filing cabinets and smothered desks jammed together, barely room to move. Half-obscured in all this sat a girl at a typewriter.

'This is Clare,' said Brenda. 'She comes in the evenings to clear the office work.'

The girl was older than the other helpers, maybe thirty, very thin, no make-up, short hair, shallow jaw like the flap of an envelope and a thin rip of a mouth.

'Throw those books off that chair,' said Brenda. 'Just a few details for the records.' She pulled out a sheet of paper from a drawer. 'Did you bring your Child Benefit book?'

'It lives in my handbag.'

'You'd be surprised how many arrive here without their handbags. Have you got an Income Support book?'

'Not yet. They've been sending me a giro.'

'And you didn't give anyone this address?'

Kathleen shook her head. 'My friend who helped me get away was a bit put out when I wouldn't tell her.'

Clare leaned across her typewriter. 'Did you write it down on anything?'

'Only on a piece of paper I put in my handbag.'

'Weren't you told under no circumstances to write it down?' demanded Clare. 'Your husband could have rifled your handbag.'

Kathleen grew tense. 'I'm sorry...'

Clare eyed her coldly. 'What evidence did you produce of your husband's violence?'

'Photographs and a report from the hospital.' This is interrogation, she thought uneasily.

'So why did the judge refuse you an injunction?' demanded Clare.

'Because he believed my husband's version.' Kathleen felt the dust of tears.

'That's enough, Clare,' said Brenda. 'I'm sorry, Kathleen, we have to be sure. We had one woman all made-up with fake bruises and an arm in plaster. Turned out she was the wife of a mate of the husband of one of the women here. She rang him after she got here, and he came round with his mates and dragged his wife off, knocking quite a few of us about in the process. So we try to keep the place secret as much as possible.'

'Would you go back to your husband if he promised never to hit you again?' asked Clare.

Kathleen, nose embedded in tissues, shook her head vehemently.

Clare's expression relented a fraction. 'How could you have stood him for so long? Men like that ought to be castrated.' She shuddered as if her whole being was revolted.

'We'll talk about practical things in the morning, Kathleen,' said Brenda, putting an arm round her. 'The DSS, that's the first hurdle, to keep the benefit coming. We have to ask for whatever we can get off you to keep us going. Let's go and get some tea now.'

In the large expanse of the coach-house women were moving round the tables. Some were seated, knives and forks ringing on plates, orchestrated to the hubbub of voices and shrill chatter of children. This is like being back at school, thought Kathleen, seeking out her own family. She found Sarah and another small girl either side of Polly, each absent-mindedly accepting spoonfuls as they listened to a story. 'Sit here, Mummy,' cried Sarah, optimistically pointing to where there was no room whatever.

'I'll come back in a minute,' she promised, as someone handed her a plateful of potatoes, sausages, cauliflower, peas and gravy. She found an empty seat beside David.

'It's not like I expected, mum,' he said.

'It's not what any of us expected,' said a voice on her other side. It was the pregnant woman with apple cheeks who had met them when they first arrived, blond hair loosely pinned up. She told them her name was Penny. 'I was bloody scared when I first arrived.'

'When was that?' asked Kathleen.

'Seven weeks ago. Look,' she said, holding out her left hand. There was a livid scar across the back. 'He stuck the bread-knife through it, pinned it to the kitchen-table. That's Derrick for you, manners of a paratrooper. I've only just got the use of it back. I thought this place was worse than a gypsy camp. I wanted to turn round and run. Now I'd be sorry to leave. You've a lot on your hands with three. I'll have the same when this comes,' she added, patting her belly. 'Tracy's sitting there with your older girl. And you met Martin before.' She nodded towards a group clustered before the enormous new-looking television set.

'Monica brought that a few weeks back,' continued Penny. 'A

man delivered it to her office, said it was for us. She reckoned it was blood-money.'

'Who's Monica?'

'She's our social worker. It's a muddle getting to know everybody. Especially with the helpers coming and going. I got ever so confused at first. You don't know what to expect. I was in a state, anyway. He'd hit me, but never done anything like that before. Blood everywhere. The pain was crushing, I couldn't use the hand for weeks. So I was doped to the top of my head. What happened to you, then?'

Kathleen explained briefly. 'The same thing happened to Dawn,' exclaimed Penny. 'Wait till I tell her. How can these people be judges and not know what's going on in the world? They must be bloody wankers. Here, d'you want some pud? I'll get you some, it's apple-pie tonight.'

Kathleen turned to David. 'Have you met anyone yet?'

'A boy showed me some bikes. They make them up out of old bits.' He paused, his voice dropped a semitone. 'He said there is school. A minibus comes.'

Vicky had already left the tables and gone off with Tracy and a jug-eared girl of about her own age. Kathleen had no qualms about her; Vicky was a sociable animal.

The meal had never been a set-piece with everyone sitting down together spooning and forking one course after another. It was fragmentary, people sat down and ate, came and went, absorbed in routines that might seem esoteric to a stranger. This haphazard activity made Kathleen feel insecure, for although there was no pressure on her yet to perform any particular function, she could see no trend to follow.

But gradually the winding-up of the meal and the putting-to-bed of the smallest children began to implement a pattern. She helped to clear plates, then decided to take the whining over-tired Sarah upstairs. Much noise was coming out of the bathroom. A woman with a small boy came up as she waited outside the door. 'For God's sake we haven't got all night, go on, there's no privacy here, not with so many.'

She had not taken in before that the bathroom was designed for communal use. There were two baths, three washbasins set into a work surface, and two lavatories side by side, both occupied. 'D'you mind?' said a voice with heavy emphasis. 'You're standing on Tony's clothes.'

'Sorry,' she said hastily, taking Sarah over to a free basin, sitting her on the edge and pulling off her dress.

'Stop that, you little bastard,' a strident voice rose over the hubbub. 'You ruddy well do as you're told.' The sound of slaps on flesh turned into a shrill howl. 'Shut up, will you?' The woman sounded at the end of her tether.

Sarah peered curiously round her mother, while Kathleen ran lukewarm water, rubbed her quickly with a flannel, concerned only to get out. Polly rose from kneeling by the bath, the ends of her long oaten hair all wet. 'Gary can come and have a bath with Martin if you like, Angie. You go and have a sit down.'

As the blubbering boy was lifted into the bath, Kathleen glimpsed small strawberry buttocks, and was reminded of her own face in the mirror after Mark's attack. Is this how brutality is handed on, she thought? By mothers?

It was a relief to be back in the peace of their own cramped room. Someone had left a pile of sheets and she made up the beds, unpacked suitcases, put out Vicky's and David's nightclothes, hung up some of her own clothes, making the room seem more their own. She found the Mother Goose book to read Sarah a nursery story, but the child was already all but asleep with exhaustion. At least she adapts, Kathleen thought, relieved.

When she returned to the main coach-house there was no sign of Vicky or David. The tables were cleared but there was still activity in the kitchen area. She went over. 'Can I do anything?' she asked.

A thin woman with a scarf round her blonde hair looked up from cleaning down the working surfaces, stared. 'Where've you been then, while we've been slaving our guts out?'

'Come on, Dawn,' said a large woman with short black hair. 'She's only just got here.'

'I'm sorry,' said Kathleen. 'I've been putting my youngest to bed. She was very tired.'

'I'm tired and all,' snapped Dawn, undoing her apron, flinging it onto the floor and stalking off.

The black-haired woman picked it up. She had pear high cheeks that made her eyes oval as almonds, the flesh covered in tiny pits. She winked. 'PMT. Dawn gets it like a kick in the head.'

A thin girl of hardly more than twenty, with curls like a mass of carrot peelings, slid a stack of clean plates beside another stack. 'I'm Sue. What's your name?'

'And I'm Paula,' added the big black-haired woman, finishing off sponging the tables. 'You'll meet us all soon enough. Fred's left us some of his home-brew, and Joyce spent half her child benefit on plonk. We have some good get-togethers of an evening. You've got two, haven't you? Three is it? I've only the one. Sue had her first six weeks ago. Her old man couldn't take her being pregnant so he set fire to the house, her in it and all.'

Sue smiled self-effacingly as it was something to be ashamed of. 'He thought it was somebody else's, you see,' she began, then stopped. 'I'd better go and see if the baby's all right.'

Kathleen went to search out Vicky and David. Through the back was an overgrown walled garden, part of which had been cleared to grow vegetables. Vicky and her new friends were playing on a patch of ground between a row of runner-beans and the compost heap, deeply engrossed in the complexities of balancing on one leg while shifting pebbles from one square to another.

She discovered David in a doorway watching two boys riding a saddleless bicycle, wobbling it round the stacks of timber and bricks, roaring with laughter each time they collapsed. It was nearly nine, getting dark, the sort of time she would normally have sent him to bed. She pressed a hand on his shoulder and walked on.

Half of her craved to find a phone and ring Linda, to discover what had been happening. The other half preferred to do nothing, pretend the past had never existed.

She looked up and saw a face at an upstairs window. It was the blond woman, Dawn. She did not appear to be looking at anything in particular, the muscles in her throat rippling as if she was weeping. Kathleen turned away, re-entered the coach-house. The first person she saw was Angie, the woman who had smacked her child in the bathroom, her elbows on one of the tables, as she jerked words dispiritedly out of the side of her mouth to the red-haired helper, Maggie.

Kathleen backed out quietly, crossed the yard, passing between the stacks of junk, and went out beneath the archway. She walked under the overgrown shrubbery towards the huge bulk of the old shut-up mansion. She was close to hopelessness and misery herself, struggling to prevent them overwhelming her. Her unhappiness was compounded by the feeling of loss, however much her life before had been worse than this. It was ridiculous to want to retrieve something rotten. Yet why did it appear nostalgic in retrospect? Was it all those lost hopes she'd been treasuring through adversity like an ageing spinster who still fills drawers with materials for her dowry? Tears pricked her eyes.

Dusk was blurring the colours, darkening the overgrown laurels and philadelphus and long arms of buddleia that pointed like folded umbrellas. A figure on a bicycle with a clattering mudguard pedalled in from the road. There was a large cardboard box in the basket. She did not recognise who it was till the rider dismounted beside her.

'God, I hate the bicycle,' panted Brenda. 'But it's the only exercise I get.' She began to push the bicycle, expecting Kathleen to walk with her. 'Even if it's only to the pub to fetch some beers. We collect a little kitty for most evenings.' Still short of breath, she eyed Kathleen. 'You're not teetotal, are you?'

Kathleen laughed, and told Brenda about Mark's accusations, the binbag of bottles, and the judge's visible distaste as if a lush was ten times worse when a woman. 'I don't know why I'm laughing,' she added.

'Where would we be without a laugh?' said Brenda. 'Mind you, I wouldn't have blamed you taking to the bottle, living with one like that.' She leaned her bicycle against the wall outside her office. 'Would you ever bring this stuff in while I lock the bike up inside. Otherwise the lads here'll have it in bits.'

Maggie and Polly crossed over to the battered Mini. They waved to her as they drove off with a rasp of its exhaust. Windows everywhere were glowing with lights. The children were all inside now. Kathleen found David and Vicky watching television and persuaded them it was bedtime. She came up with them. Sarah was a small lump in her bed, fast asleep.

'How long will it be before we go home, Mum?' asked David, as he self-consciously dallied with his undressing.

'I don't know,' she whispered, a finger to her lips to keep his voice down. Considerately she turned her back and helped Vicky, who was also having difficulty undressing. In her case it was eagerness leading to frustration. She wanted instant transformation from clothes into pyjamas so that her mother would sit beside her and read to her.

'I like it here,' she said. The moment she was freed from her dress, she tore off her pants and socks, her skinny naked body wriggling like a lizard into her pyjamas before she grabbed the chosen book and flung herself into bed.

'What about the bathroom?' asked Kathleen.

'Couldn't I do it in the morning?' she grumbled, getting out of bed. 'D'you know something,' she said as her mother handed her a towel and washbag. 'When I drink blackcurrant juice, my pee still comes out yellow.'

Vicky's uninhibitedness abashed David, who had done a rapid change but had no intention of going to the bathroom till she returned. He sat dejectedly on the bed and his mother squeezed round and sat beside him, put an arm round him. Very slowly he inched closer, let his head slide down onto her breasts, till he was enfolded within her arms, then with a squeak like the air being let out from a bicycle tyre, he wept. 'I wish we were at home,' he sniffled.

After the children were settled she went back downstairs.

The interior of the coach-house was dimly lit, the kitchen area in darkness. It wasn't cold, but in the fireplace flames crackled off splintered boards, sparks flew up the chimney. Chairs had been pulled round it, a couple of old standard lamps with burn marks on the shades illuminated women's faces, arms and laps, threw glints on the glasses in their hands. A couple remained watching the television, its burble mingling with the murmur of voices.

'Come and sit here, dear,' said Brenda, patting the empty place beside her on a sofa. 'Kids settled down all right? Difficult for them in a strange place, uprooted, so many new faces. Did you get the plastic sheet all right? This sort of thing always seems to bring on a few wet beds. What'll you take? It's lager or red wine?'

Kathleen chose wine.

'None of the rest'll sit beside me, you notice?' chuckled Brenda.

'It's because I'm the symbol of authority, the male role, d'you see?'

'But we still love the bastards really,' said Paula.

There were a few titters.

'You speak for yourself,' scoffed Brenda. She laid a hand on Kathleen's arm. 'Who haven't you met? Don't worry if you can't remember their names. I forget them myself sometimes.'

'I'm Joyce,' said a thin, bespectacled girl who sat with jeaned legs tucked beneath her. 'How'd you come to be here, Kathleen?'

She suspected this was what they were waiting to hear as she explained once more.

'That's like Dawn, isn't it?' said Paula. 'Some of these judges seem to think that unless we're carried into court on a stretcher, we're putting it on. Where is Dawn by the way, is she OK?'

'Said she'd be down later,' said Sue.

'D'you know what the judge said to Dawn?' Paula continued. 'A strong woman like you should be able to defend yourself, you don't need an injunction. Never mind the fact she's half my size and her husband laid her out with a beer bottle. Then the arsehole said to her, how am I to know you didn't get your injuries falling downstairs?'

'Injunctions're a waste of time,' said Joyce, cigarette stuck in a V of fingers. 'Everyone said don't bother, learn karate or get out. Pete used to nip up every bit of skirt that could be lifted for a couple of vodkas. Out all hours night after night. I'd be grieving on a sodden pillow, and in he'd creep stinking of somebody else's perfumed BO, and drop off to sleep like I was the mattress. I didn't object because the one time I did he broke my arm in two places and cracked three ribs. After that I only had to breathe in and he took it as sign of complaint and smacked me in the mouth. One day I took two black eyes and jaw like a steak to a solicitor. No bother getting an injunction, the judge was a dear old boy, ever so concerned. But a few nights later Pete comes knocking on the door, darling, forgive me, you're the only one, and all that crap. You can't call the old bill when your bloke's on his knees blubbering. So we had a big cry and a cuddle and then it was you know what, and for a fortnight everything in the garden was sunshine. Then one evening, bingo, I'm on the floor again, growing bruises like a crop of beetroot. But no more injunctions this time. I'd had my ration. We're not like the Benefit Office, says the judge. Dishing out free hand-outs to all and sundry. You women don't seem to know your own minds. I wanted to shout at him, you try being us, I'd like to see what you'd do.'

'You can't expect judges to accept that there are men around who've the instincts of killers,' said Paula. 'Because they're fuckers themselves. All right so I'm pretty solid, but my old man used to go for me like I was a lump of wood that wouldn't split. It's no good people telling us to learn a bit of self-defence, when we don't have the aggression. Tom'd come home three hours late for his tea, tanked to his ears, and I'd slap his dinner on the table.' She wagged a finger. 'All right, I met a psychologist who said that was an act of aggression. What else I was supposed to do? It's fucking burnt, he'd scream and hurl it on the floor. Now clear it up, he'd bellow, and bang me on the side of the head with the teapot.' She lifted up her hair to display crimson skin tissue spilling up into her scalp. 'That was boiling water. I wasn't so bloody stupid to start on him as he came in the door, where've you been, why're you late, like some cows would. But same as Joyce I soon found out that if I said nothing, he'd read that as criticism too, or if I said all friendly, hallo dear, he'd belt me just the same. Then in the morning he'd be all sorry, you know me, love, when I've had a few I'm not myself. And since he was all I had, I remembered the good times. I always had a bit of hope sitting inside me like a phantom pregnancy.'

'Depends what you were brought up to expect,' said a girl called Carol.

Kathleen had already noticed her, thinking how beautiful she was. The skin of an Easter Lily, lips round as Hamburg grapes. But all set in an expressionless mask. Even when she spoke, nothing moved, as if all emotion had congealed like cold wax.

'Go on, Carol,' said Paula, nodding her head in encouragement. Everyone in the group must have known full well what was coming, but all seemed to want to hear it again.

'When I was little,' said Carol tonelessly, staring at the fire. 'My dad beat me like I was a mat he could never get the dust out of. I'd say something wrong, or spill some food, forget what I'd been told, and he'd be unbuckling his belt. I didn't know life was any different. One night he came into my room and pulled the blankets off, grabbed me by the ankles, swung me out through the open window, hanging me upside down and saying he was going to drop me. Another time he came in when I was in the bath, pushed me down and held me under the water. When I was twelve he got into my bed and told me I was old enough to be fucked. The next day I ran away, but the police picked me up and brought me back. I'll only get another hiding, I told them. But you wouldn't want to be taken into care, they said. That's much worse. So I thought maybe home can't be that bad. Mum was all right. She never hit me. But she was afraid of him, too. Every night I prayed to Jesus as I lay in bed that He would let me die and come to Him, and be safe. I wanted to kill myself but I knew it was a sin, and then I mightn't get to Jesus. My dad was quite good-looking really, with a long moustache and curling hair. He used to breed show birds in an aviary in the garden. I can still see him holding them in his hands, stroking their feathers, talking soothingly to them. I knew I must be bad.' She fell silent.

'Then at eighteen you met and married Jimmy,' prompted Paula, nodding her head in encouragement.

'Everybody thought Jimmy great,' said Carol, her voice low and monotonous against the crackling fire and the still-muttering television behind them. However many times everyone had heard her story, they listened in rapt silence. 'He was like my dad, curly-haired and a moustache. He'd stroke me and call me pretty names like my dad did with his birds. After we were married and he began to hit me, I thought, this is what they all do, what else did I expect? But when I talked to other women at the clinic I discovered their husbands never hit them. So I knew then it was me, there was something bad in me that had to be punished. One day I bought a hundred aspirin and swallowed the lot. I thought maybe Jesus'd understand. But I sicked them all up. Somebody told me afterwards I should have taken them a few at a time. I felt so ill I collapsed into bed. When I didn't get up to cook his dinner, Jimmy pulled me out of bed and dragged me round the house, kicking and punching me. My screams made the neighbours phone the police. They brought me here.'

'One thing for sure, Carol, dear,' said Brenda. 'There's nothing bad about you. But there's a lot of sick men about.'

'Some say we're the unlucky ones,' said Penny, waving her scarred hand. 'Like people who buy cars made on Monday morning, we got the duff models. Then you're lumbered with them.'

'You feel you've got to have a man,' said Joyce. 'If you don't have somebody nobody'll respect you. Better a shit than no one at all.'

'You always hope,' said Sue, the young girl with a mass of brown hair. 'I'd think, I'm leaving this time, definitely, no changing my mind, this is it. But pain don't last for ever, and I'd see all the difficulties of leaving, where'd I go, what about money, how would I manage. Then the bugger'd cry like a little boy and I'd be hugging him and thinking, he's not so bad really. A few grains of love's worth a mountain of hatred. Sometimes I wake in the night now.' Her voice broke. 'And still think I love him, the bastard.' She paused, wiping her eyes. 'He was a sadist. That's the only word for him. It made him feel big and strong when I was screaming. When I told him I was pregnant, he swore it was someone else's. He tied me to the bed, said he was going to heat up the poker with a blow-lamp. There came the sound of explosion and him shouting and then the smell of burning. By rights I should have died that night with the house on fire. But you can be better than Houdini when you're shit-scared. I was out of the ropes and through the window and a ten foot drop to the grass below before I'd time to think about the baby inside and that I hadn't got a stitch on. The firemen found me blubbering in the shed, wrapped up in plastic bags. I couldn't tell them what happened because the baby was coming.' She paused, sniffling. 'He could be so nice when he wanted, make me feel real good inside. I wish I'd died in that fire.'

Brenda went over to her, put her arms round her. 'Don't say that, Sue. That's never going to happen again. You're safe here with us.'

'It's not the same,' sobbed Sue, covering her face with her hands. 'It's not like being wanted by a bloke. It's only kindness.'

At that moment there came a loud knocking on the coach-house door. The door was always opening and rattling shut, as women or children came and went. But this was a peremptory, intrusive sound. A shiver of alarm ran round everyone. Some twisted in their chairs, and others half rose, their fear turning into a bristle of defensiveness.

'It's only me,' said a woman, pushing open the door. 'Sorry to barge in so late.'

'Geraldine,' exclaimed Brenda, already halfway across the brick floor.

Geraldine was tall, expensively dressed, with silver hair.

'She's a solicitor,' Paula whispered to Kathleen.

'Have you room?' asked Geraldine. 'I thought we'd just chance coming as it was all a bit of an emergency and we weren't near a phone.'

'We'll find somewhere,' replied Brenda.

A woman carrying a baby in one arm and clutching a small girl by the hand came in. The hiss of breath as we all gathered round was like a tree felled. It wasn't just that the woman's face was bruised, but the small girl's face was purple as a summer pudding. 'This is Charlene Williams,' said Geraldine. 'And this is Sam. We're going to court in the morning, but it wasn't safe for them to remain.'

Mark Clement rose from his seat and went over to the window. His instinct was to throw it open wide and suck in lungfuls of fresh air, his head choking with the images she had created of the refuge.

'How could any human being treat a child like that?' Kathleen shook her head as if to flick the memory away. 'She was the same age as Sarah. In fact the bastard was arrested the next day and remanded, so they were able to go home.'

He was close to shouting, that's enough, I don't want to hear any more. Instead he went to fetch the coffee-jug from the cabinet.

Kathleen sat slumped with exhaustion. 'You can understand why we were like a sisterhood of rage.'

'There are times when I feel disgusted with my own sex.' He was aware of being in need of reassurance himself. 'I'd understand if you saw all men as monsters.'

She sipped her replenished coffee, frowned. 'Maybe women like us share some common factor that aggravates men.'

He knew she wasn't listening, that she did not realise how shocked he was. 'It makes me feel guilty to be male.'

'We did share one thing. Our family was everything, we didn't exist outside it, yet we couldn't take hold of what was going on inside it.'

He went back to the window, pressed his fingers on the sill, stared out. Voices of children playing entered the open casement, mingled in his head with distant echoes of Respighi's The Birds. He drew in a deep breath. 'So would you say that you live your life through other people?'

She looked at him warily. 'Is that a bad thing?'

He turned round. 'What would happen if your children were taken from you, and you were left with nothing?'

Her expression contracted as if he had struck her. 'I dread that more than anything in the world.'

'But you'd manage. You told me you were a solitary child when you lived in Ireland; that you found distraction in books and your imagination.'

'That was different,' she exclaimed. 'I knew nothing else then.'

'Most of us live much of our lives through other people. You could say that I live through other people's problems.' He glanced at his watch. Nearly six o'clock, half an hour past the allotted time.

'I'm glad we share something,' she said quietly, her smile hooking across her face, her eyes searching his.

He nodded abstractedly. 'The human condition is based on interdependence. Which makes us all so vulnerable to our fellows' pronouncements.'

She hitched her bag over her shoulder and stood up. She was still regarding him. Her eye-contact is getting much stronger, he thought.

'This talking is beginning to give me a sense of perspective,' she said. 'It was all so jumbled before.'

He put his notes into his briefcase. 'Then we're making progress.'

He stood observing the mid-blue blouse she was wearing, the way it billowed carelessly over her breasts, had a drawstring collar that accentuated the narrow column of her neck. Below she wore a dark-blue skirt that hugged the spheres of hip and haunch, and revealed white-tighted calves of shapely legs. This is an inventory of lust, he thought as he held the door open for her. What was he thinking of?

'I couldn't identify you with those sort of men, you know,' she said as they went downstairs together. 'I feel you're on my side.'

'You may not entirely see me as a man,' he said as they reached the hallway. 'The role of counsellor being supposed to be caring, I might appear more as female.'

They found the outer door locked and he had to use his keys to switch off the burglar alarm to let them out. 'Besides,' he said, holding the door open for her. 'Old men are less likely to be a threat.'

'You're hardly old,' she protested.

'Old enough to be your father, if you remember,' he murmured, as they set off along the pavement.

'Surely it's the person who matters,' she said. 'Not their age?'

This was hardly the pinched, anxious woman of a few days ago, he thought. She was flirting with him. He was not sure that he wasn't shocked, as if someone in her situation oughtn't to remain properly depressed.

'Such kind words.' He pointed towards the sign-board of the Dancing Bear down the road. 'If you have a few minutes to spare I'll buy you a drink.'

'I'd like that.'

He brought her a glass of white wine and himself a pint of Adnams. 'There's nothing so good for the ego of the elderly male as to be seen in the company of a pretty young woman.'

He thought he might be overdoing it. But he could tell she was pleased.

She drew in her chin. 'If only it was true.'

'So you're calling me a liar?' He elevated his eyebrows to indicate it was only banter.

She lowered her eyes. 'It was nice to hear you say it.'

'Then I should say it more often. You should know what you are.'

But her animation had drooped. 'You're trying to boost the confidence of your client, aren't you?'

He could see that her self-assurance was still only skin-deep. 'Look how you've improved since we started the sessions. A few days ago you were a wilted rose. Now you've blossomed, begun to reassert yourself. You possess far more inner strength than you realise.'

She frowned. 'You don't have to go on being professional.'

He shook his head and stuck his chin out at her. 'I'm responding to you as a person. You are a very attractive person.'

She sipped her wine, gazing at him over the top of the glass, not speaking. Just like Nicole, he thought.

'I think you're attractive too,' she said. She coloured, then as if not knowing where to look, glanced at her watch, became anxious. 'I ought to get back.'

She drank off the rest of her wine, and as she turned, about to rise, met his eyes again. In that moment he became aware that in the intensity of her gaze burned more than ordinary regard.

As if caught off balance by the realisation of what she was expressing, she fumbled with her clothing and handbag, became embarrassed.

'My landlady's looking after the children. She only expected me to be away a couple of hours. I'll see you... tomorrow?'

She turned at the door to look back at him, her cheeks suffused, her lips parted with a smile he had never seen before, then she was gone.

There were more people in the pub now, faces bubbling with chatter and laughter. He could have misread her expression, he thought. Perhaps he ought to gulp down his beer and rush after her, clear up the matter at once. But what would he say to her? Look, our relationship is and must be purely professional. And what might that do to her progress? He must be more circumspect, he thought. Clients could become dependent as lead waterwings. He must clear a space between them, keep sufficient distance; even if the underlying relationship was affecting her recovery. It had been his male susceptibility that had allowed her to move in close. He should never have invited her for a drink. Yet what was it that was pleasing about her? A woman with dependent children, her family life in chaos, still married to a maniac? The physical chemistry, he thought. Operating subconsciously. The fact was that he liked her. How stupid of him. It was all very well for those who can only live by rules to say professionals should never allow personal feelings to intervene. Unaffected, controlled emotions could indicate an inflexible intellect. It might be best to have her transferred to another therapist.

These thoughts kept recurring as he walked home. Once inside the house, his anxiety was calmed by the familiarity of its disorderliness, the comfort of its chaos. Such disorganisation appealed to him like a neglected garden where man-bred plants reverted to their own free spirits. He went into the bedroom and sat down at the piano, not so much to drive out his thoughts as to heighten them, inflate them with adrenalin. Rachmaninov came to his fingers, the pianist's pianist, the vigorous virtuosity halfway into the C sharp minor Prelude, he could hear it all crystal-clearly. The damper pedal welded the sounds together, burred off the rough edges. His digital ability was like the skater who whirls into a double axel, falls on landing and his momentum spins him back up onto his feet again, whereby falling becomes part of the choreography.

Then the phone rang.

It was Nicole. 'It's two months old now. Seven months to birth or one to execution. Terence is as patient as an owl, can't see what all the flap is. D'you think there's something wrong with me that I can't make up my mind? Worrying's making me ill. I don't think I'm cut out to be a mother. What do you think?'

For a moment his mind whirled in panic as if he was confusing different client problems.

'Depends how you look at it,' he replied, gathering his thoughts. 'You may have considered you were making love when this happened. But you were also making babies. That's what fucking's for. And the first word babies say is mama, the Latin for breast. So women as far as babies are concerned are simply breasts to suck milk out of. Birth remains a primitive business, don't lose sight of that.'

There was silence. 'That's disgusting.'

'Don't forget that of all animals human females suffer most sickness when pregnant and most pain at birth and have least control over their offspring.'

'I never expected such prejudice from you,' shouted Nicole. 'Or are you playing games?'

'Try making a balance sheet,' he suggested mildly. 'Pros and cons. See which comes out longest.'

'I already did. Murder came out tops. Wipe the sheet clean, carry on the great work unburdened, be free to take up whatever opportunities aren't offered graduates any more. But my doctor's pro-life so I may have to go private. It'll cost me £250 and I haven't got it.'

'I'll put a cheque in the post tomorrow.'

There was a prolonged silence. 'No, dad,' she moaned at last, sobbing mingling with her words. 'I don't want thirty pieces of silver. Don't you understand?'

'Sorry. Why don't you come down and I'll practise fishing on you.'

'Fishing?'

'Dangle the bait. The answer's in there somewhere.'

'Play some Chopin for me tonight.'

Of all composers he could make Chopin sound the most authentic; the passionate expressiveness, the bounding cadences, the florid phrasework, all lent themselves to his bunches of fingers. It would be untrue to say that accidental dischords never vibrated in his cochlea. But because he heard the music perfectly in his head, any notes out of focus heightened the intensity of the flood. So he could play the Mazurka in F sharp, threw his fingers down the keys to pelt the Polish resonances round the room till he was dizzy with emotion. One neighbour had genuinely asked why he didn't give concerts. Someone else had said, like Florence Desmond? But he didn't know whom the man meant.

The truth could be that Mark Montjoy Clement was no different from dipsomaniac, junky or voodoo dancer. He needed to extract his ecstasy from something, and as a murderer may pluck the entrails from his victim as easily as a surgeon from his patient, so the piano had no option.

The front-door bell rang, rang again, continued to ring as if it knew it had to persevere.

'Forgot my key,' said Madeleine as she slapped her lips over his face, took his arm and guided him to a chair. 'You're in a state. Sit there while I make some coffee. I could hear the Chopin half a mile away. Had you forgotten we're going to the Tom Stoppard tonight?'

He sat shivering on the pile of magazines which hid a chair, echoes of the music rippling through him as if his nerves were the piano wires still reverberating. 'What's it all about?' Madeleine called from the kitchen. 'Something got under your skin. Was it a client?'

She knows me too well, he thought. She brought the mug of black coffee, held it to his chin. 'It's not too hot. You're in such a state.'

He was forcibly reminded of infancy, the assumption that the incapable child must be thirsty, liquid slopped into his throat, down his chin. 'Nicole's pregnant,' the half-drowned man spluttered.

'It's hardly the end of the world,' said Madeleine, good-humouredly, and over the menopause. 'Why don't the young take precautions?'

Soon afterwards he was reclining in the basalt vinyl interior of her car with its firefly digital displays indicating fuel in its belly and the heart-rate of its engine. 'Nicole plans her life very carefully. This was an accident. It's thrown her out of gear. Her mother was an organiser too,' he added.

'If only we could all plan everything down to the last detail,' sighed Madeleine. 'Why, we might even be able to out-manoeuvre the lunacies this paranoid government paralyses us with.'

He forebore from pointing out that goverments might feel the same about recalcitrant councils which tried to wreck their policies. He did not remember much of the play, though the naked secretary on her trapeze was a vision he found singularly erotic. It made him wonder what Kathleen looked like without her clothes, so that he instantly became mortified with guilt for such a basic conjecture.

He only surfaced from his anxiety after they had taken their seats in a restaurant. A glass of claret emptied its earth-and-fruit-clad liquor down his throat and slices of flesh fell apart between his teeth like perished rubber. Another evening swallowed in a few singed mouthfuls with a feeling that there had been no time to catch up with himself.

'You never talk about Veronique,' Madeleine was saying. 'It's almost as if you want people to believe you had three daughters by immaculate conception. I mean I'm always blathering about Desmond as if he's like some old favourite dress hanging in my wardrobe that I no longer fit, but cannot bear to throw away. You once said to recall Veronique was like disinterring a coffin full of worms. I was so revolted by the image I didn't want to enquire further. Though I could never understand why you of all people would want to keep it buried inside you.'

He sighed. 'My fear is that I have no real feelings left, that I am merely a recording apparatus.'

'Mark, darling,' she exclaimed, pushing aside the basket of bread-rolls to grasp his hand. 'You are full of feeling. You play the piano with such passion.'

'Have you ever thought that real beauty might be nothing more than pain?' he said. 'For the fleeting, the unattainable, for that which must perish, is lost? A composer writes his anguish into the bars of his music, and we say, how beautiful. I was looking out of the window the other day and I saw a woman standing in her doorway, staring after a departing car. Then she clung to the jamb with one hand, covered her face with the other and wept. Although

I knew she must be unhappy, my first thought was, what a beautiful image she made.'

'I know Veronique caused you a lot of suffering.'

He flicked his eyebrows resignedly. 'You know what happened. I thought we were happy, that life was good. Then I woke up one morning alone. It was an indescribable shock. I had been living a lie. All those months I had been loving her and thought she had been loving me, when in reality she had been despising me and loving someone else. I'd been kissing her and putting my cock inside her unaware that someone else's had been there a few hours earlier. It made me feel like a replica. I was the book of which someone says, I think I read that once, can't remember a thing about it.' His voice began to rise. 'I kept asking myself, what was it about me that drove her into another man's arms?'

'Shall I tell you?' said Madeleine, licking chocolate dessert off her lower lip. 'It was because you're afraid of women.'

'No I'm not,' he protested indignantly.

'You want their good opinion of you, you want them to like you, so you overdo trying to be fair to them. You won't make demands on them lest they resent you. You're much more unsure of yourself than you appear.'

He pointed a finger at her. 'We all have our weaknesses.'

'Oh yes?' she demanded.

'You're bombastic because you're afraid your intellect is insufficient to win you the argument.'

She laughed out loud. He picked up the bottle to split the remains of the wine between them. But she reached out and made sure most of the bottle went into her own glass. 'That's enough for you, or your performance later will be affected. As I'm going to be away for the next few days, I need it to be good.'

'And your rampant sexuality is because part of you is still a child and needs masses of tactile reassurance. The next few days?' he echoed in surprise. 'Where are you going?'

'You're hopeless. I told you weeks ago. The symposium in Budapest.'

'Of course. About how to adapt the outdated buildings of ancient cities for modern people. As our city council housing expert you're going to tell them about the mess you've made of ours.'

'I haven't done too badly, have I?'

She was always eager for his approval, he thought. It seemed on the one hand a demeaning aspect of so strong a personality, and on the other an endearingly childlike quality. Three-headed Hydra and trinity of transactional analysis, the child mother of the woman. Could he ever stop seeing people as collections of subconscious reactions?

'You mean like allowing those hideous office blocks to disfigure the city? Those damned shopping precincts. Handsome old buildings torn down for vested interests to throw up their concrete charnel-houses.'

'That all happened before I was on the council,' she protested.

'Sometimes I used to think that if I'd found out before she left, I might have strangled her.' He saw Madeleine's startled glance. 'Veronique, I mean.'

They argued over the bill when it came, whose turn it was to pay, almost tearing it in half. 'You bought the theatre tickets,' he hissed as she uncapped her pen to write a cheque, and he slapped down a bundle of banknotes on the plate. He always preferred to pay with actual money, relishing the sense of trade, exchanging fine engravings of the Duke of Wellington and Florence Nightingale for goods and services. Scribbled notes of demand to a bank on scraps of paper did not appeal to him.

He thought of trade that night, providing his sexual rod and seminal fluid to stimulate the white cornucopia of Madeleine in return for a brief orgasmic signature. Was he being more than cynical, he wondered, as he slipped from the bed onto the piano stool, paced reassuringly up and down the Goldberg Variations. The variations of his own were like unintentional splashes of colour, radio interference, accidental syncopation, confrontations of cats, schematic alternatives that even Bach might have cast a wry smile upon.

He was feeling jaundiced, he thought, as if an unexpected light source had entered his spectrum and shed illumination on the flaws in his life.

On and off during the next day between seeing clients, writing reports, discussing cases, he worried about how he would manage Kathleen when she came again. Half of him insisted that he was creating a ghost out of a creaking floorboard, and that he had entirely imagined her interest in him. The other half considered how to reset the perspective of their relationship to allow him to continue assessing her. He argued that it could be a severe set-back to regaining her confidence if he had to transfer her to someone else. One more rejection, one more punch into the soft susceptibilities of her mind. Poor unfortunate woman. Surely a man of his experience could control the situation?

When Kathleen arrived for her appointment, her appearance took his breath away. She had gathered her hair back with combs to display her long neck. She wore discreet yet manifest make-up. She was wearing a slim, waisted dress of thin stripes of shades of mauve, with red shoes and bangles and a thin coral band round her throat. All this damned allure, he thought dismally, is living proof.

'Everything all right?' he asked, trying to sound businesslike.

She nodded, the warmth in her face shivering behind taut uncertainty.

Just when I ought to be telling her how attractive she looks, he thought, to commend her appearance, give credit where it's due, boost her confidence as she puts it, I can't for fear of being misinterpreted.

A fly buzzed on a windowpane. In a window of a house across the street an adolescent girl leaned out, a cigarette in one hand. On the house's television aerial perched a one-legged seagull. The Waltz of the Toreadors was in his head today, as persistent as the fly.

'Where did we get to yesterday?' he heard himself ask.

Her smile hooked up briefly, as if she understood him perfectly.

At least, he thought, they were client and therapist again.

'**EVERY** night Sarah insisted I read her the Three Little Pigs. It must have seeped into my brain. I kept dreaming about them. The wolf prowling about outside, snorting, growling, scratching at the door. Then I'd realise the children weren't in the house. And I'd hear them in the distance, squealing with laughter, coming closer, not knowing that he was waiting for them.

Like others there I grew attached to the refuge. It was a relief that there were other women in the same boat, that it wasn't just me. But it was also the sense of involvement. I've heard people talk of the purpose and camaraderie generated in a war.

When women arrived in bits, weeping, dragging themselves about as if they were dying, with miserable, wailing children in tow, they were like the wounded returning from the front. Brenda was the hospital matron revitalising them. We'd see them restored in a few days from crumpled wrecks into full-blown women again, and the kids'd be laughing and playing. Not always, of course. One woman had a nervous breakdown, an ambulance came for her and her children were taken into care. Another slashed her wrists, blood like red wine all over the bathroom. But we found her in time.

There were difficult ones like Dawn. Quarrels would blow up about nothing, about who should have second helpings or who should sit where, resentment over the slightest sign of favouritism. Some of the children were very disturbed. One dragged another off the rocking-horse and nearly started a civil war.

Some, like Paula, were irrepressible, always saw the irony. We had to laugh at ourselves, pile on the self-ridicule.

One night a carload of cat-calling men rolled up and started heaving bricks at the windows. Children were screaming, Brenda phoned the police, while Paula and Joyce rushed out and threw bricks back. The men were taken by surprise, the car driver started to back out, afraid of it being hit. That encouraged the rest of us out there like raving lunatics, hurling anything we could lay our hands on. The car reversed into the police coming up the other way, and then there was a real punch-up. We all danced round cheering and yelling. Our blood was up.

Afterwards we had a post-mortem. It was obvious from the name shouted out that one of the men was the husband of Sharon, a trinkety blonde who'd been with us a week, and that it was she who must have given away the address. There was an overwhelming vote to chuck her and her kids out there and then. The poor girl was crying her eyes out with everyone yelling at her. Then Brenda started stamping around breathing hellfire, lecturing us about the sisterhood of women, how we should stand together, that we shouldn't behave like men, we should show forgiveness and understanding. Anyway what the hell did we think we looked like, screaming and throwing bricks, worse than yobs? We were even more shamefaced later when it turned out it wasn't Sharon's fault at all, her husband got the address off a mate in the police.

I don't think a place like that could manage without a person like Brenda. Some thought her too fussy, too bossy, too nosy. But she kept us going with that mixture of grumbling encouragement. We knew she cared, that she'd get things done. She had my Income Support organised within a week. Even got my solicitor going.

He'd laid a complaint that much of our evidence had been completely overlooked by the first hearing. So they gave us another. It took a good few weeks to happen, of course. Mark never turned up, so I got my Non-Molestation Order reinstated. But it was too late to get the house back. Mark had handed in the tenancy.

I'd been keeping in touch with Linda. She'd seen Mark collecting mail from the house. Then one morning a pantechnicon backed up outside and three men started emptying the house of furniture. She told them it wasn't Mark's, but they wouldn't stop so she phoned Mr Onion, but he wasn't there, she tried the police but they said it was a civil matter. Two weeks later new tenants were in. So when I got my injunction Brenda and Monica went to work on the Council to give me a house somewhere else.

It was a little mid-terrace. There were some Chinese cooks on one side, whom I never saw but sometimes heard hawking their throats in the middle of the night, and an old lady on the other, Mrs Mathews, nearly ninety and with arthritis in her neck so she could only look at her feet. She said the local shops were too dear, so she'd snail-pace bent-necked half a mile into the city to do her shopping. You have to admire the tenacity of the old.

Council houses, of course, come unfurnished. Fred found me a cooker, an old telly and a few sticks of chairs and Brenda got me a grant from the DSS for bedding, and I sold a ring of my mother's to buy a fridge and some crockery. The first night we had a great party; Penny, Paula and Joyce came together with Sue and Brenda, and Clare and Linda came as well.

The house was drearily tatty, so I used to take Sarah off to look for bargains in sales. I bought a twenty-five litre drum of white emulsion at an auction for a quid. Eight rolls of Laura Ashley paper at a jumble sale for 20p. Two lampshades for 10p. The place began to look quite homely. though I would have liked my family pictures back and the few knick-knacks. Mr Onion had written to Mark about them, but of course there was never any reply.

All I knew of Mark during this time was that he was living in the farmhouse he'd bought a few miles from Ipswich, near Hintlesham. Mr Onion found that out so he could sent the divorce petition there.

Despite being lonely and often thinking back to the good times, it began to feel as though I might really be free of him at last.

WHEN the front-door bell rang, Kathleen glanced at her watch. Three o'clock. Monday. Linda, she thought, putting down the palette knife she had been using to ice David's birthday cake ready for the next day.

A man stood in the doorway half-obscured by a number of parcels and a bunch of flowers he was clutching.

'Kathleen darling, how lovely to see you. How are you?'

She stood petrified as if a great crocodile was rearing up on the doorstep.

'I've brought a birthday present for David. Plus some little things for the girls, so they won't feel left out. And some flowers for you.'

He moved forward as if assuming his right to enter. 'Just want to wish him many happy returns when he gets back from school.'

'No,' she faltered. 'You can't come in. You know that. The injunction. You're not supposed to be here at all.'

'Surely you can't object to me bringing my son a present on his birthday?'

'His birthday's tomorrow.'

He frowned, put-out for a moment, then recovered himself quickly. 'I can't come tomorrow.' He smiled agreeably. 'All right, I'll wait in the car, if you'd prefer.' He took a step down the path and turned back. 'You don't have to worry, you know. I accept that the marriage is finished.'

She was still rigid with alarm. That last sentence echoed in the back of her mind with unexpected pain: *...the marriage is finished....*

'I'm sorry, of course,' he said, still smiling. 'I think you're making a mistake.'

Each word seemed weighed down with regret. But she thought she recognised the undercurrent of incipient threat, and shivered inwardly.

'The kitchens are going like a bomb,' he said, chuckling. 'I'll be a millionaire soon if it goes on at this rate.'

She dared not comment.

'There're a few things we ought to talk over,' he said casually. 'Like making arrangements about contact. You're not going to object to me seeing the kids, are you?'

She shook her head. Apart from her ingrained proclivity for fairness, she was too scared to object.

'We may as well be sensible. Sort out as much as we can between us. Bloody solicitors.' He rolled his eyes heavenwards. 'It's all very well for you, being on Legal Aid, but I have to pay an arm and a leg for every minute.'

Listen to him, just listen to him, she thought, feeling her skin prickle at the memory of his lies in court. I know the sound of his patter so well. Why do I feel so helpless when I hear it?

He looked at his watch. 'They'll be back from school soon. If I come in for a minute, then I could give David a surprise. And while we're waiting we could fix up a date for me to take him out.'

It seemed a harmless enough proposition; and she wanted to seem reasonable. 'As long as you promise you'll go immediately afterwards.'

He followed her into the dining-room, put the parcels and the flowers on the table.

Sarah ran up to him uninhibitedly. He picked her up and sat down with her on his knee. 'A present for you, too, darling,' he said, handing her a parcel.

She tore at the paper. 'David's birthday tomorrow, Daddy,' she said, pointing at the cake in the kitchen. 'You come to party?'

Kathleen, making coffee, strained to listen. Would he take advantage of Sarah's invitation? What would she do if the children wanted him to come? She shivered, already regretting her rashness allowing him in.

'Daddy's busy tomorrow, darling,' he replied. 'Another time.'

She relaxed half a degree. Sarah ripped the paper off and pulled out a toy furry kitten. 'Are you going to say thank you?' she called.

She brought in two cups of coffee. Remembering that he took a spoon-and a-half of sugar had caught in her throat.

'What about this weekend?' asked Mark as they watched Sarah giving the kitten a meticulous anatomical examination. 'I could collect David Sunday morning and bring him back at teatime? I expect you'd like a break from all of them, but I'll try and fix something up for the girls later. Don't want any of them to lose touch with their dad.'

'As long as I know in advance,' she said, amazed to hear herself speak so unemotionally when inside she was knotted with apprehension.

'If Sunday's inconvenient, I could manage Saturday, only I could be called out.'

His reasonableness made her ache with tiny lesions of regret.

There was the scuffing of shoes on the path outside, voices shrieking like squabbling blackbirds. As the children burst into the inner room, their argument froze in mid-utterance.

'Dad?' exclaimed David, breathlessly.

'Here,' said Mark effusively, rising with the parcel held in outstretched arms. 'I've brought you a little present. Many happy returns.'

David was lost for words. Almost cross-eyed with uncertainty, he kept glancing from one parent to the other as he clutched the parcel.

'Go on, then,' urged his father. 'Open it.'

He hesitated. 'But my birthday's not till tomorrow.'

'We don't mind, do we, darling?'

Mark's use of the word "darling" and his leer filled her with alarm. She could barely move her head.

David began to pluck eagerly at the wrapping. Sarah watched with goldfish mouth. Vicky had squeezed round to lean close to her mother. Exclaiming with delight, David lifted out a model army vehicle together with radio control-box. It looked expensive to Kathleen, far more than she could ever afford. There was also something repugnantly corruptive about it, as if Mark was offering his son a cigar to learn smoking.

'It's remote-controlled,' Mark explained, leaning over to press a switch. 'They put in the batteries in the shop.' He showed David how it operated.

Sarah discarded her kitten and moved close, frowning. Kathleen put an arm round the silent watchful Vicky.

The toy vehicle began trundling across the floor, small engine whirring, David clutching the control-box, eyes bright with excitement. 'You've got the hang of it,' said Mark, looking at his watch. 'I must be going.'

'Is this other parcel for Vicky?' Kathleen asked as he headed for the door.

Mark turned, striking his forehead with the palm of a hand. 'Vicky darling, sorry. Of course, this is for you.' His foot trod on something and he looked down. 'You've dropped your kitten, Sarah,' he exclaimed, picking it up off the floor.

But Sarah had gone back to the kitchen where she had been engaged in the manufacture of murky little buns from the residue of David's birthday cake mixture.

David went out with his father to say good-bye. Kathleen remained standing by the table, looking down at the flowers, a patriotic mixture of white chrysanthemums, blue irises and pink carnations. It was difficult to conceive of such beautiful blooms as anything but an innocent gift. So why did they make her feel ill?

Vicky sat at the table, her parcel unopened, frowning at her mother. 'You said Daddy wasn't allowed to come into the house because of what he did to you.'

Kathleen started, stung by her reproach. 'It was a special occasion, darling, because of David's birthday present.'

'Emma told me at the refuge,' said Vicky tearfully, 'that her father wasn't allowed to come in the house in case he killed her mother.'

'It's not like that now,' said Kathleen, soothingly. 'Things'll be better now. He'll come round sometimes and take you out for a treat.'

'Will you come too?'

Kathleen shook her head.

Vicky jumped up wild-eyed and clutched her, crying. 'No, mummy, no, I don't want to go with him, I want to stay with you.'

This is my panic too, shivered Kathleen, hugging her, we're equally paranoid about the man.

She hardly slept at all that night, Vicky having nightmares which upset Sarah, so that Kathleen had to take them both into her own bed to comfort them.

That Friday Vicky came running into the house from school, alone, white-faced and breathless. 'David's gone into the car with Daddy. He wanted me to, but I wouldn't.'

Kathleen found herself beginning to tremble.

Half an hour later David came in, flushed with excitement. 'Daddy took me for a drive. Vicky's such a crybaby. He only wanted to arrange a time for me to come out.'

There seemed little wrong with that, except... 'David, you're supposed to be in charge, not leave Vicky to come back on her own.'

'It was her own fault,' he scoffed. 'She wouldn't come in the car. Besides she knows the way. I've trained her.'

There boasts his father, she thought. Anyway, she'd trust Vicky ten times more than him.

Her trepidation grew hour by hour as the time of the outing drew nearer.

Mark arrived half an hour late. Throughout the time David was away her nerves were pinging with anxiety. She could concentrate so little that she started a wash and left out the soap powder, found herself putting a bottle of bleach away in the fridge.

In the end David was left back an hour early. The only jarring aspect was Mark pushing into the house again. She had hoped he would remain in the car or come no further than the front-door, but he swept in proprietorially. She felt it would spoil the air of geniality to make a fuss over the rules of the injunction. But all the time he was in the house her chest was squeezed so tight she could hardly breathe. Vicky fled upstairs.

He wanted to make arrangements for a further outing. 'I thought of going on the river, hiring a launch. Perhaps we could all go out together?' he suggested, regarding Kathleen meaningfully.

He seemed to have forgotten his debacle on the river. Her stiffening expression was sufficient response.

'Surely we can do something together as a family? For the sake of the children?' He turned back from the door when about to leave. 'What's the matter with Vicky? She's always running away from me. And David told me she wouldn't even open her present, he had to do it for her. Have you been saying things to her?'

'Give her time,' said Kathleen quickly. 'While we were at the refuge, several badly-beaten and hysterical women came in, and she's picked up some of the fear that everyone had for fathers.'

'I should have guessed,' he muttered, and she could see him

suppressing his annoyance. 'Don't let me catch...' He broke off. 'All that sort of thing's finished, isn't it? Try to make her understand.'

Later that evening she overheard David remonstrating with Vicky.

'You're stupid. What're you afraid of Daddy for? He never really hit Mummy, not like those other women from the refuge were beaten up by their husbands. Why should he hurt her? He loves her. She got those bruises from falling over. He'd like us all to live together again, like other families. Daddy's good, he loves us.'

Cold fear chilled the listening Kathleen and she shivered with dread as she leaned to catch Vicky's response.

'You're stupid. You'd believe anything he says. You know perfectly well Daddy hit her. You just like him because he gave you a big present. Daddy's always liked you best because you're a boy.'

The little girl's acumen was some relief. But over the next few days the relationship between David and his mother began to deteriorate. He became unco-operative and rebellious, filled with a newly-found resentment. On several occasions the friction overrode her natural patience, flared into conflict and tears. 'If Daddy was here he wouldn't make me go to bed now... Daddy'd let me stay up and watch that programme... I hate rice, why can't we have chips, Daddy always has chips... Daddy said this shirt's pansy... You're always going on at me... I hate you, you're horrible.'

Kathleen agonised over these outbursts, trying to see how she could have acted any differently, how she could have avoided the conflicts. There was no reasoning with David, it was as if he had suddenly reverted to a frightened wild animal to whom kindness is a waste of time.

Mark Clement stood waiting by the percolator for it to fill. The burnt caramel colour in the bowl had the same tincture of anticipation as the red of a glass of claret.

He had noticed that she would on occasion clip two fingers and a thumb about her chin as if grasping her concentration by the stem, then allow her forefinger to run along her lower lip, never quite putting it into her mouth.

'I thought of something I wanted to tell you last night,' she said. 'An incident in my childhood. One of those things that remain unexplained, stuck in the mind.'

'Go on,' he said.

'There were paddocks behind the yards at our house, some of them not much bigger than tennis courts. Most had grown into each other, the hedges worn away by the passage of animals. Some of the gaps were studded with hawthorn trunks twisted like gnarled harps. In other places the hedges had spread out like copses, and over them loomed big unkempt ash trees and oaks. The land had that arcane, ancient feel of passed centuries, of history eroded by time, melting back into the soil. Usually it was inhabited by horses, sometimes a few cattle, a tatterdemalion Eden, ragged bridal with mayflower, the banks pocked with rabbit-holes and covered in primroses and violets, wrens no bigger than walnuts flitting silently about the roots and a heron like a halberdier stalking down the stream.

In one field there were a row of old stone sheds used for keeping winter-feed in. The end shed had a stable-door. Passing it one day I heard noises, and wondered what animal was shut inside.

On going a bit closer I was shocked; the noises were words. They were something like: "...bloody bastards, bloody bastards, what the hell d'they think they're at, Good Lord Jesus, will you for Christ's sake do something, can't you hear me, it's not right, it's not right at all..."

All the bolts on the door were shut fast. "Is there somebody in there?" I asked.

"The devil there is, this is somebody all right, will you let me out of here quick."

I hesitated, my mind filling with tales of fairies and dwarves and goblins. Could this be Rumpelstiltskin himself, or was I in the position of Pandora about to expose terrible troubles upon the world if I opened the door?

Whoever was inside must have been observing me through a crack in the wood. “There’s a good little girl, I’ve been shut in here by a terrible mistake, and I’ve shouted myself hoarse and I’m near dead with starvation, you just let me out now, there’s a good girl...” and his voice ran on like that while I fetched an old bucket to stand on to reach the top bolt, and then I pulled the two bottom bolts. The doors flew violently open, knocking me onto my back.

I saw a tailless creature with smooth white skin flee across the field as fast as its scrawny backlegs would carry it, its globular haunches rippling. For a few seconds I was convinced it was a goblin, some night creature caught out of its habitat. It was only as it twisted sideways to get through a gap in the hedge I realised it was a man, and that he was completely naked. By the time I’d got up, he had vanished. My heart was thumping. There was nothing in the shed but trampled straw.

The next day there was a strange grey pony poking its head out of that same shed. We had plenty of vacant stables in the yard so when I saw D’Arcy, the groom who looked after my father’s horses, coming up to the kitchen I ran to ask him.

“It’s one of McKeever’s. Jumped out of their land. Been in there a week back and they still haven’t come for him. He had all the mares in a lather.”

“He wasn’t in there yesterday.”

“Don’t be talking nonsense, of course he was.’

I was never one to argue. But I thought that he might say something to Mrs Jones the housekeeper after I’d left, and tiptoed back to listen.

“It must have been her let him out, damn the child. We’ll never get the money now.”

“I’ve got his clothes all dried and pressed. What’ll I do with them?”

“Burn them. He’d never have the nerve.”

I never heard anymore about it. I didn’t tell anyone because my father always grew irritable whenever I tried talking to him. I knew my mother would dismiss it as another of my stories. Parents bring their children up on fairy tales, and then never understand why their reality may get confused with fantasy. It was only after telling you about being locked in the attic that it came back to me.'

'Prophetic, wasn't it?' Mark Clement was carefully opening two small tubs of milk and emptying them into the mugs of coffee. 'Would you describe yourself as a fatalist?'

Accepting the proffered mug, she shook her head. 'I may recognise events fatalistically. But gradually I've learned not to accept them.'

'Or does fate force you to react?'

'I've only begun to realise lately that I have to make choices,' she replied. 'You've made me very conscious of that. My father always used to say, we'll have to wait and see. Another of his sayings was, give it time, all in due time. There was a retired man who lived in the village who'd studied medicine for twenty-five years at Trinity College in Dublin and never got his degree, till out of desperation they made him superintendent of a mental home in Terenure. He wasn't stupid, he just wasn't bothered. He was an easy-going sort of man, and his house was covered in roses. I remember thinking this is another way of life. Things have to happen of their own accord, why waste time struggling to fight them. It's taken me a long time to learn to react.'

ONLY four days had passed since Mark had taken David out, and here he was again, in the early afternoon, a bottle wrapped in tissue-paper in one hand and a briefcase in the other, easing his way familiarly into the house.

'Hallo, darling, I've just come from my solicitor. Everything's signed now, accepting all that you've asked for. But before the divorce goes ahead I thought we ought to go over some points that my solicitor suggested. No problems, it's mainly about the contact with the children.' He looked round. 'Where's Sarah?'

'Linda and her mother have taken her and Tessa out for the day. They've gone to a wild-life park.'

There was something odd about the way he looked round, as if he had planned the gesture, as if he already knew the answer, perhaps David had mentioned to him Sarah would be away, as the outing had been arranged since last week.

'Why didn't you go?' he asked casually.

'So they wouldn't have to hurry back for the end of school. Barry's coming here with David and Vicky.'

He nodded and put the bottle down on the table. 'I thought we might celebrate our amicable settlement. How about some glasses?'

'A bit early in the day, isn't it?' Faint alarm bells were ringing. The style was so smooth. Could he have put something in the wine?

'I thought it would be a nice way to seal our agreement. We ought to try and remain friends,' he added as she still hesitated. 'For the sake of the children.'

I don't trust him, she thought. But she wanted to appear reasonable. She fetched two glasses and a corkscrew from the cupboard.

He pulled out the cork and filled the glasses. 'Here's to our independence, and I hope, darling, our continuing... friendship.' He drank half his glass and put it down, then sat down on the sofa, opening his briefcase.

She realised that she had been waiting for him to drink first just in case... How ridiculous, she thought.

He took out a sheaf of papers. 'Come and look at these. Just check that I've agreed to everything you wanted.'

It took an effort to seat herself beside him. 'Look, you see, he suggests we have joint residence, but they live with you on a weekly basis, and we could change it if they wanted. That's what most people do nowadays. Maintenance of £70 per week. Hoping the kitchens still swim along. Contact is the other thing. What do you say to them all coming to me one weekend a month? I'm desperately busy, but I'd like to put one weekend aside and give them a really good time.'

'Will you be able to manage all three?'

He laughed lightly. 'Perhaps not at first. But old Plover said it was best to have it written out that way as something to aim at. If we agree, it keeps them happy.'

At first she could not understand what was happening. One moment he was talking and the next he was gasping for breath, a hand up to his throat, his face white and rigid. The papers spilled everywhere, the briefcase fell off with a heavy clunking sound and he began to topple slowly onto her. Then as she put out her arms to hold him, he jerked with what she thought was a convulsion.

As his right arm encircled her, she realised too late, it was all a deliberate ploy. He caught her left arm with the speed of a striking python and twisted her away from him, then thrust her face down into the seat of the sofa, kneeling across her pelvis and yanking both her arms behind her. As she struggled and shouted into the muffling cushions and tried to wrench her hands from his grip, she could not prevent him tying her wrists together.

'You thought you were going to get away with it, didn't you?'

He pulled her up and shoved her back against the sofa, grabbed the wine bottle and sat astride her thighs, pushing her head back, his fingers gripping her jaw so that he could insert the neck of the bottle into her mouth. 'You've really messed me about,' he snarled.

'Stop,' she gargled and bubbled, trying to twist her head away. 'What are you do...?' The words were drowned, wine was spilling down her neck. She tried to spit it out, but he squeezed his fingers tightly over her mouth and nostrils. She had to swallow to avoid choking. Then as she tried to shout he crashed the bottle against her teeth, hurting her so that she opened them in pain, and in poured more wine.

Each time he held her nose to make her swallow. 'Drink, you bitch. Things are not going to work out the way you thought.'

However much she jerked her head and spat out, however much was spilled, she knew a lot was going down. All the while through her terror raced one great comet of regret; why had she been so stupid, why had she trusted him, believed all that blarney, whatever possessed her to allow him into the house?

He had emptied the wine bottle, produced another from the briefcase, twisted its cap off, but this was different, burning. Whisky, she thought, clenching her teeth, twisting her head about frantically, trying to wrench her hands free, throw herself sideways.

But he punched her in the stomach, so that she gasped involuntarily and he got the bottle past her teeth again. When he held her nose she had to swallow to draw breath, and then afraid of drowning, gulped. The liquid burned her throat, made her cough. He poured more in. She could feel herself becoming dizzy.

'You thought I'd agree to your petition, their residence with you, didn't you?' he snapped, the muscles in his neck taut as cords while she weakened and sagged against the back of the sofa. 'But I'm going to contest their living with you on the grounds that you're a drunken slut.'

He had brought out another bottle. The briefcase must have been full of bottles, she realised. Hidden under the papers. More wine, she thought, relishing the cool liquid to soothe the burning whisky, and took the bottle like a baby.

Her mind was swimming now, there was a buzzing in her head, her thoughts slipped about like soapy fishes. He's very kind really... to keep opening the bottles... but he frowns a lot, the fucking-clever awful daddy bastard... giving his little girl a drinkie, so she'll sign everything over the hills and far away... goodbye everything, it's so nice of him to want to look after the children, so generous... because I cant lift a finger any more.. lost my hands, can't find them anywhere.

She hardly noticed the change back to the whisky bottle, only the increasing glow inside, guts a hot-water bottle filled with Madras curry. No need fire in the winter... central heating installed in the belly already... head big as a church... balloon with lips. The words lengthened in her mind like long ribbons, trailing and floppy, extending and fraying, breaking into different coloured fragments.

She dimly remembered the forced drinking ceasing, his getting off her, so that she toppled sideways in slow elongated motion like a building falling, subsiding into the soft depths of the sofa. As she lay thinking how strange that her hands were growing out of her back, she found herself being turned over, her hips lifted up, knickers sliding down her thighs, hands parting her buttocks, something sliding up her rectum, chilling nerves like a bottle's neck, a little joke puffing into her strato-cumulus mile-wide mind that she was being pumped with wine from the other end, just to make sure she was properly full, but she knew really it was him like a dog leaving his message.

Minutes, hours, days later voices were dragging at her like heavy chains. There was an overpowering stench of vomit and the smell of whisky as if someone had turned on the gas-fire and forgotten to light it. Her throat was sore as if clogged with broken glass, her tongue and gums were aching. All she wanted to do was to be still, to curl up around herself to mitigate the dreadful sickness inside.

'It's disgusting. Fancy the children coming home and finding their mother in this state. Empty bottles under the sofa, half-full ones hidden in drawers.'

'She's in a terrible state.' Linda's voice was shocked. 'That my Barry had to see this. I've never known her like it before. I'd always thought her husband planted the bottles. But just look at it all.'

As her body arced on its ribs to vomit more, iron-hard hands yanked roughly under her armpits, half-flew her to the bathroom, held her over the white china bowl with its pool of water shaped like a slice of bread. Then she disfigured it with further kaleidoscopic contents of her stomach. The flushing water spun dissolving, restoring it to pristine whiteness, that clear little pool where her family's turds were wont to float. She felt as if her throat was lacerated with a thousand cuts. Her stomach heaved like a rotting cabbage. Her entire consciousness was imprisoned within her aching nausea. When she was lifted, she felt herself held like a two-handled jug.

‘She’s in no state to look after herself, we can’t leave her like this. What about her husband?’

‘There’s a Ouster Order against him. He’s not supposed to come into the house.’

Kathleen snorted like a pig, mumbled words in her nose, unable to enunciate.

‘I think we’d better get her to hospital.’

The voices passed high over her head like migrating birds. She could see the black shapes of the words as they flew out of mouths. Why would nothing come out of her own mouth, to tell them what had really happened? What did it matter, she didn’t care. But there was one sound echoing in the dim recesses of her mind that distressed her. She knew what it was, but her mind was unable to grasp it.

She remembered when she woke in the hospital the next morning. It had been Vicky crying out. A note of fear. Her elder daughter was the only one who’d recognised the handiwork.

But as she lay in her bed she could not summon the anger she wanted, she was too exhausted, her body too washed out, her mind limp. The disapproving diagnosis was simple: alcohol poisoning.

They pushed her out mid- morning and she returned to an empty house like a ghost come to survey the scene of her undoing. The mess remained untouched. She felt deadened of all feeling. There could be no hope now. The children would already be with Mark. She remembered the voices as she lay on the sofa, one of them an authoritative woman’s voice, someone official no doubt sent in by Mark to record her humiliation. Nevertheless she went down to the call-box and telephoned her solicitor.

‘Why did you let him into the house, Mrs September?’

She forbore from admitting exactly how Mark had conned her. ‘He’s bigger and stronger than me. I’ve no phone. My neighbour on one side is nearly ninety, and the others are Chinese cooks who are only there in the middle of the night. What was I supposed to do?’

Mr Onion sighed. ‘One of the problems with injunctions. They’re not easy to administer. I’ll inform the court at once.’ He sounded weary. ‘Your husband seems to have planned it all very carefully. The way he brought the allegation of drinking to the attention of the court at the first hearing. Then setting it up so that there were witnesses to the empties, all done presumably to show that you're incapable of looking after the children. I should contact Social Services or your friend about their whereabouts. Let me know.' He sighed as if he would have much preferred to be dealing with a snappy piece of conveyancing.

She was about to cross over to the cornershop for change to phone Social Services when she heard her name being called. There in the distance was Linda. Surrounded by children. Her heart wobbled and she ran to meet them, falling on her knees on the pavement to gather Vicky and Sarah to her, tears gushing from her eyes with relief and joy.

'We've just come from the hospital,' said Linda. 'Looking for you.'

'I was about to ring you. Damn, look, I've ruined my tights.'

'You won't leave us again, will you, Mummy?' pleaded Vicky.

'I kept her back from school, she was too upset,' said Linda, as they turned towards the house. 'David was all right. He went off with Barry. That social worker who came to the house, Mrs Coe, was going to take them all into care. It was a close thing. I expect she'll be round soon to check if you can cope.'

'I'm ever so grateful, Linda.'

'I didn't know if I was doing the right thing. Are you... OK?'

'I don't feel too good,' said Kathleen as she pushed her key into the lock and opened the front-door. 'God, the smell,' she exclaimed, wrinkling her nose. 'I should have started cleaning it up the moment I got back. But I wanted to know where the children where. I was afraid he might have got them. How am I going to get rid of this awful smell of whisky? It's like a pub lavatory.'

'I'd have thought you'd enjoy that,' said Linda, grimly.

Kathleen turned, a hand across her mouth. She had been aware of a slight edge in Linda's manner. 'What d'you mean?'

'Seeing the rate you seem to be knocking the stuff back.'

'But I didn't...' Kathleen turned and went into the kitchen, took a bucket from under the sink and began filling it with hot water. A great weight had suddenly descended on her, pressing down, a fear that made her shake, so that she had to hold onto the metal flanges of the sink tightly. Surely Linda wasn't taken in? She couldn't bear it if Linda turned against her.

'You'll lose them, you know,' said Linda, gesturing in the direction of the children's voices upstairs. 'Mrs Coe reckoned it looked serious. All those empties everywhere. I mean, what's it doing to your liver?'

Kathleen looked down into the water splashing into the bucket, added some washing-up liquid, squeezed her eyes shut. Nobody knew, she thought. No one seemed to realise that Mark had contrived it, except Vicky and Mr Onion. For how much longer would he believe her? 'Have you ever seen me drinking, Linda?' she asked.

She carried the bucket and sponge past her into the sitting-room, and knelt down, trying not to gag at the smell. Savagely swabbing at the mess was the only way she could control the turmoil within herself.

'I didn't believe it till yesterday,' said Linda. 'Then I started to think about Mark's evidence at the hearing. It all began to add up.'

Kathleen could not see what she was sponging, blinded by tears. She took the bucket out to change the water. It was difficult to keep her voice level as she tried to describe what had actually happened.

Linda interrupted her. 'Am I supposed to believe you'd be so stupid as to let him in?'

'I know, I know,' cried Kathleen, in agonised tones. 'But he was so reasonable. He said he just wanted to settle a few details about contact with the children.' She lifted her shoulders. 'Of course... I should have known what to expect.'

She could tell Linda remained unconvinced. 'How could he force all that stuff down you? Nobody can make you drink if you don't want to. You could have spat it out.'

'Why won't you believe me, Linda?' Kathleen stood up, arched her back, dropped the sponge back into the bucket. She was weary beyond anger.

'It's too fantastic. You still had a bottle clutched in your hand when we found you. Mrs Coe said she'd never seen anyone so bad.'

'How did a social worker get here, Linda?' cried Kathleen. 'Who told her?'

'Probably David telephoned his father, and maybe he contacted

Social Services. Why don't you ask him?' She shrugged. 'I've got to get back. Tessa,' she called up the stairs. She stood in the doorway. 'You worry me, Kathleen. Can't you see your stories are too far-fetched? Mark told David when you were drunk you chased away his customers, that you'd get so incapable you'd fall over, then blame the bruises on him. That's why you were in hospital when you told me that fantasy of being locked in the loft. I never could quite believe that story. And David can remember you drinking bottles of yellow stuff, scotch presumably.' She shook her head. 'I don't believe Mark was here at all. Nobody could force another person to drink that much.'

The children were coming downstairs as Kathleen, shocked at the treachery of her son, was about to explain that it was Shloer David had seen her drink. But just at that moment Vicky ran across to the sofa and pulled something out from under a cushion. 'Daddy's tie,' she said. 'Did he tie your hands with it?'

'God what a family,' exclaimed Linda. 'You see what you've done to Vicky? Come on, Tessa.' She turned towards the door. 'I'll see you.'

'Thanks for looking after the children,' said Kathleen quickly.

'I only hope I did the right thing,' Linda called back as she hurried down the path.

Later Kathleen made lunch. The three of them were sitting round the table when there came a knock on the door. She froze.

Vicky ran to look out of the curtains. 'It's the lady who was here yesterday.'

Kathleen opened to the door to a middle-aged woman with round cheeks, uncomfortably penetrating eyes and a sharp critical smile.

'Betty Coe,' the woman announced. 'Social worker. I was here yesterday afternoon.' Her short brown hair fitted round her skull like a wooden clock-case, and a pleated skirt curtained her calves as she turned from Kathleen to survey the cleaned if damp sofa and carpet.

'You look a bit better than when I last saw you.' She smiled. 'You've got the girls back, then. Vicky's not at school, I see. I didn't really expect her to be. She was very upset yesterday. Hallo, you two, all right are we? Glad to be back home? You finish your lunch then, while I talk to Mummy.'

She guided Kathleen back into the front-room. 'I hope this isn't going to distress you, Mrs September, but a message came from the school to say that your husband has taken David away.'

'I've been afraid of this all along,' cried Kathleen. 'What happened?'

'He left a letter explaining that the boy was very upset by your drinking, so he has taken him to stay with his sister, and will return him to school next week. I'm on my way to check it out now. If that is where David wants to be, then it might be better not to disturb him over the next few days till we sort things out.'

Kathleen put her fists into her eyes to block her tears. 'I have not been drinking, Mrs Coe,' she said quietly. She explained what had happened. 'You may not believe me, nobody else seems to, and I know I was extremely stupid to have let my husband in.'

Betty Coe's smile was not unkind. 'Your story would explain why there was so much alcohol spilled all over your clothes and the sofa. But I'm not here to take sides at this stage. Often when a marriage goes wrong unpleasant allegations are flung about. My main concern is the children. They come first. I should certainly prefer to believe that you are not a dipsomaniac. Both the girls seem devoted to you.' She perched on the arm of a chair, nodding at Kathleen to sit down. 'I've seen the probation officer's court report and the photographs of what your husband is alleged to have done to you. So I appreciate what you describe could easily have happened. But why on earth did you let him in?'

Kathleen sat down. She desperately needed Betty Coe to continue to believe in her. 'He's such a smooth talker. And I did so want everything to be right.'

Betty Coe looked at her. 'You're afraid of him, aren't you?'

Kathleen nodded. 'I never know what's going to happen. He's charming one minute and violent the next. He doesn't seem to have any conscience.'

Betty Coe's voice remained level. 'As I've said, I'm not making any judgement on what happened yesterday. But you must appreciate that in any situation where the children could be in any danger because of what their parents get up to, we have powers to intervene. I should like to be certain there's no real drink problem.' She stood up.

After going to say goodbye to the children, she paused at the front-door. 'I shall have to meet your husband. They say hell hath no fury like a woman scorned, but what about a man, eh?'

Kathleen shivered.

'Why did she come here?' Vicky asked anxiously after Mrs Coe had left.

Kathleen bent down to wipe orange juice off Sarah's face. 'She came to tell me that David has gone to spend a few days with Daddy.'

'He's such a wimp,' groaned Vicky in perfect emulation of adult disgust. 'He believes everything Daddy tells him. Like that men never hit ladies, but sometimes they get confused and run into a door and bang themselves. I told him I'd seen Daddy hit you, and he said, no, you haven't, you haven't, because he never has.' She put her head on one side. 'D'you think he needs glasses?'

Kathleen wanted to laugh, but the pragmatic vision of six-year old Vicky was insufficient consolation against the pain. What was going to happen next? What was happening to David? Why this early ingrowing self-protection of delusion? Was this like father, like son?

During the afternoon she cleaned the house, occasionally distracted by the needs of the children. But all the while she remained detached, floating above them like a hot-air balloon, seeing across a vast expanse, and dotted over it, signs of terrible depredation. She felt quite alone, close to despair, closer than she had ever been before, even when locked in the darkness of the loft. For so long Linda had been her chief support. Now that was gone. She wished she was back in the refuge with Brenda and the sisterhood in adversity. She could be sure that somewhere out there, Mark was scheming the next stage.

At one point in the afternoon she found herself opening the cupboard under the bookshelves where the glasses were kept, reaching in and lifting out a bottle. This what she would be doing if Mark was right, she thought, looking at it in surprise; Manzanilla sherry. It was all there was in the house and she could feel the thought forming in her mind, as if she was actually saying to herself... pity there isn't something stronger. She started up, shoved the bottle back, slammed the door, alarmed, blushing. Did she really have the inclination? She could not remember doing such a thing before. Unless there was another self, standing inside her body, sharing it with her, one that she hid from, one who was a secret drinker? Could this have been her first glimpse of the person who was the truth of Mark's allegations? Cold terror crept into her. Not only did she have no control over outside events, but perhaps not over her own thinking either. She stared uneasily at the cupboard.

'I can hear the ice-cream van, Mummy,' said Vicky. 'Can I get one?'

Kathleen nodded, looking round for her bag, then stopped, hand to mouth. The image had suddenly come into her mind of Vicky running along the pavement towards the ice-cream van, and a white Sierra swinging alongside her, the door opening, an arm reaching out... 'No, no,' she cried, then dropped her voice. 'We'll go to the corner-shop in a minute for something for tea, and get an ice-cream then.'

'Want to go toilet,' said Sarah. Must they use that word? Mark used to say with pained expression.

'You can manage, darling, can't you?'

'You come.'

This was their insecurity, she thought, following her to the bathroom. They gave up managing when they were tired or anxious, they regressed to total dependence, food cut-up, buttons undone, hair brushed, bottoms wiped, and clinging to her like a pair of koalas. They relied on what little strength she had. This made her feel intensely guilty that it was she who had taken the steps that had broken up the family.

When Sarah was finished she gave her a hug and sent her off so that she could sit on the seat herself, barely warm from the child. Surely she wasn't a bad mother, was she? She never consciously considered her role, it was instinctive to... God, they're in the sitting-room and the front door's unlocked. She felt her laddered tights finally rip in her haste to hurl herself from the room. She leaned breathless against the doorpost, looking at them with relief, hands still arranging her clothing. 'Let's go shopping, then,' she said, trying to sound natural, thinking that she must take hold of herself.

TO FIND himself sitting in his chair in his consulting room was like the lights going up in the cinema at the end of a heavy movie, the orchestra still playing in his head, Bartok's Music for Strings, Percussion and Celesta.

'That was a cruel blow,' he commented, arching his back to ease his stiffness. 'Linda letting you down.'

'I've never understood why. She seemed such a good friend. Though I suppose you'd say it was more like a dependence,' she added.

He was on the defensive, reducing eye contact to as little as possible. At least the lure of her new decorative presence had failed to erode his concentration, he congratulated himself. Perhaps he should view her as bedecked in the warpaint of a warrior recounting exploits of battle.

'How would you describe your relationship with her before?'

She frowned. 'I'm beginning to think like you, you know. Looking for motives everywhere.'

'There's nothing odd about interdependence. We all need companionship, communication. Take your children for instance. However much you love them, they need you. And maybe you need them too?'

She sucked in her breath. 'Of course I love them, they came out of my body, they're little, they're my life, they...' She stopped and looked pleadingly at him. 'There I've given my dependence away, haven't I? But surely love itself is the most important of all? You never answer me.'

He looked down at his hands, ran a thumb over a knuckle, thinking of what he imagined she wanted him to say and what he ought to say.

'We keep allowing it to intrude when we shouldn't, because we fail to consider the consequences. Love ought to be logical. As a plover knows a pigeon isn't a suitable mate. But too often it's as you said the other day, more like a dream which we all wander round clinging to like a childhood teddy bear. A dream that somewhere out there exists this perfect condition. As if it's the real purpose of life. But most of the time it's no more than shelving our inadequacies onto someone else's problems instead of strengthening our own independence.'

Her voice rose plaintively. 'Why must you always make it sound so basic?'

It wasn't just the discomfort of the chair, he thought, it was the tension he was under, attempting to erect a discreet wall between them without her noticing.

'I'm trying to set it in perspective. It's my business to show people how to recognise themselves, how to understand their needs, to handle their strengths and weaknesses, so that they can cope. Or so they won't be caught out so badly the next time.'

'But we're not rational human beings.' There was a flush on her cheeks. 'We can't help our susceptibilities.'

He shook his head. 'As children we were susceptible to running out into the road and being knocked down by passing cars. But we learned not to.'

She was disappointed, he could tell. Would she take it as a rebuff? Or see it as a gentle warning? As long as the strands of trust had taken the strain. But it was a strain that he could feel stretching taut within himself.

IN THE morning a letter arrived from her solicitor.

Dear Mrs September, We are in receipt of your husband's answer to your divorce petition. He is disputing your request for the children to live with you, and makes a number of allegations about your unsuitability in order to substantiate his own claim for residence. Please telephone the office to arrange a time to discuss the matters arising. Yours sincerely, Graham Onion.

The words threw her into a panic, and she lost no time in hurrying out to phone his office, nearly forgetting to tell him what mattered most of all, namely what had happened to David.

'That won't go down well with the court,' muttered Mr Onion. 'I'll inform them right away. We'll discuss it further when you come in.' She could hear him rustling papers. 'It's curious. In your husband's answer there is reference to a social worker finding you in a drunken coma. Allowing for the post, it's interesting that he should appear to know about it in advance. See you on Thursday.'

For once Mr Onion is on the ball, she thought. At least he's still on my side.

Early the next morning Betty Coe, the social worker arrived.

Kathleen could barely contain her impatience. 'Is David all right?'

'He appears contented,' Betty Coe replied, and sat down on the sofa, settling herself in a businesslike manner. 'Tell me, was he happy here before he went off with his father?'

'He was a handful the last week,' admitted Kathleen, ever truthful. 'It began soon after his father started meeting them outside the school. Vicky says he started to believe everything his father told him.'

'You haven't mentioned what happened to your solicitor yet, have you?'

'Of course. I told him yesterday.'

Betty Coe frowned. 'You promised me you'd wait till we discussed it further.'

‘I had to, Mrs Coe. My solicitor says my husband wants the children.’

Betty Coe’s mouth was tight. ‘If the court becomes involved things may be taken out of your hands.’

‘At least a court might consider a man who uses his fists to get his way, a man who is a consistent liar, a man who has no scruples to be a poor influence on a growing child?’

Betty Coe shook her head in exasperation. ‘You should realise that courts are used to hearing colourful denigrations from both sides in family disputes. What they concentrate on is what’s best for the children. Children are the innocent parties, yet they suffer just as much if not more so.’

‘I do understand that, you know, Mrs Coe. That’s why I worry about what’s happening to David.’

The social worker took a deep breath. ‘You must understand that David doesn’t want to come back here. He said he’d run away if we made him.’

Kathleen sat stung. ‘How can he have changed so much?’

Betty Coe leaned forward and touched her hand in an attempt to be reassuring. ‘I’m afraid it happens all too often, my dear. Circum-stances like these force children to take sides.’

There came a knock on the front door. Kathleen got up to see who it was. As she swung the door open she felt herself lock solid as if she’d turned into a pillar of ice.

Mark stood smiling, lean in jeans and open-necked blue shirt, clutching a slim zip-case to his chest. ‘Hallo Kathleen, darling,’ he said breezily. ‘How are you?’ He was just about to ease his way forwards, when he saw there was someone in the room behind, and as if suddenly mindful of correct behaviour, stepped back. ‘I just popped round to try and arrange to see the girls at the weekend.’

Betty Coe came up behind Kathleen. ‘You must be Mr September,’ she began cordially. ‘I’d hoped to meet you at your sister’s. I’m Betty Coe, the social worker assigned to the case.’ Kathleen felt herself pushed aside as he reached forwards to shake the woman’s hand.

Mark beamed. ‘I’m so glad to meet you, Mrs Coe. My sister told me how helpful you’d been. I should have liked to explain to you myself about David, that I only took him because he asked me to, and because he had been so upset by... what happened here. I realised it might cause problems, but I thought it was best for him.'

'I do understand, Mr September,' she simpered. 'I'm sure we'll be able to sort something out.'

'You must be very experienced in this sort of problem, Mrs Coe,' continued Mark. 'Children caught up in their parents' disagreements. I'm only sorry that we've been such a nuisance to you.'

Kathleen's eyes flicked from one face to the other. She felt barely able to breathe.

Betty Coe's fingers were absently patting her curls down behind her ears. 'It's just routine, Mr September. This is our business. By the way, your sister said she'd talked to the headmaster of the school her eldest attends.'

'Isabel's going to take David along tomorrow morning. It's a good little school, almost in the country, too.'

'Yes, I've heard very good reports of it,' said Betty Coe effusively.

Kathleen felt faint. Mark's smile remained sickeningly amiable.

'I called round this afternoon to see if Kathleen and I could arrange for me to take the girls out.'

Betty Coe nodded approvingly. 'We don't like to see children deprived of the paternal connection.' She turned to Kathleen, her eyebrows lifted. 'I'm sure that should be no problem?'

'There is an injunction, Mrs Coe,' replied Kathleen evenly. 'It specifically bans my husband from all contact with me and the children.'

Mrs Coe narrowed her eyes sharply. 'Haven't you virtually negated the Order by allowing your husband into the house on several occasions?'

Kathleen gasped, too angry to muster response.

'It'll only be for lunch at Isabel's,' said Mark, placatingly. 'I'll bring them straight back. There's nothing to worry about.'

She shook herself. 'You've lied to everyone, you wormed your way in here with false promises, you know perfectly well why I'm worried.'

Mark raised his eyebrows at Betty Coe as if to imply he knew she was sensible enough to appreciate the nonsense of such allegations. 'I'm only concerned for the children. I feel it's important for them to keep in touch with the rest of their family.'

'All right,' exclaimed Kathleen turning to Betty Coe, her anger coming to the boil. 'Why don't we ask them? You notice they haven't exactly rushed to greet their father. This house being so small they'll hardly have missed his voice.' She called into the house. 'Where are you two? Daddy's here.'

There was no response. She went through into the next room, beckoning Betty Coe to follow her. Both children were standing the far side of the dining-table; Sarah sucking a thumb, Vicky white as paper, eyes and mouth like three little scrawls.

'It would be nice to see your brother, wouldn't it?' asked Betty Coe. 'Just to go with your daddy to have Sunday lunch at your Aunt Isabel's, then come home to Mummy? You'd like that, wouldn't you?'

Vicky was round the table in a trice, throwing herself into her mother's arms, the words coming out in squeals of fear. 'Mummy, no, no, don't let them take me away, no, no.'

Sarah came running after her, infected by the panic, bawling in unison.

'My God,' shouted Mark over the noise. 'What's got into them? What's she been poisoning their minds with?'

'It couldn't possibly be what you've done, could it?' exclaimed Kathleen, clutching the two crying children to her.

'Mr September,' said Betty Coe quickly, taking his arm and steering him out of the room. 'This is not going to get us anywhere. You shouldn't be in the house. Leave this with me. I'll be in contact.'

'Quite right, Mrs Coe. What a sensible person you are. Of course I'll go at once.'

After he had gone, Betty Coe returned. Kathleen was sitting on a dining-chair, the children caught up in the folds of her skirt as she hugged them to her. Betty Coe sat on another chair, rested an arm on the table. 'You've been making them afraid of him, haven't you?'

Kathleen rolled her eyes upwards. 'Why don't you ask Vicky?'

Betty Coe switched on a smile, pulled a chair in beside her, patted its seat. 'Come and sit here, dear.'

Vicky remained clinging to her mother.

Betty Coe's smile persevered. 'You're not afraid of your daddy, are you?'

'He hits mummy.'

'Even grown-ups have quarrels sometimes. As I'm sure you and David or you and Sarah do as well.'

'He hit her with a plate once, there was blood all over her neck. Another time he broke her arm in the door.'

Betty Coe winced. 'But he doesn't hit you, does he?' she interjected.

'He doesn't like me. He only likes David because he's a boy.'

Betty Coe reached across and patted her hand. 'I think you'll find he loves you all, dear.' She turned to Kathleen. 'You should make an effort to calm their fears rather than exaggerate them. It'll only make things more difficult for them in the future. The court will want some kind of reasonable arrangement between the two of you.'

'Even if the court knew the kind of man he is?' cried Kathleen.

Betty Coe stood up. 'You're seeing him in a black light because the marriage has gone bad. But he's no different from any other man.' She turned at the door. 'Isn't it about time Vicky went back to school?'

Kathleen was very low that night. After the children were in bed and she had cleared up, she went and sat in the sitting-room, turned off the lamp and sat in the gloom, a dull glow percolating through the curtains from the streetlights. Shards of light rolled round the walls each time a car passed. Weightless voices floated by outside. There was a murmur in the walls from Mrs Mathew's television.

She sat as still as if her body was one more piece of shadowy furniture in the otherwise empty room. She thought back to her childhood friend, Carmel Clinton, all freckles and breath that smelled of boiled ham, and the occasion they had followed the fashion of proving friendship by mingling blood. She had taken a Stanley knife blade wrapped in wax paper from a drawer in her father's study. She could still see the blood issuing like wine from the nick she cut in her thumb. The blade slicing easily, the crimson fluid swelling into a glossy bead. They were both convinced their blood had been exchanged as they pressed thumbs together.

Whatever had become of Carmel? She was a relic of her childhood. She thought how her parents' sudden death on the Naas road had snuffed out more than their own lives. Like a vivid wind lifting a frog from a pool and depositing it five hundred miles away, she had been snatched away from childhood.

She would be afraid of the pain, of the blood and mess to use a blade like that now. There were other ways. When she was a child, a woman at Monasterboice had climbed up into the loft of her cow shed, put a rope halter round her neck and attached the end to a rafter and jumped. She was not found for three days. Her brother, searching for her, had never thought of looking upwards. While the balance of her mind was disturbed, said the coroner. Then there was the body washed up on Annagassan beach only a week before the summer holiday. It had been a young woman who had waded out into the sea at Laytown after her baby died. She would do nothing like that, she thought. As her marriage descended into its grinding misery, there had always been the children to sustain her. But without them she would have nothing to live for. If the court awarded them to Mark, she knew what she would do. She would buy a bottle of aspirin and a bottle of wine, take them in her handbag on a bus out into the country. She would go deep into the woods where nobody would find her, sit down with her back against a tree, and leave the world behind.

And yet... it was curious how recently the city had seemed to her crowded with covetable men. Her eyes hungered after their passing faces, her senses tingled at their innate nubility, her groin ached for the power of their maleness. She had found herself sick with envy at the sight of couples hand in hand. Such intimacy seemed as intensely a desirable acquisition as the sight of a girl bouncing along the pavement might be to an old woman like Mrs Mathews taking an age to hobble homewards. She had felt yearning at the sound of male laughter rich as her uncle's, the way he used to abandon himself to the relishing of a joke, put his arms round her to share the humour, instil in her a sense of companionship.

That night wasn't the first she cried herself to sleep. It wasn't the first she'd been woken by Vicky crying. It wasn't the first she ended up with both children in bed with her, Vicky's thin legs wrapped round her as if she was scaling a pole, and Sarah's small bottom like a ball in the pit of her stomach. But it was the first night she dreamed of her death. She knew she was dead because she was outside herself, looking down at her body laid out on a table, a wreath of lilies on her breast, her mother's locket lying at the base of her throat. Mark was standing there among the mourners. She tugged at his sleeve, thumped his shoulder, shouted at him, but he ignored her, remained staring down at the empty body.

HE COULD not help being stirred by the image of her need.

'How would you describe what you felt? When you found your suicidal depression being countered by this awareness of the promise in other men?'

She hesitated. 'It was like a pain.'

'A sort of despair?'

She lowered her eyes. 'More like longing.'

He nodded. 'Better than death, surely? What would that have brought you?'

She shivered. 'No more being hunted. No more being disbelieved. No more humiliation. No more terror.' She waved a hand dismissively. 'But I can't think like that now. You've done so much for me. I feel so much more hopeful.'

'What is it that you hope for now? Can you visualise what it is?'

Colour rose up her cheeks, she was obviously caught out by the questions. He shouldn't be on this track, he thought, what was he thinking of? He was losing his way.

'Tell me what attracted you to Mark in the first place,' he interposed before she could reply.

She thought for a moment. 'He could be very charming. He seemed so different from my father, someone who could cope. I was wrong.'

'Suppose you hadn't stopped loving him?'

'D'you mean that if I'd loved Mark all along, none of this might have happened?'

'From what you've described, that wouldn't have been love, it would have been submission. Maybe that's what you were conditioned to give. If we have parents who don't have enough time for us, we grow up clinging to the smallest favour. Then later it might make us throw ourselves at someone who duplicates our parent's indifference, because we felt it was our fault that we failed to awaken love from our parents, so when we transfer to someone similar, we're still blaming ourselves.'

She frowned. 'So am I likely to make the same mistake again? Is that what you're saying? But the way you describe love, it's just selfishness, nothing but taking from each other.'

'So how would you describe it?'

She leaned back in her chair. He could see the muscles of her throat working. 'What about feeling good about someone? And warmth, affection, passion?' She shook her head angrily. 'You're trying to draw me out, aren't you?'

He laughed.

'What about what you're doing for me?' she continued, colour patching her cheeks. 'You're helping me. Is that selfishness on your part?'

'Of course. I'm getting paid.'

She bit her lip, looked away. 'I can't believe that you don't care.'

A sudden sense of exhilaration swept through him like an unexpected gust of warm air, overcoming him with recklessness, eliminating all concern with the consequences.

Every knock at the front-door triggered alarm. They were like a trio of deer listening to the long grass rustling, imagining a stalking tiger. The postman with a parcel, the milkman for his bill, the meter-reader, all sent apprehension stiffening through each of them.

This time the knock was Sue with her little baby Paul asleep in his pram.

She and Kathleen hugged each other like old campaigners. 'Felt like stretching my legs,' said Sue, her abundant hair swaying about her face like the branches of a summer tree. 'Thought I'd look you up. Hallo, darlings,' she greeted the children.

She lifted out the sleeping Paul to show him to the girls. 'Jo's been sent down for five years. Never thought I'd feel so relieved. D'you want to hold him, Vicky? Mark you, Geraldine wasn't too pleased. He got done for arson, not for what he did to me. His solicitor found some psychiatrist to make out he was an emotionally deprived child. And the judge was one of those, you know, reckons all the troubles of the world are down to Eve. Never mind. It's a breather for me.' Paul began to pucker his tiny winter-apple face and squeezed out bagpipe wails. 'Let's have him, Vicky, the little blighter's got a thirst on him like my dad, you should see the beergut he has already.'

The two girls watched in fascination as she unbuttoned and pulled out a breast as if it was a melon she kept inside her blouse for the baby to gnaw. 'You'll hardly believe it, Kath, but I've got a new fellow.' Sue giggled. 'He's lovely, his name's Mickey, a fitter who came to mend my gas-leak, got a nose like a blood-hound, a dab of perfume behind my ear and he can find me blindfold in the supermarket. He's half the size of Joe, but his you-know-what's twice as big, so I get half the weight for twice the pleasure. He's sweet as a tin of peaches. He has a baby, too, Tina, well, a toddler really. His wife said she wasn't cut out to be a mother, and took off with a bus driver. So his mum looks after her. Hey.' Her face widened with intensity. 'Did you hear about Carol? Took an overdose of tranquillisers. Been in hospital a week now.'

The satiated Paul had fallen asleep. Sue buttoned up her blouse. 'So how are things with you, Kath?'

Kathleen flicked her eyes up with self-disparagement and told her about letting Mark into in the house, being forced to drink and all that had followed. 'As a result he's got David now, and he's trying to get them all.'

'Jesus,' swore Sue, wide-eyed. 'What's your solicitor doing, Kath, why don't you go to Geraldine? She wouldn't stand for that. I don't know, most solicitors just seem to stand around and let the porridge burn. You should have had Brenda fix you up. Here, we'll talk about this another time, I must run.' She bundled the baby into his buggy. 'Write down my new address. 13 Paradise Place. I've got to dash, I'm supposed to have Tina this afternoon, and Mickey's mum's a funny old girl, I don't want to get the rope in a tangle with her. Bye, Vicky, bye Sarah.' She hurried away, weaving the flimsy pushchair before her like a metal-detector.

Kathleen felt depressed after she had gone. She felt she ought to be pleased for Sue's sake that she had found someone else. But the clouds remained. She knew she was jealous. She couldn't help suspecting Sue had been anxious to leave lest her happiness be contaminated by someone else's misery.

When she came home from shopping in the afternoon wheeling Sarah's push-chair packed with carrier bags of vegetables, bread and cartons of orange juice and fruit yoghurt, Mrs Mathews uncranked her stooping figure from prodding weeds in her garden with a trowel and hobbled over to the fence. She peeled her lips like a rubber glove off her grey teeth. 'I must tell you, dear,' she quavered, rotating her head sideways like a bird, pushing strands of silver hair out of her anchovy eyes. 'A nice young man came looking for you a short while ago.' She pointed her trowel at Kathleen's front door. 'Left a note. Came and helped me pull up the dandelions, and tied up the rose for me.' She waved the trowel in the direction of the pink blancmange blooms that frothed up the wall beside her own front door. 'A charming young man.' She leaned on the fence. 'He said if ever I needed a nice easy-to-work kitchen, he could fix one at a special rate for pensioners, and he showed me some lovely pictures.' She shook her head. 'Such a considerate young man. Wouldn't stay for a cup of tea. But we had a nice chat all the same. Quite restored my faith in human nature.'

Back inside the house, Kathleen stood reading and rereading the note, while Vicky carried the packages and bags into the kitchen. She felt faint. There were just a few words in pencil on a torn piece of notepad, rough capitals such as a child might have scrawled. *You won't get away with it.*

He's mad, she thought with a shiver. I know he's mad. But she knew he was cunning, too. The note was useless as evidence of harassment. She could hear them saying she wrote it herself, or got one of the children to do it.

There was a letter lying on the mat as well. It was from Mr Onion.

...Social Services and your husband's solicitor have persuaded the court to convene a special hearing Tuesday week. Please telephone the office to arrange to see me as soon as possible...

I'm going to see him tomorrow anyway, she thought. But what about the children? Mr Onion viewed small children as akin to rabid dogs and was consequently always agitated in their presence. She could ask Sue. Or Paula, who lived much nearer. 'Come on, you two. We're going out again.'

It was about ten minutes walk to Paula's. After ringing the bell twice, she was about to turn away, thinking no one was in, when the door opened a crack. 'Kath,' exclaimed a thick voice from inside, and the door was pulled wide. Paula's face was like a joint of meat, one eye swollen shut, mouth caked with blood.

'Christ, Paula,' gasped Kathleen. 'What happened?'

'Shush, you haven't seen anything,' slurred Paula. 'Come down to the kitchen and I'll make you a cup of tea.'

'You sit down, Paula,' said Kathleen, pulling the children in behind her. 'I'll make the tea. Let me have a look at you first.'

'Glad you came by, Kath,' sighed Paula, slumping into a chair. 'Can't say I'm feeling too good.'

Kathleen organised Vicky to find mugs while she switched on the kettle, filled a glass with salt and water, brought over a bowl. 'Rinse out your mouth. Any loose teeth?' She found a clean cloth, made a pad and soaked it in cold water for Paula to hold over her eye. ‘Got any aspirins?’

‘Your two must have seen all this before,’ mumbled Paula as she swilled her mouth out. ‘Going to grow up with a queer view on life, aren’t they, poor little sausages? Like some orange squash, darlings? God, this salt doesn’t half sting. Tell us your news, Kath.’

Kathleen made a pot of tea and filled the mugs. Each time she repeated her story, it seemed to her to rub in her stupidity. But Paula grimaced as if this was the sort of bad news she expected of her friends. ‘He’s a real bastard if ever I heard of one. As for Betty Coe, I know her. She’s a man’s woman. If your bloke cut you up into little pieces and buried you in the garden, she’d say, poor man, he must have been driven to it. You should have got onto Monica. She’d never have fallen under the bastard’s spell.’

Kathleen laughed. ‘Thanks for calling him a bastard. Nobody else does. Listen, you should see a doctor. You might need the evidence?’

Paula shook her head. ‘Not going through all that. My own fault anyway. We all do it, don’t we? Fall for a little reasonableness and let the buggers back in. Can’t do any harm to let him collect his gear, I thought. Couldn’t stand losing, that’s Ted’s trouble. Look, darling,’ she said to Vicky, pointing to a tin on the dresser. ‘There are some fancy biscuits in there, if Darren’s left any. He should be back from school soon. Really sorry about David, Kath. Kids can be funny. And dads are important to boys. The macho to identify with. Hope your solicitor’s going to put up a good fight. I’ll look after these two for you tomorrow as long as they don’t mind. Do I look a fright? Like a witch out of Hallowe’en, wouldn’t you say, Vicky?’

‘You take it easy tomorrow, Paula. We’ll manage.’

‘Nonsense, nothing wrong with me that a good night’s rest won’t fix. Would it be best if I came over to your place?’

‘Supposing Mark came?’

The grin in Paula’s swollen face was like an axe cut. ‘I’ll see him off, don’t you worry. Broke Ted’s collarbone one time. He wouldn’t have done this to me if I wasn’t off my guard.’

‘See how you feel first.’

‘I’ll be all right. Been through worse. Have them on the day of the hearing, too. You know if you hadn't come round I'd have sat here miserable as a hedgehog flattened on the motorway. Aspirin's working a treat. You're a real comfort, Kath. D'you hear about poor Carol?'

Kathleen looked round cautiously when they left. In her mind white Sierras stood out like the great white sharks lurking in the shallows.

Secretly, lest presumption trip her, she allowed herself a small resurgence of confidence as they walked home. Just to know there were people on her side. There were times when each passing face brewed with malignant intentions, footsteps stalked like predators, buildings threatened ambush from every window, and she scuttled past nervous as a mouse. But with one brush of optimism, she was conscious of birds singing, a pensioner with toupee askew being dragged past by an eager Skye terrier, a figure with a huge red bubble for a head sputtering by on a moped, female only by her stockinged calves. 'Would Paula like me to read to her?' asked Vicky.

But there was no sign of Paula the next morning. Fifteen minutes before her appointment, Kathleen gave up waiting. She hurried the children to the bus-stop. The traffic was glutinously slow. Once at the solicitors she could see that Mr Onion didn't mind her being late half so much as the prospect of having children loose in his office. He clutched nervously at his collar.

'What with your husband claiming the children, Mrs September, his taking the boy, and Social Services flapping about you being found unconscious among the whisky bottles, it's all been brought forward.'

He leaped from his chair, arms outstretched, as Sarah strayed from her mother's side to pluck at a pink ribbon round a folder.

'Important papers,' he muttered, whisking it away and shoving it onto a high shelf. He sat down again, swallowed, smoothed his thinning hair, laughed nervously, while Kathleen quietly retrieved Sarah.

'Anyway, courts tend to favour mothers, and they usually leave children with the parent who has possession. Unless there are obvious reasons to move them, such as the parent is incapable of managing because they're handicapped or lesbian, or they drink...'

He giggled with embarrassment. '...that sort of thing. Or indeed if a parent forcibly removes a child as your husband has done. We can assume his main case is going to be that you are an alcoholic. He's already contrived things so that the court records will show a number of alleged examples. Could he produce any other evidence?' His eyes constantly flicked to check that Sarah was still in place. Vicky sat locked against her mother, listening to every word, sucking her thumb.

'God knows what he's cooking up,' Kathleen replied uneasily.

'Of course we'll make a lot out of the drinking incident, but the court will want to know why you let him into the house, flouting their Order. No,' he cried, catapulting himself across the room as Sarah reached down to touch the brass catches on his brief-case. He whisked it away onto another shelf. He was breathing heavily as he sat down again. 'How're you getting on with Mrs Coe?'

'Not very well,' replied Kathleen. 'She eats out of Mark's hand. You know how convincing he can be. She believes I've poisoned the girls' minds against him.'

'I do wish you'd exercise some control over them, Mrs September.' He stood up anxiously.

Sarah popped her head out from under his desk. 'Nice house.'

Kathleen lifted her up to sit on her knees.

Mr Onion wiped his brow limply with the back of his hand. 'Has Mrs Coe suggested they might be taken into care?'

The interview did little to restore her sagging confidence. On the bus heading back out of the city, she decided to remain on the two extra stops so that they could call and see if Paula was all right. The three of them stood on the doorstep while she rang the bell. There was no response.

The lace-curtains of the bay window next door lifted. Moments later a thin-lipped woman in her forties appeared. 'Is it Paula you're looking for? She was ill in the night. We phoned for an ambulance this morning. Probably be back tomorrow.'

'Did they say what was wrong?'

She shook her head. 'They ought to arrest that man. He wouldn't be safe looking after cattle.' Her thin lips whipped out the sentences.

'What about Darren?'

‘We telephoned the sister. I don’t like to see a good woman hurt by a bit of rubbish like that man.’

When they arrived home there was a note protruding from the letterbox. A cold shiver went through Kathleen. She knew what it would be. The same childish pencil scrawl. *Why don’t you give up? I’ll win in the end.*

She hurried through the house, half-expecting to find signs of intrusion. Of course there was nothing. But the note was like an infection taking hold, unsettling her, debilitating her. She couldn’t help imagining, however irrationally, that he was behind Paula being taken to hospital, spreading his malignancy, denying her friends.

The next day Kathleen rang the hospital. They were laconic, nothing serious, Paula should be out in a day or so.

She was nervous, lonely, in terror of a knock on the door, constantly expecting a shadow to fall across the window. The one that came was Mrs Coe.

‘Why isn’t Vicky back at school?’

Vicky had asked the same question herself, causing her mother to groan inwardly, knowing how she enjoyed school, how gregarious was her inclination, how animated she became with her small friends.

‘I’m scared he’ll snatch her,’ she replied. She could see Betty Coe sniffing, looking round the room for the slightest evidence that she might have been drinking. ‘I’ve been doing a lot of reading and writing with her. Anyway, the holidays start next week.’

‘He wouldn’t do anything so stupid as to snatch them,’ Betty Coe retorted tartly. ‘He’s not likely to jeopardise his case at the hearing.’

Kathleen froze, horrified by the implication. ‘D’you mean that he could... win?’

Mrs Coe was not to be drawn. ‘It’ll be the court’s decision. But they’ll certainly be concerned about the drinking, and the children coming home and finding you incapable.’

‘You know that wasn’t what really happened, Mrs Coe,’ exclaimed Kathleen. ‘I don’t drink.’

‘There’s no smoke without fire, my dear,’ said Betty Coe.

Kathleen bit her lip to hold back her anger, afraid to antagonise her. 'But he broke the Court Order.'

'Didn't you invite him in?'

'He forced his way in, Mrs Coe.' There were tears in Kathleen's eyes. 'I don't understand why you're on his side all the time.'

Betty Coe was preparing to leave. 'I don't take sides. But I do believe that men get a raw deal over residence. Many would probably make better child-carers than their wives if given the chance.'

Upon that note she left.

The dark void of fear closed in on Kathleen again that night. Was she ever going to escape from this torment? Was it Mark's power to dupe people that she was up against, or was there some intrinsic flaw in herself? Was she being punished for her failure to take charge of her life? She kept her misery from the children, cried only in the dark of her bedroom. What was going to become of them?

When there came a knock on the door the next morning she began to tremble, stood there paralysed, till Vicky ran to look out of the window. 'It's Clare,' she said. Kathleen burst into tears with relief.

'What's been going on?' exclaimed Clare, hugging her. It all came out again, while she in her turn sat Kathleen down, organised the children to go upstairs and play, made a pot of tea. 'It wouldn't have surprised me if you had taken to drink,' she said. 'What a nightmare. Mark is either the most scheming bastard I've ever heard of, or he's mad.'

'Either is as bad as the other. Clare, I'm so glad to see you.'

Clare's face was concentric with roundness, peachy cheeks, semi-circular eyebrows, amber button eyes, plum chin, domed forehead, all contributing an effect of self-containment. 'I shall have words with Linda. Fancy her reacting like that. When did she ever seen you drunk?'

'It must have been pretty convincing, vomit everywhere, the reek of drink, empty bottles all over the place. And nobody will accept that he could have forced the stuff down me. It's very scary to have nobody believe you. You begin to doubt yourself.'

'You should get right away from this part of the world,' said Clare. 'You'll never have any peace otherwise.'

'But where could I go? How could I leave without David?'

'What about your uncle and aunt?'

'They're old. They haven't been well. Anyway Mark knows where they live. They never approved of him, they'd be saying, we told you so.'

Shrieks of laughter were coming from upstairs. They went to investigate. Vicky had got out paints and painting books. But apart from what had spilled on their clothes and the carpet, it was all on their faces.

'I made Sarah and John look like they've been attacked by a man,' explained Vicky. 'Like Paula and you, Mummy.'

Clare and Kathleen looked at each other.

Kathleen explained about Paula in the kitchen as she prepared scrambled eggs, toast and a salad.

'Let's go round and see if she's back after lunch,' said Clare. 'What is it about these men?'

'Has Bill never hit you?'

'He wouldn't see me for dust if he did. Mark you, he's left home a couple of times himself. Couldn't take my PMT. He can never understand that I'm not aiming at him personally, that I've just got to shout at someone. I made the mistake once of suggesting there was no smoke without fire. There was no hope of convincing him after that.'

Kathleen shivered. 'I hate that expression. That's what Mrs Coe said to me about the drink.'

'I don't know how you've stood up to all this, Kath.'

'I'm beginning to worry that I might have a tendency for alcohol which I shut out of my mind and refuse to accept. Maybe I don't even know I'm doing it.'

'Rubbish. That's auto-suggestion. Don't let these bloody people work on you.'

After lunch they put the cleaned-up children into Clare's 2CV to drive round and see if Paula had returned from hospital. The door was opened by Darren. Paula was in the kitchen doing a wash. She seemed to have lost stones in weight and her face was spectacularly coloured with blotches of purple, cinnamon, green and yellow. They couldn't help giggling.

'Didn't think I was that funny,' exclaimed Paula. 'Look at them,

Darren, you'd think I was something out of the circus.'

Kathleen put an arm round her and explained about Vicky painting a battered woman's face on Sarah. Paula shook her head. 'Kids are so quick. You hope they won't notice, but there they are, busy taking notes like bloody journalists.'

'What's been going on, Paula?'

'Here, Darren, take some biscuits and show them your new Lego set your nan bought you. I'll put the kettle on for some tea. Concussion, that's all it was. X-ray showed what might be a hairline crack, so they kept me in for observation. Got to take it easy for a few weeks. You know me, that won't be difficult, it's what I do normally. The doctor reckoned a skull like mine should have broken a man's fist. Didn't say, but he knew what had happened. Mrs McGovern next door told me Ted was round while I was away, so she popped out and told him I had a fractured skull and the police were making enquiries. He went pale as a piece of cod and couldn't get away fast enough. Really sorry about that morning, Kath. Did you manage all right? I'll have them the day of the hearing, no problem.'

They sat drinking tea till Clare looked at her watch. 'I'd better be getting back. Bill has been away a couple of days at a conference, so he'll be home soon, exhausted and expecting sympathy.'

It had started to rain. She dropped Kathleen, Vicky and Sarah off on the way. 'Good luck at the hearing. I'll come round anyway, but if there's anything I can do, phone me at once.'

Kathleen felt lifted out of her loneliness that evening, listening to dinning of the rain. Friendship was a tenuous commodity, she thought. Each had their individual lives to fulfil, each had their own dependencies, but every contact, however brief, was like sunshine to the tundra.

'SOMETIMES I see my entire childhood depending on the weather. Grey wet days that barred me in the house or sunshine that liberated me. When it rained the house seemed desolate as a prison, monitored by ticking clocks whose sole purpose was to eke the day around their dials second by second. Sometimes so slowly that as I stood at my bedroom window and watched the horses grouped beneath the holm oaks in the paddocks, their coats stained with water as they tried to shelter, I felt that we were fixed in time as if we'd become the photograph of ourselves. From the other side of the house, I could look down from the top landing on cars and lorries passing beyond the front garden, glistening with rain, sending out sprays of water as they swished through the puddles, windscreen wipers like metronomes, misty people reclining inside, heading towards Drogheda or Ardee. So many busy people, I would think. With so many places to go to, so much to do. I longed to bean adult to become part of that busy process.

The top floor was my favourite part of the house. Nobody came up there, except occasionally to clean. I shared it with the hissing water tanks and three empty guest rooms that used to be the maids' rooms. There was an old lavatory where the water raced across a flat porcelain plateau like a hydro-electric dam. It was very clinical if you wanted to examine the efficiency of your digestion. One of the guest rooms had a great brass bedstead with a pale-green satin-finish bedspread like ice on the skin. The bed made strange musical jinglings that sounded in my room beneath. It was amazing the orchestral crescendos some guests could extract from it. I thought they must be telling each other funny stories and shaking with laughter.

Only up there or outside in the fields or in the garden of the burnt house was I free from vigilance. The sole function of parents seemed to be to criticise. Their eyes were like horse-flies, settling on me the moment they saw me, to bite complaints about the state of my clothes, my hands, my hair, or accuse me of being late, of spilling glue on a table or trampling on a flowerbed.

Parents were just another form of weather. Generally overcast, given to persistent downpours, often stormy, rarely sunny. I felt like an untidy mess they wanted to clear away. I supposed all parents were snappy; with each other too, the way cats would arch their backs and spit, flick their tails when they met. D'Arcy, the groom, with his greasy flat cap and stained breeches wide as elephants' ears, was the same, no respecter of anyone, forever grumbling. I didn't mind him, everyone expected him to crab, whereas my parents were charming to everyone else.

One day I compared the sheen D'Arcy was rising on a horse's coat to the shine on Father Flynn's nose, and he nearly split himself cackling. From then on we were friends. In indulgent mood he might show me how to plait a mane or treat a swollen fetlock, and out would pour a stream of scurrilous gossip. He knew everything about everyone for forty miles. I was mesmerised by his hair-raising profanities, and by the way his tongue would nip in and out among the stumps of his few remaining molars like a pink eel.

My parents never told me anything about anyone. Should I chance to enter a room while they were talking, they clammed up immediately. They would appear embarrassed by my presence, cough, straighten their clothing, then make some suggestion about my homework needing doing, or send me with a message to Mrs Jones. Mrs Jones did the cooking, though it was doubtful if cook was the right description. Food-boiler, perhaps. But then preparing meals was only part of her employment. She was also housekeeper and maid, though there was a girl who came into help with the cleaning.

I thought of my parents as my parents only because they were there. I belonged to them like the house did. D'Arcy had a wife and children who lived in a cottage on the Slane road, but he only ever spoke of them contemptuously, as if they were possessions he was ashamed of. Mrs Jones had a photograph she claimed was her husband. Whenever she looked at it, a tear would seep into the corner of each eye. And she had a son in Boston, Massachusetts, whom she maintained had sent her the red anorak with the St Brendan label, which everyone knew was from Dunne's Stores in Drogheda.

I accepted that my mother had produced me out of her body, but I never really believed it. I could understand hens were responsible for eggs which hatched into yellow chicks which in turn became hens again. That's what they were there for. I'd seen foals slip from their mothers as from envelopes. It seemed natural enough. But my parents didn't seem remotely like child producers. I was sure I'd been there all along, like the furniture.

I thought of my parents as indestructible, as permanent as the house itself. They were predictable, intransigent, they took all the decisions. They lived on a higher plane from me. Then suddenly and quite arbitrarily they were gone. Summarily sucked away as if they'd been caught by some giant vacuum cleaner passing down the Naas road.

The greatest shock was not their loss, but that it could happen to them. If they were ephemeral, then the house and all those years of my existence could be swept away. How long could I remain untouched? When I was taken over by my aunt and uncle in an effortless baton-change, that made it even more difficult to rationalise. I acquired parent-substitutes who were far more loving and caring than my real parents had ever been.

I only accepted my mortality when I became a mother myself. When babies emerged out of me, little hands like nerine lilies, buttocks like hot-cross buns, eyes like little sapphires, and gorgeous smiles that would melt you into your boots. There are no words sufficient to describe my sense of involvement. They were beautiful, they smelled intoxicating, they were miniature god-creatures. They weren't bits of furniture that had always been around, pieces of paper from an envelope, calves from a cow, eggs from a hen. They were made inside me, they endorsed a purpose I had never really considered of myself. And yet they were entirely separate creatures, almost frightening in their individuality.

It was Mark whose particular seminal-pen had written them into existence. As apparently my father had done to my mother to set my being in motion. That made Mark special to me for a long time. In the beginning he wasn't Mark, the dark presence lurking out there that he is now, the cunning werewolf threatening my sanity. That's why in the early days of our troubles I clung to him, was never able to view him as the two-faced amoral male that others saw.

Recently I've worried about David. There's something special about the first-born. He was the prototype I cut my teeth on. All this while just a child. But what's happening now? Is he being formed into another of those demon figures? Another greedy monster, sugar-iced bully, another manipulator of susceptibilities? I can see the frailty of his developing mind, seeking guidance, illumination, the whys and the wherefores. I, his mother, the fatalist, too passive, too easily pushed around, the wrong sign for a boy to follow. In the last few months his father had suddenly come to the fore, the apparent man of decision, a forceful businessman, a guiding light for that thrusting male power in their genes; a father to admire, not knowing, of course, that it's all built on sand. Will it be a terrible let-down when he finds out? Or will he just twist it aside to his own benefit, like his father does?

I wanted to keep the little boy, the toddler always trying to extend himself, demanding to be lifted onto walls to walk along the parapet while I held onto him, to run along park benches and finish with a big leap down, wheeee... watch me jump down the stairs, Mummy. Or making waves in the bath, that sudden moment of exhilarating fear as they lurched up to his face. But sentimentalising isn't going to bring him home. If Mark was me now, he'd be devising schemes to get him back. But I can't engage my mind like that. It requires an innate deviousness I lack. Perhaps I'm like my father, saying, wait and see. He didn't possess the bite necessary to be a hard-nosed businessman. He allowed others to squeeze him out, to further their interests at the expense of his. The other directors of the bakery had sold their shares privately in a deal that left him the odd man out, his shares suddenly valueless. He had been part of a syndicate that had purchased a valuable stallion, ostensibly to serve their own mares. The other members got foals out of the project but when it came to his turn an infection had made the stallion infertile. Thinking about my parents always fills me with regret. Their dying had reversed the roles, and I look back on them as if they had been my children whom I never helped enough when they were alive.'

ON THE day of the court hearing Paula arrived early. 'Had to show I wasn't going to let you down again, Kath.'

Kathleen took a bus into the city in a state of numbed dread, certain that her worst fears were about to be enacted. Her case was due to be heard at eleven-fifteen. By eleven-thirty Mr Onion had not appeared. She began to shake with anxiety. What would happen to her if he didn't turn up? He arrived at eleven-forty quite unconcerned, and two minutes later they were called into the judge's room.

Mark sat beside his solicitor, so smart, so assimilated into his navy-blue suit that he was like a waxwork. It unnerved her to have to sit so close. He looked the sort of man a judge would give every ounce of credit to, she thought. The wolf of Arcady so trimmed and polished and immaculately tailored as to pass for an ivory pillar of the establishment. She had never known this man.

The judge was different, too. He also wore a navy-blue suit. His eyes appeared separate in their sockets like stones in dried-up apricots, and the grey hair around his bald head was like a ring of ash. He dominated the proceedings, his eyebrows raised, not so much in surprise at what he read from the notes on his desk, but more as if it was all so commonplace. He was as matter-of-fact as if he was dealing with a disputed boundary through a back garden.

'...if these allegations are correct, it is a matter of concern to this court that a Non-Molestation and Ouster Order has been totally disregarded by both parties. But I notice that the plaintiff does not pursue the matter. Were some of these allegations to be substantiated it would be a matter for the police. No doubt we'll return to this later...'

Kathleen was puzzled. She thought Mr Onion had said he was going to make a formal complaint to the court.

'...after reviewing some of the points raised,' continued the judge. 'The report from Mrs Coe, Social Worker, states that in her opinion Mr September seems to be level-headed and caring, whereas Mrs September has hysterical tendencies that are not conducive to family stability. She also states that she found the two smaller children, at present living with their mother, very repressed...'

Kathleen felt dazed, sickened at such words, seeing her last hopes fade.

'...There is also the matter of Mrs September's drinking. Allegations were made about this in Mr September's original affidavit as well as in Mrs Coe's report. But these you have refuted, Mr Onion, as quite unfounded, being based on one incident alone, when you allege Mr September entered the house against the Court Order, and forced his wife to consume a large quantity of alcohol.' He raised his eyebrows even further. 'A somewhat bizarre and incredible extreme. However I note Mr Onion's point that in Mr September's answer to the petition, dated prior to the day the incident is alleged to have occurred, he seems to have remarkable prior knowledge of the matter. He glanced at Mark, who gave a brief shake of the head.

'Mr Onion also states a number of occasions when Mr September flouted the court order and harassed his wife. Also that he removed their son David from school and has taken him to live with his sister; although I note the court does not seem to have been informed of these alleged transgressions. However, I assume the fact that the Non-Molestation Order was granted to Mrs September in the first place might suggest there was no smoke without fire. I also have the Probation Officer's report that assisted her case at that hearing, in which he could find no evidence of her drinking and considered her an excellent mother.'

The judge constantly shuffled the papers in his hands like an accomplished dealer at a card game, always seeming to know exactly what he was holding. It was evident that his habit of keeping his brows stuck halfway up his temples was a feature of his applied concentration rather than disdain.

'...Mrs Coe complains that Mrs September is keeping her elder daughter back from school. I would have thought her action reasonable in the light of what happened to her son. Also I am given to understand that the school holidays have now started. As regards the boy, David, and his father taking him, Mrs Coe states in her report that she considered no action should be taken since the boy strongly expressed his preference for being with his father, and she felt the mother was not providing a stable environment.'

The judge put the papers down, intertwined his fingers and gazed at Kathleen. 'Now Mrs September, it would make life easier for all of us if we could clear up the matter of this drinking. The inferences are that it is habitual, that it severely inhibits your responsibilities as a parent, and that it is very disturbing for your children. What would you like to tell me about it?'

Kathleen's heart was throbbing, her throat stiff as a stalk of celery. 'I don't drink... I mean I might drink... a glass or two at a party... that's all.'

'Quite.' The judge nodded as if he expected no other answer. 'So the problem we have here is conflicting claims and opposing reports. If the allegations are true it would place in my mind serious doubt that you are competent to manage your family, Mrs September.' His eyebrows rose higher again. 'It is also my experience that in these circumstances the consequences of perjury do not deter combatants from stating serious falsehoods. However I am not satisfied that we have yet discovered the truth. The looking-after of the children is the principal concern of this court so I shall postpone my decision till further investigation. I should like the Probation Officer to arrange for a psychiatrist's report.'

However relieved that the outcome had not been worse, Kathleen still felt faint. All she wanted was to get away, to avoid any confrontation with Mark. Mr Onion seemed pleased with the result. 'Old Middleton takes things as they come. He'll see this sorted out.'

'It doesn't seem right,' she said to him. 'That lies are treated like facts. You'd expect a court to be able to recognise the truth. I can't understand why you didn't make an issue out of the court orders being flouted and David being taken.'

Mr Onion looked pained. 'Didn't you notice that Plover never pursued their allegations? That was why I was late. Plover wasn't too happy about the consequences if his client's story didn't stick, and my feeling was that your husband's lying skills could have made his a better case than ours, so I agreed to a deal. We would hold back if they did. It was a risk, but it worked.'

Kathleen stared at him dumbfounded. 'I didn't know you could do things like that,' she exclaimed.

She said the same to Paula when she got home.

'Horse-trading,' said Paula, her bruises now in pastel shades. 'Not much cock, is it? Still lets the bastard get away with it. At least that probation officer, Fulcher, put in a good word for you. Not like that licker of male arses, the Coe woman. Anyway, what can a psychiatrist find wrong with you, darling, that a nice hot plate of fried plaice, chips and peas won't put right? We had ours earlier.'

'What would I do without you, Paula?' she said, sitting down to eat.

Paula brought over a pot of tea. 'Got to stick together and help each other. Everyone else's so wrapped up in the rest of the world's doings, the country's debts over the moon, people at each other's throats in the name of Islam, Christianity, Jewry and others I can't pronounce, shit getting into the water, poison in the atmosphere, so nobody's got time for the pollution of what men keep doing to women. Equal rights and feminism are getting louder, but they're still kicking us in the slats from here to kingdom come.'

'But why does it have to be like this?'

Paula shrugged. 'It's their little world, isn't it? That doesn't change. Males are stronger, they never have to get pregnant and they think they're in charge.'

She poured out two cups of tea and sat down. 'I enjoyed your kids today, you know. Wish I'd had a little girl. Don't understand how Betty Coe could say they were repressed. Of course they're afraid of their bloody father. So would I be. You're too nice, Kathleen, and they're the same. It's no good being nice. That's what men want us to be, so we'll comply with their wishes. Maybe what you should really be doing is putting your two through an SAS course.'

Back at home that evening Kathleen set a wash going, the old machine grinding and gushing in its endless turmoil. She ironed by the table in the dining-room listening to an Irish pipe band playing. The wailing jigs drew her mind back to the nostalgic corner she kept for her old home. Not that it was music that her parents had ever listened to. Her mother had liked Peggy Lee and Ella Fitzgerald, and her father, who had sometimes played the organ in the little Protestant church that was a replica of Kings College

Chapel in Cambridge, had only listened to Bach fugues. She wondered if the house was still there in Collon, and who was living in it now, if the ruin still stood in its lost garden.

She folded away the ironing-board and went into the front-room, turned on the television, the volume low, as if to keep it at a distance.

She was aware of the occasional street noise, a car passing like the gurgle of water emptying from the sink, a twitter of voices from people walking along the pavement. Then periods of nothing save the rapid patter of repartee from the television programme she was too tired to concentrate on.

The shocking din that suddenly interrupted was for a moment unidentifiable.

Then it clarified into the violent clanging of breaking glass behind her. She jerked her head round and saw the curtains billow out in elephantine curves. As the cool night air swept in on her, she screamed, leaping away, spinning round, her back against the chimney breast.

She stood pinned there, a hand across her mouth, watching the curtains swaying in the new draught, as more pieces of glass cascaded down from behind them onto the floor, breaking into smaller fragments. A black brick lay on the carpet just in front of the curtains. The programme on the television continued quietly, an unabashed box of bright colours, little people in another world, unaffected by this one.

She stood rigid with terror, not knowing what to expect next. Each swirl of the curtains suggested someone about to enter. There was a new volume of sound now, the hum of the city intruding into the room. Her heartbeat thumped the seconds away as she waited.

Cautiously she slid along the inner wall to the door, watching the curtains all the time. She stood in the doorway at the foot of the stairs, listening to hear if the children had been woken, wondering how, if nothing else, no one of the neighbours had appeared to enquire about the noise.

Eventually she worked up enough courage to unlock the front door, her skin prickling with anticipation, as if the night itself might burst into the room in a black deluge.

The little front garden was empty. Street lamps glowed

steadfastly, shone diamonds of reflection on the roofs of parked cars. Along the dark terrace of houses glowed buff rectangles of curtained light. Somewhere down the street a car's engine was chafing as its owner parked it, then at last switched off. In the distance the faint cry of an ambulance siren strode long-legged through the city suburbs. Her pulse was buzzing, her temple throbbing, yet the scene all around seemed calm and undisturbed. It occurred to her that had she been murdered a few moments before, nobody would have known, not a single soul would have responded to her screams. They would probably have thought it was a scene on television.

Inform the police, she thought, suddenly energised. But she would have to leave the children while she ran to the phonebox. Perhaps that was what he wanted her to do. Cautiously she stepped out along the path. A soft furry shape wrapped itself round her ankles, purring. Mrs Mathews' cat Timothy. She saw a strip of light down the edge of a curtain in the old lady's bay window. Mrs Mathews had a phone. She went round and knocked. She had to knock several times before the door opened a crack, and Mrs Mathews' face appeared over the chain. She felt guilty that she might alarm the old lady. 'What is it?' Mrs Mathews quavered.

'Please, don't be scared, it's only me,' pleaded Kathleen. 'Somebody threw a brick through my window. I don't want to leave the children to phone the police. Could you phone them for me?'

'Oh my goodness, Oh God, what are we coming to, what a terrible thing, no one's safe anymore...'

Kathleen groaned inwardly. 'I didn't want to bother you...'

'I heard noises,' said the old lady, still reluctant to undo the chain. 'Drunken hooligans, I thought. It's not right, disturbing innocent folk. You want me to phone for you, do you? It's 999, isn't it? I've never dialled it before. I hope it'll be all right.' And she closed the door.

Kathleen went back inside, crept upstairs to check on the children. Vicky's eyes shone like a cat's in the light from the landing. 'What was all that noise, Mummy?'

'A window got broken. Probably some drunk passing by.'

'Was it Daddy?'

'I don't know. The police are coming in a minute.'

The wait was agonising, listening to every sound, not knowing if Mark mightn't be out there somewhere, or even have already entered the house. She had no faith that the police would come, yet minutes later there was a knock on the door. She looked out from her bedroom window before running down to let them in.

The policeman was young, matter-of-fact as a meter-reader, despite the hour. 'You're on our Power of Arrest list. A Non-Molestation Order. We'll check round.' A second policeman stood out on the pavement.

Kathleen was still trembling. She waited in the dining-room, clutching the two children, for neither would leave her side. They listened to the sounds and voices of the policemen as they carried out their search. She felt paralysed. Her fear now was for the eternal presence that Mark had instilled, whether he was physically there or not. His threat was like a leakage of gas poisoning the air, it hung in the shadows, clung to the walls, an invisible malignancy permeating the house.

The two policemen came back inside. 'Didn't expect to find anything,' said the first one laconically. 'They don't hang around. D'you usually keep a binbag full of wine bottles leaning against your back door?'

Numbed, Kathleen shook her head. 'That's his signature,' she said.

The other policeman was making cups of tea in the kitchen. 'We'll get the window boarded up for tonight. You won't want to be here on your own after that, will you? We could take you to the refuge if you like?'

The hot cup of tea revived her a fraction. 'I've a friend a few streets away,' she told them.

'We'll take you there, then,' they said. 'This is council property, isn't it? We'll report it now, so it'll get done first thing.'

FOR several moments neither spoke.

'Do you have any religious conviction?'

'Why do you ask?'

How small her hands were, he thought. They'd have difficulty stretching an octave.

'I wondered what else sustained you. Apart from friends.'

'I'm not very religious. But I've always believed there's something out there.'

'I know what you mean. It's difficult to accept so great a variety of life-forms developing on earth without some outside force. On the other hand, how could any single entity have created such complex creatures?'

Ravel's Introduction and Allegro revolved through his head as he admired the brown plumes of hair crowning her forehead, the cream cusps of her cheeks, the pasta texture of jaw neatly angled to neck.

'I'm surprised you have faith left in anything after all that happened to you.'

'Perhaps adversity becomes like a vaccine. Mark was always mocking. A bit like you sometimes. He'd say things like: there's no such thing as altruism, good deeds are for purely selfish reasons like wanting others to think well of us. Pity is nothing but saying, thank God it isn't happening to me. Whenever I argued back, he'd put me down. He was so cold he'd have me close to tears.'

She fell silent with the unhappiness of her recollection.

'You didn't really believe him?' he urged her.

She shook her head angrily. 'I know people care because there's an influence that exists outside ourselves. Jesus Christ showed how faith in what was good was more important than suffering. But the institutional Christians reversed it, didn't they? Concentrated on the suffering because they had no answer to poverty. I don't believe in worship. That's us imagining what God as a man would require of us.'

He imagined stringing his fingers through the lacy curls of her hair.

‘So you are made of the stuff of martyrs?’

‘You’re mocking me,’ she bridled. ‘Just like Mark did. What do you believe in, then?’

This was his chance, he thought. Encourage her to identify him with Mark. If she could transfer her anger onto him, that might burn away her desire.

He was overcome instead by an inclination to say something endearing. He could hear himself saying; look, I’m here now, I’ll be your ally, you don’t have to worry any more, let me take care of you, let’s drop all these pretences...

‘I think religion is one of the banes of civilisation. Too many people determined that other people’s faiths are wrong and theirs is right.’

‘So what should we believe in, then?’ She stared at him intently, as if trying to challenge him to make an inescapable admission. ‘Love?’

He felt that same shiver of insuppressible excitement that he had felt before.

‘But does it work?’

'I WENT back early to the house the next morning to be there when the council men came to repair the window. They didn't arrive till eleven o'clock, but immediately started making a mess and cracking jokes connecting breakages of windows and sexual frustration. Then one of them shouted through the din that there was someone to see me. It was Mr Fulcher, the probation officer. He didn't seem surprised to find the council men at work. When I told him what had happened he pointed out there was no proof it was Mark. I mentioned the bag of empty bottles, then wondered if that had been wise. But I hadn't had time to dispose of them, and he was always nosing about. He could see I was agitated. I told him I didn't think I could take much more of Mark's attacks. But there was something else on his mind.

'Are you sure you're telling the truth, Mrs September? It wouldn't be the first time an unhappy wife has invented being attacked. I knew a woman who became ill with severe poisoning. It turned out she'd taken weedkiller herself, hoping to incriminate her husband. Could it be that you broke the window yourself and collected the empty bottles in a bag so that you could blame your husband? I don't think you drink, Mrs September, you don't behave like a drinker. But you are in a very nervous state. It's not unlike suppressed hysteria. I did wonder earlier whether you, yourself, might have set up the drinking incident?'

I flopped down onto a dining-chair and burst into tears. I could see him hovering near for the final confession. 'Why won't anyone believe me?' I sobbed.

He frowned, as if unsure of his ground now. 'It's just that I've never known a man persist in this way.'

He buttoned up his coat. 'Anyway, I've made an appointment for you to see a Mr Clement at the St Giles Clinic.'

'It's Mark who ought to see someone,' I shouted at him as he left.

I told Paula when I got back to her house. 'He's been watching too much television,' she said. 'Anyone with half a brain could see that Mark's trying to turn you into a gibbering wreck to prove you're unsuitable to look after the children.'

'I don't know how he gets away with it,' she mused. 'Why don't I come and stay with you for a few nights? There's never been a witness to his little schemes. That'd give the likes of Coe and Fulcher some real evidence. Darren and I could sleep in David's room.'

Kathleen paused, glanced across at Mark Clement.

'You said yesterday that I have more strength than I realise. But it's women like Paula who are the strong ones. They're the ones who take action. They've a flick-of-the-fingers determination I lack. Perhaps I choose my friends because they're tough. Any strength I have is from them. All the time I feel like a bad swimmer struggling to keep afloat. Maybe some of them chose the wrong men, too. Maybe they loved them once, as I loved Mark. You never think of those words at the wedding, for good or for bad, that it'll ever go bad. I thought bad meant hard times, lack of money, shortages. We had plenty of those.

I realise now since talking to you, that my father was one of those who got by, but couldn't really manage, who put his problems in a drawer and tried to forget them. Mark's like that in the sense that he can't take the real world, and twists reality to suit himself. But he takes others with him, and they become his victims, whereas my father only deluded himself, so that he ended up the victim. Both their worlds are illusory. Brenda described Mark as a psychopath. Someone without any morality. I wish I'd known that long ago. I wish I could have been prepared somehow. Maybe I could have changed things, helped him in some way. But I don't suppose it would have worked. Leopards don't change their spots, do they?

On the way to our house that evening Paula and I bought a bag of fish and chips for supper. I was opening the cupboard to get the ketchup down when I saw the whisky bottle. He's been here, I screamed. It was half-full. We searched and found five bottles in all, another in a different cupboard, one at the back of a drawer, one under the sink, another in the airing-cupboard... I was hysterical. Mr Fulcher was right in that respect. I can't tell you how terrifying it was, knowing that Mark had freely entered the house while I was away. It wasn't just that revulsion people feel on finding their privacy has been violated by a burglar, it was knowing that he had so much control, that something was driving him to keep persecuting me, that I was never going to be safe from him.

Paula reckoned he stayed around last night after he heaved the brick, waiting to see what would happen, then as soon as the police took me and the children round to her house, he came back, got in through the broken window and planted the bottles, arranging for Fulcher to get word in the morning. Only Fulcher, thinking I was setting up my own incidents, believed I'd sent the message, and didn't bother to look.

We went round tightening all the window-catches, making sure all the doors were locked. She tried to cheer me up. 'We might as well have something stronger than a cup of tea, Kath. Since the bastard has been so kind as to provide it, who are we to complain it isn't the best Highland Malt?'

I didn't care for the stuff, especially after he'd poured so much down me. Suppose it was poisoned or drugged? 'Don't be daft,' she said. 'The bastard's not that stupid. He'd realise if you were found poisoned he'd be the first suspect. I'll brew us up something that'll fold up your nerves and send you to sleep like a baby.'

It was a punch with lemon juice and honey and hot water added. Not bad stuff. Good thing Betty Coe didn't come on a spot check. We sprawled on the sofa, got maudlin and wallowed in childhood nostalgia. Paula's dad lost an arm in an accident at work, and became the only one-armed conjurer in the business, did children's parties with dreadful trick arms that fell off when you shook them by the hand, a balloon one that got bigger and bigger, one that turned into a snake. They never had any money because he spent every penny he made constructing new ideas for arms. She used to help him in his workshop, holding nuts and sawing bits of metal, while her mother used to sew him special jackets full of extra pockets and tubes. Great days. He died when she was twelve, and she could never forgive him that a man so full of inventive ideas could let himself be taken off by death.

We had two peaceful days.

Then I was woken up in the middle of the night. There was a noise like a rat gnawing at the woodwork. Raising my head cautiously, I couldn't believe what I was seeing, yet knew already what it was. The curtains in the bedroom were thin, and they glowed from a street lamp that shone through a gap in the houses behind. A dark shadow was silhouetted across them. I lay there petrified. But at least he was still outside, the window still constituted a barrier. I slid from the bed and crept across the landing to wake Paula.

'Leave off will you,' she kept muttering. 'Leave me alone, it's the middle of the night, for God's sake go back to bed.'

I was in tears pleading with her. 'That's the trouble with being large,' she grumbled, as if she'd forgotten why she was there, swinging her big white thighs out from under the duvet. 'Everybody thinks you can toss bloody-minded males over your shoulder.' She plonked her bare feet down heavily onto the stairs, went into my room and peered in. 'Where is he then? Can't see anybody?' She crossed the dimly-lit room to have a closer look at the window. 'Are you having me on, Kath? Looks more like you were dreaming.'

I was about to enter the room after her when a dark figure emerged from behind the door right beside me. I screamed with fright as it cannoned into me, knocking me down. 'Come back, you bastard,' yelled Paula, tripping over me. She scrambled up, turned on the light and pounded down the stairs as the front door slammed. I heard her wrenching it open and shouting into the night.

I was still sprawled winded in the doorway when she returned. 'No chance,' she panted. 'He went down the pavement like a greyhound.'

The children had appeared, white-faced, eyes puffed with sleep. Paula looked solid as a wrestler in her black bra and pants. 'He must have been as surprised as we were. He won't try that again.' She helped me up. 'Are you OK?' Sarah began to cry and she put her arms round her and Vicky. 'There, there, darlings, it's all right, Mummy's not hurt.'

Darren was plainly mystified. 'Was it Daddy again?' asked Vicky.

'You can't keep anything from the child,' said Paula, chest still heaving. 'Wish I'd caught the bugger. Such excitement, my heart's thumping like a bus engine. Couldn't see his face, I think he had some kind of balaclava on.'

'What's this?' asked Vicky, picking up a brown plastic bottle from the stairs. It was full of some liquid, but had no label.

Paula unscrewed the cap and sniffed. 'Phew,' she grimaced, wrinkling her nose and jerking it away. 'Stinks. Ether or something. He must have dropped it.'

We looked at each other.

'What am I going to do, Paula?' I cried.

'Come on, kids,' she said. 'Excitement's over, back to bed.'

They wouldn't stir from my side, clutching onto me like marsupial offspring. 'You see,' I said. 'This is what happens. I'll take them into my bed.' But I was shaking so much I couldn't move.

'Let's go and make a cup of tea,' said Paula. She had to help me downstairs.

'Just a minute,' she said as the kettle started to sing. She went out of the back door. We all sat there in a huddle, fear reviving. There were several muffled noises. She came back in, grinning, went over to make the tea. 'We've got a wooden ladder, the bottle of ether and me as witness. I'll put some clothes on and phone the police.'

They were twenty minutes coming. One of them was a policewoman. I was glad to see a woman, a sergeant who spoke her mind. When we'd finished explaining, she looked at her watch. 'If we get permission to ask Ipswich to go to his address, and if there's an available car, by the time they get there they might just find his engine still warm. It could be circumstantial evidence at three o'clock in the morning. OK, Tom? It's worth a try. Break-in and attempted assault.' The policeman went out. 'A patrol could take hours to find an isolated farmhouse in the middle of the night. It's not going to be easy. From what you've told me it's unlikely to be anyone else but your husband, but since it was dark and neither of you got a butcher's of his face, a court won't condemn on possibility. The ether could come from anywhere, and the bottle'll be dappled with your fingerprints. His lawyer'll say you were trying to discredit him, his client was fast asleep in his bed. What d'you suppose his intention was, Mrs September? Same as last time? Make you unconscious, dump you on the sofa downstairs, splash some of his hidden whisky around, stick a bottle in your fist, and there'd be another example of your bad habits? He sounds a number one weirdo. I think we ought to shake this case up a bit.'

Even after they'd left, promising that someone would be round in the morning to check the window and the outside, I was still shaking.

'It's no use, Paula,' I said. 'He'll talk them round. He always does. I can't take any more. I've got to find somewhere he can't find us.'

'I was thinking the same,' she replied. 'It's ridiculous, but if the law can't protect you, you're going to have to take steps yourself. You come round to mine. He doesn't know where I live. And at least there'd be the two of us.'

'I don't want to keep imposing on you, Paula,' I said.

'You haven't any choice,' she replied.

I rang Mr Onion in the morning. He managed to express horror and legalistic delight at the same time. 'This could be our lucky break. He had to make a mistake sooner or later. And you've got a witness. Wonderful.' I didn't have his faith. Then I rang Clare and she came over to transport mattresses on the roof of her car for us to sleep on. We made sure no one was watching.

She came over again three days later.

'A man rang this morning. "This is Mr Fulcher," he said. "Court probation officer. I'm trying to find where Mrs Kathleen September's moved to, I believe she is a friend of yours?" But I recognised Mark's voice. "You're going to end up in prison," I said. He put the phone down. It's all right,' she added, seeing the alarm in our faces. 'I parked in the Unthank Road. You're going to have to get right away, Kath. I've got some friends in Scotland, would you like me to contact them?'

Maybe I should have agreed. But I didn't want to go so far away.

Two days later I opened the front door to put out the empties... and there he was. He was sitting in his milk-white Sierra with the window down, arm on the sill, wearing dark glasses.

'Hallo, darling,' he said. 'I wondered where you'd got to. It's cost me a lot of money to find you. You're not looking too well. Is your illness catching up with you?'

Then he drove away. Paula found me slumped on the doorstep, clutching my chest.

Illness? What was he talking about? Was this going to be his next line of attack?

A little voice inside me was saying, how can you let him have such an effect on you? You've got to pull yourself together, you're making a fuss about nothing. It was like the voice of Betty Coe. I felt terrible, as though I had flu.

It was frightening to feel as if everything tangible and solid was close to disintegration, the ground crumbling under my feet, everything I gripped coming away in my hands. What would happen if my mind really slipped over the edge? Would I become a screaming, gibbering maniac? Would I actually fall apart? How could I hold onto sanity? I said all this to Paula, collapsed over the table, clasping a cup of tea.

'It might be an easy way out for you to go bananas,' she said. 'But don't forget the girls. What would happen to them?'

'But I can't stay here, Paula, can I?' I cried.

She snapped her fingers. 'I bumped into a woman I know a few weeks back. She was buying a big bag of oranges in Gateways, that's how I recognised her. That and her red hair. When I was a probationer at the hospital before I had Darren, she was a ward sister, ever such a nice woman, but always eating oranges. We still exchange Christmas cards. She told me her family were grown up and had moved away, but she missed the company and was thinking of taking in lodgers. Sandra Kussetski. She lives near the waterworks, not far from the ring-road.'

Eat while the bread's fresh was Paula's dictum. So we set off there and then. We were careful now, watching in case we might be followed, realising Mark might be employing an agent. We doubled back on our tracks, went through a cemetery, just like in some detective story.

With all our detours we took forty-five minutes. It was a large terraced house in a quiet street. Sandra was tall, but not big the way Paula was big, her clothes hung from her shoulders like curtains. Her hair was still a striking shade of red, and she had strong front teeth and a small pointed chin. She told us she'd done nothing about taking in lodgers yet, but as she was getting fed up with hospital pay she'd thought of setting up on her own and taking in disabled people. She looked a bit dubious when she heard my story.

What sane person would want the risk of maniacal husbands invading in the middle of the night? But suddenly she agreed to take us. Paula reckoned it was because she fell for the girls. She told us the rooms weren't ready yet, that she'd try and sort them out for next week, but when we told her how urgent it was to move in immediately, she agreed.

Sandra was a stroke of luck. She'd been married to a Polish lecturer at the university who'd gone off with one of his students five years earlier. You could say she was on my side from the start. She dotes on the girls, spoils them as if they were her own. We did have a few problems about money. How was I to persuade the Council to pay rent for somewhere else when I already had a perfectly good council house?

I went to see Monica, the refuge social worker, and she contacted Mr Fulcher. Mr Onion had already told him of the police interest after the latest incident, and I think that finally persuaded him to help. And course it was Mr Fulcher who fixed up for me to see a psychiatrist for the court report. Which, I suppose, is where you come in...'

Mark Clement blinked. With those words they were suddenly back in the bare cubicle of his office. It seemed startlingly empty with just the two of them, as if they were the only survivors of her story.

'I'm not a psychiatrist, though,' he said. 'Greg Fulcher's gone off psychiatrists. He says the language of psychotherapy is less obscure.'

'I didn't care what you were,' said Kathleen. 'When I walked into this room it seemed like you were my last hope.'

IT WAS late. Panic began to edge along his nerves as if he knew a distant bell would shortly announce the end of class. Soon his brief would be completed, the clinical status terminated and she would walk out of his life.

'Could you see yourself acting any differently now?' he asked, trying to sound composed. 'How would you handle Betty Coe, for example?'

'D'you mean the way I allowed her to treat me like a naughty child?'

'What do you feel about that?'

'Annoyed with myself for being so weak and ineffectual.'

His eyes fed constantly on her face. 'But remember that you've taken a tremendous emotional and physical battering. Your whole life has been turned upside down. At times it must have seemed that everyone was against you.' He paused. 'But you've survived. That doesn't sound like someone weak and ineffectual, does it?'

'I only just survived.'

'You can't change Mark, can you?' Were these necessary questions, he wondered? Or were they uttered to keep her there as long as possible? 'And the law hasn't proved much help if he's intent on hounding you. So what else is there?'

She looked at him uncertainly, head tilted.

'There's only you,' he continued. 'The changes have to come from you.'

Her face lost colour, her shoulders sank. 'Am I the problem, then? Have I been the cause of the trouble all along?'

He shook his head impatiently. 'Come on, now. You know I don't mean that.'

She straightened up with a shiver. 'I have wondered, you know, if it might be me. When everyone believed in him, how could they all be wrong?'

It was so easy to imagine enfolding her in his arms and hugging reassurance into her.

'But don't you see?' he said. 'You've already changed considerably. Just in this week alone.'

'In a week?' she exclaimed, frowning incredulously.

He nodded his head insistently, willing her to accept. 'I'm telling you.'

She shook hair off her face. Her throat seemed to ripple with the effort of speaking. 'If I've changed it's because of you.'

For a moment they sat looking at each other, blinking as if unsure what to expect.

Then she leaned forwards, reaching her hand out. Their fingers met fumbling like short-sighted many-legged creatures intertwining.

His head became so awash with feeling he felt dizzy.

'You gave me a hard time,' she said, her small hooked smile beginning to spread. 'I wouldn't have understood if you hadn't restored my confidence.'

For God's sake let her go, a little voice warned, say good-bye, avoid complications, just wind it all up normally. 'I'm sorry it's over,' he said, getting to his feet as if to dismiss her.

She rose, too, and he found himself suddenly and blindly enfolding her in his arms, hugging her body tightly against his, feeling her heart thumping. He tried to tell himself it was no more than a farewell embrace, a dissemination of comfort and reassurance.

'O God,' she intoned into his neck.

Then his voice was murmuring, 'Darling, my sweet girl,' rushing out endearments which he seemed to have no control over, while she lifted her lips upwards, responding in kind, 'My dearest, my love,' and they clung and kissed, writhing hungrily, sighing and groaning away their relief and excitement at having at last discarded the barriers.

'I've wanted to do this so much the last few days.'

'I thought I'd die if something didn't happen.'

After a while, she spoke into his ear. 'I have to go. Sandra's doing an evening shift all this week.'

He went down the stairs with her, hardly knowing what he was doing, his face hot, his body floating along the pavement beside her.

They stopped among the brick flower-beds on the pedestrian way, swung face to face. 'You won't need me any more then?' she asked, her smile hooked teasingly.

'I'm afraid I'm going to have to go over your case again and again,' he replied. It felt painfully treacherous to think that he had to write his report on her in the morning. 'Can you get away during the lunch hour tomorrow?'

'I'll arrange it,' she whispered.

He could not help being aware of the slenderness of her body enclosed inside his arms, so easily held, so fulfilling in its touch.

As he watched her walk away he stood consumed with boiling delight. He wanted to unwrap a certain word, smooth it out, wave it like a banner. But was afraid that after he had so often kicked it about, used it as a rag, scorned it, it might be moth-eaten and threadbare, fall apart at the first attempt to use it.

He shook himself to clear his head. Was this really him, standing here, thinking these thoughts?

There was a pain in his chest, a muffled knocking within, his breathing congested. What a hideous irony if he was to suffer a heart-attack, he thought, just when all that he had been resisting, all that had been caged behind her eyes and boxed inside his brain, was freed.

He did not remember walking home, climbing the stairs. Beethoven. The Appassionata. All that mattered was the music belling inside his head, never mind the wires embedded in the spine of the ebony Steinway. The clashing notes could have cracked the plaster for all he cared.

No Madeleine tonight, away in Budapest. He felt guilty at the relief. At least the pain and congestion had gone.

He had to attend a meeting of the clinic management committee that evening. He wondered if his state of mind might show, that they would notice his feet were inches off the ground, that his concentration was drifting like a patient on stelazine, that he kept smiling distractedly to himself like someone on a high dosage of tepixol.

Later, several members of the committee went round to a nearby pub. He would have resisted going if a friend hadn't persuaded him. He felt he was still in a state of shock. Or perhaps exhaustion from suppressing his feelings for so long, for not even recognising they were there. Professional conduct was like being mummified before you were dead.

Elliot Powell was a lecturer in development studies at the university, and possessed a gravelly Michael Flanders patter that Mark had accompanied on the piano at a few late nights. After a few beers his untidy playing acquired the fluidity of a cascade.

As they consumed their Adnams Mark ached to tell him. What restrained him was not propriety but the fact that he could not find words he felt acceptable to describe what was happening to him. Perhaps it was his age; conviction fading like disremembered counterfoils. His cynictsm contained him like an audience around a second-rate comedian, heckling what others might see as a ridiculously unsuitable infatuation. He could hear himself say to Elliot, listen, I've met this wonderful... Wonderful? After so many years he knew that no one was wonderful. Delightful? She delighted him, but would she delight anyone else? In fact what exactly was it in her that pleased him so much anyway? But he had only to think of her and he felt faint, barely conscious of what he was doing, his pulse throbbing uncontrollably like a flat tyre at seventy miles an hour.

Elliot waved a hand in front of his eyes. 'What is it this time, Mark? Chopin? I can always tell when a piece of music's going through your head, your eyes mist over like apple puree. Not falling for a client, are you?'

Mark choked into his beer. 'I don't have nubile students like you, Elliot.'

'I don't fall in love with my students,' scoffed Elliot. 'Bask in the glow of their admiration, perhaps. Any erudite father figurehead goes to their heads. They're so screwed up and tense, poor little things, it's more a case of emotional massage. All part of the teacher's overworked brief.'

The banter trampled underfoot any inclination to reveal.

Later that night he wondered what could have prompted him to try and bring the matter up with Elliot in the first place. Some nagging disquiet perhaps? He was so drunk that he imagined perfect verisimilitude to the transposition of the Vivaldi Lute Concerto. When he finally closed the lid, his head was ringing with notes as if the firmament was popping with stars.

The next morning he had only one case before the time allotted to write his report. The case had an echo of Kathleen's about it.

An apparently able and honest man had made a disastrous partnership to raise finance for his business, which had then collapsed because of the partner's overspending. He had been forced to sell up his home to pay off a loan, whereas his partner still managed to maintain a large house with a swimming-pool and keep his Granada. He felt the principal creditor, the bank, was in collusion with his partner to cheat him and strip him of every asset he possessed. The bank refused to communicate, his solicitor could get no response from his partner, the receiver kept saying he was powerless to intervene over a private arrangement to secure a loan. The man was convinced that the business in itself could still be made viable. But he could not gather his wits together to formulate a constructive plan, he was too obsessed with the injustice. All he could do was seethe with bitterness.

Above all, the man was angry with himself for being taken in, was ashamed at the loss of his home, that symbol of security and position, felt he had lost the good image of himself among family and friends. His loss of confidence was sapping his ability to be objective. He was convinced he was in the grip of a jinx.

As Mark sought ways of rebuilding the man's confidence, he felt as if he was fighting a duel, that his prowess as a fencer was being stretched to its limits, sweat seeping inside his shirt. At times it seemed to him that he had exhausted every trick, that he was parrying with a destitute defence. Then, without any noticeable turning-point, he felt his perseverance regain the ascendancy, the muscular thrust of his attack scoring points, which in their turn forced the man to become more combative and retaliate with vigour. He was stirred with excitement. As the man was about to leave and turned to shake Mark's hand, he seemed to have gained inches in stature.

Kathleen September, Kathleen September... it gave him pleasure just to write her name. He would rather be writing about the phenomenon of his feelings, than a report analysing her person.

Kathleen September, Kathleen September is an attractive woman... he couldn't put that in the report. Why was she attractive to him? He was conditioned to respond to certain facial proportions, conformation, mannerisms, habits, actions, he could tot them up like a profit and loss account... the reasons were probably simple enough. She was right, of course, wise girl, the susceptibilities were always there.

...if the picture of her position the subject described is accurate, she has shown remarkable endurance throughout a series of unnerving disasters. During the sessions she was encouraged to narrate a detailed account of her childhood and married life. I found her consistent, no trace of hysteria, and however bizarre the tale, no obvious indications of fantasy. At the start of the sessions she evinced a degree of depression that would be consistent with any normal person suffering the reverses she endured during the past year. This depression had been heightened by the amount of incredulity offered her by authority generally, and by her failure to convince them of her version of events. As to the truth of these, there seems to be little doubt of the physical brutality inflicted on her since it has been well documented in the doctor's reports. There is no indication in them that the type of bruising could have been inflicted by a fall or accident in the home, as was claimed during the court hearings. None of the medical reports mention any history of alcoholism, nor could I find any sign of an inclination in that direction. Her delivery and responses were straightforward, her eye-contact good, she appeared to remain objective even when recalling moments of acute stress. Wherever she appears to have acted indecisively or unwisely, such actions seem consistent with her particular background and conservative upbringing, especially in her belief in the traditional family role of the male at the centre. Unfortunately for her, the male in this context as he appears in her narrative, was an abnormal one. The portrait she produced is that of a psychopath. A mentally unbalanced subject may fantasise about their problems and circumstances, or about a person they are having difficulties relating with or bear great resentment against, even transferring their own characteristics onto them. But I am certain nothing like that applies here. Despite the string of adversities she appears to have suffered, she remains a rational, well-balanced person...

The report was completed by midday. He added a rider that it could be significant to obtain a psychiatrist's report on the husband.

But he felt depressed as he reread it. There were unanswered aspects of the case lurking like unpaid accounts thrust out of sight into a drawer. Would any woman remain so long with a man as malevolent as she portrayed her husband? Secret drinkers manifest extraordinary cunning to hide their habit. There are always two truths in every human contention. But these could be the rumblings of his own cynical mind. The most depressing aspect was having to dissect her to such a degree, reducing her to a box of bits. Such abjection opened out his own stock of guilts; towards Madeleine, about his own subconscious manipulation, his conduct, quite apart from being old enough to be her father, and deluding himself that he could be a haven for her from her nightmare. But as he kept telling himself, at least the professional contract was completed, he was now free to fall flat on his face.

She had been ten minutes late at the wine-bar. He was beginning to chew his fingers. Had she decided it was all a mistake? That he was too old? Could the other Mark have caught up with her again?

His first thought when he saw her was that he wanted to go to bed with her. It came to him like the compelling need for relief in the middle of a movie, the signal from the bladder overriding all compunction to remain.

She came into the bar, nervous, freshly-washed hair like auburn chrysanthemums, dressed simply in a jumper and skirt of hues of cream, a pink scarf at her throat. Her eyes were wide, darting anxiously to find him. She reminded him of some perfectly formed creature in the wild that at any moment is liable to be seized by a predator and reduced to shapeless meat.

Then she saw his wave, moved towards him. She has an elliptic grace, he thought. Like an unhurried alto who just reaches the beat. His depression had vanished.

He reached out a hand, standing up from his barstool, and her arm slid along his sleeve up to his shoulder, round his neck. There was no doubt about her impelling will to kiss him. There can be perfection in a kiss, he thought. A whole summary of adoration recorded in one precise data stamp, all the sensuality of mind and body gathered at the mouth.

'I nearly didn't make it,' she said. 'Vicky had an earache. But...' She pulled at an earlobe and blushed. 'I'd been telling Sandra about you. You don't mind, do you? She insisted I came, pointing out that she was a nurse after all, she ought to be able to cope. She's ever so kind like that.'

He had a table booked on the mezzanine, looking down over the balustrade at the curving bar below. Their hands reached out, their knees touched, they inclined across the table mats. I'm ill for her, he thought. I've caught her like a virus.

'I lay awake last night,' she said, her smile curved like the tail of a lizard. 'Thinking about the change you mentioned. What kind of person I should be. I'd like to be the person you want.'

He shuddered inwardly. His role was still there, like a shadow. 'I want you to be you,' he said. 'Just as you are. The person you are is what I find enchanting.'

'But it's inevitable, isn't it, that I should respond? Don't we all try to please?'

Their conversation went on like this through the smoked salmon salad, the bottle of Orvieto and the curaçao chocolate gateau and the black Turkish coffee.

Then they were both turning to look at the clock above an Edwardian engraved mirror. 'I always seem to be having to get back,' she said, her face crumpling with regret. 'I promised Vicky.'

'And I'm already late for my first client,' he said, equally lamenting.

They rose from the debris of the table, extricating themselves from chairlegs and tablecloth like lovers from the bedclothes. They held onto each other at every possible moment, wending through the lunchers and drinkers out into the bright afternoon sunshine. After a passionate embrace on the pavement, they parted.

A few minutes later he was seated before a woman the same age as himself. She had cheeks like turnips that squashed her mouth between them and crushed her eyes against her forehead. He listened to a picture of abysmal loneliness and longing for love. Many years ago she had been married, had children, been divorced. Over the last seven years the man she sometimes lived with had cheated her of her money, beaten her up if she refused, screwed her neighbour, was blatantly using her for his own purposes, yet as far as she was concerned he was all there was. It was tearing her apart to feel so used, so unloved, and having to cling to such an uncaring brute. Mark felt appalled, and riven with guilt. The degradation this woman went through and her desperation to keep this man were depicted in her ravaged face. She had let herself go with constant weeping and become increasingly unattractive. How could he encourage her self-esteem, make her aware that she was worth better things in life than this endless suffering, when the chances of her finding anyone else in her unattractive state of physical deterioration were remote? And here was he, the same age, over-endowed with lovers.

That evening after wading through papers to find the handphone, discovering it beneath a pile of case-notes which Mo was sleeping on, he rang the number Kathleen had given him. He could hear the squeak of excitement in Sandra's voice as she called her. 'It's him.'

'I was hoping you'd ring.' Kathleen's voice was breathless.

Its soft-bellied cadences sent tremors up and down his spine. 'I'm free tomorrow around midday,' he said. 'I thought of hiring a car and taking you and the children for a drive, a picnic perhaps?'

Afterwards he played the barcarolle from the Tales of Hoffmann. How sentimental can you get, he thought, his smile stretching the length of the keyboard, his fingers leaping and stumbling happily among the keys as if they were seaside rocks.

AT SOME stage in his rough playing the ringing of the phone pierced the purity of the music that crowded the inside his head.

'It's a good job I know your habits,' said Nicole. 'I've been trying for five minutes.' She sounded weary.

'How are things?'

'I thought of killing myself.'

The words hung in his ear as he groped silently for a response. The tendency to bring up suicide as a way out of problems had been one of her mother's habits, he thought, depressed by the revelation. How the hell had she come to inherit such a proclivity? 'Please...'

'You're not in my position,' she cried. 'You can sit there and pontificate, don't do that, try doing this, but you're not me, you don't know what it feels like to be me, I don't believe you've ever been depressed in your whole life.'

'Are you drunk?'

There was a pause. 'I'm sorry. I shouldn't have said that. I just feel the problem's insuperable. I can't kill it and I don't really want it. At least not at this moment. I feel dreadful that it boils down to such stark alternatives, it makes me feel ill...'

'Have you talked to other women who've had abortions?'

'It doesn't help. Nothing helps, nothing anyone says does any good, nothing you say will do any good.' She was crying. He longed to reach out down the miles of wire and hold her.

'Suppose I committed myself to the wanting-you-to-have-it lobby?'

'What? You're willing to take a definitive position? Is this really you speaking, Dad?' He could sense the tears wet on her mouth as she mocked him. Another small curtain of silence hung between them. 'Why?'

'You don't have to treat life as an orderly progression. If your studies are interrupted, it wouldn't be fatal. Take a year out, then pick them up again. Besides, I don't believe you when you say you don't want it.'

'I don't know what I want any more. I've argued and debated

myself into the ground. Why d'you say you don't believe me when I say I don't want it? You always maintained that our mother didn't really want us. Why couldn't I have inherited the same attitude?'

'I think you're more like me. For your sins.'

She was silent. One of her idiosyncrasies, he thought, those staged pauses while she considered. Anyone who didn't know her and carried on talking, perhaps moving away from the topic, would have their sleeve grasped while she exclaimed, hold on a minute. She felt it unreasonable not to be allowed pause to reflect. Except that people tended to assume she hadn't understood, and would launch into further explanations.

'You're saying it because you want a grandchild.'

He sighed. 'I've tried to be as objective as possible. If rational and philosophical arguments have had their day, perhaps it's time for feelings alone.'

'I'll blame you if it all goes horribly wrong.'

'What else are parents for? Our sins are visited upon our childrens' heads, so we try to demand respect to hide the shortcomings. Obviously I didn't tan your backside enough when you were small.'

She laughed, a little humour restored. 'I wish you had. My analyst can never come up with anything.'

He felt his head reel. 'You've been to an analyst?' Wheels within wheels. Everything seemed to have happened before, repeating itself like variations on a theme, something he should recognise as an extemporiser. Never mind the quality, feel the effect.

'Everybody does, Dad. You know that. Modern universities have whole departments living off student problems, regurgitating them back to us like mother cormorants. Mine's convinced I got pregnant deliberately because I didn't have a mother around when I was a kid, so I'm trying to make up for the lack by becoming one myself. They're all freaks, these tricky-dickies, they make you wonder how they hold onto sanity themselves. Why do you do it, Dad?'

He could imagine informing her of the new element in his life... I've just fallen for one of my clients, a young woman not much older than Angela. I don't know whether I'm coming or going.

'Because I like to play God. You know that.'

There was a pause. 'I hate it when you won't take me seriously. It's very holier than thou, you know. Still treating me as a child. It makes me really cross.'

The irony of that, he thought, is how easily she can make me feel guilty as a child. 'I thought we were joking.' He could not help his voice hardening. 'When you get to my age, finding reasons becomes more and more like a comedian pulling out the same old well-worn jokes.'

She groaned. 'Sometimes I think you could do with a bit of analysis youself. You spend your time listening to others. When do you talk to anyone about you? I've never known the real you inside all that chatty exponential exterior. When I was little I used to think of myself like that little dog sitting listening to the phonograph on your old His Master's Voice records. I had this fantasy of telling people when they asked what my father was, that he was a big black piano.'

Mark felt uncomfortable. Guilt again. Her words were suggestive of his failure as a father, never mind the pianist. 'I must have smothered you with rationality.'

'That's what Marianne always maintained. What's he trying to hide from? He's like an artist who draws fifteen different angles of someone's face because he can't make up his mind. No, no, I'd say, it's because he wants to explore every aspect.'

'You were always good at defending me. I've always felt closest to you, Nicole, you know that. That's why I feel deep down you want to keep your child.'

Silence hung in his ear. Small atmospheric mouse-sounds, spatial sibilances. 'Goodnight, Dad.'

She was the only one of his children, he reflected, whom he'd ever had his cock stirred by, been tempted but resisted fondling those neat upright breasts, compressing her mouth with kisses, all he'd ever done was squeeze her chubby bottom. But then she had always been the one to sit on his lap, wriggle her haunches over his thighs, drape her arms around his neck, nibble his earlobes and gaze at him brown-eyed, wet lips apart, as if trying to unleash something she was not quite sure about. She was the one who always skipped from the bathroom naked. She still did it. Safe because he was her father. And he always assumed he was more flattered by her trust than disturbed by her temptation.

Such closeness never existed with the other two. At times he felt Marianne positively disliked him, a chronic wedge of resentment across her temples. She had become adept at sarcasm at an early age, contemptuous of all, as if no one could aspire to her expectations of them, he least of all. Angela was the quiet, industrious one. In her case, he sometimes suspected it was he who did not like her. But how could anyone admit that about their own child? Especially as it might have been his fault that she had become the person she was. She was the unfortunate one on whom he had had to experiment parenthood. She was forever trying new fads, sticking to none of them for long, perhaps each a desperate attempt to seek his approval, plunging into each as if hoping at last she had found the solution to her problems. What problems? He suspected these revolved round her lack of beauty, that earnest plainness, a lack that could well be his own fault. The unloved tend to look unlovely.

He returned to the piano. Glazed in the window of the room was the deep sapphire night, yellow-lit church-towers of the city like an old photographic negative. Bach. It had to be Bach tonight. An elegant stylised pattern of the emotions, to rationalise their passion. Though he was hardly one to worry that he made the Steinway sound like a church full of bells rending at the epicentre of an earthquake.

THE HIRED car was nearly new and its interior had the tang of freshly-minted plastic. He drove down many streets of Victorian terraces to find the address Kathleen had given him. He felt both reckless and nervous, a new self; or perhaps an old one, as if he had gone to his wardrobe and put on once-dapper clothes which had slept on their hangers for decades, kept there only from nostalgia, their fibres steeped with the flavours of carnations and hair-oil.

But was this really him walking his shoes up a red-and-cream tiled path to an Edwardian porch of arched white-painted woodwork? Was this young woman who embraced him real?

The sun hung like an optic light point beaming down interrogatively from its bracket. Kathleen was ushering the children out of Sandra's house when she stopped, riveted to the path, her face stiffening with anxiety. He saw that she was staring past him, and half-turned to look over his shoulder.

'Whose is that car?' she asked, her voice fading to a whisper.

'I've hired it...' he began, surprised. Then he struck himself mentally on the forehead. The car was white. How could he have forgotten? But he always went to the same firm, and all their cars were white. 'It's not a...' But he could not even be certain of the make of Mark's car, all these modern cars looked so similar.

As she stood transfixed, muscles in her neck taut as wires, her lips moving, he cursed himself for being so stupid, for not appreciating that her frailty remained. 'I thought we'd go to the seaside,' he said quickly, trying now to pretend that all was normal, hoping to distract her. 'Up to the north coast. It's such a perfect day.'

She twisted round and hurried back into the house. He held his breath, afraid she would not return, that the day was ruined before it had begun. Should he go after her, try to assuage her fears? He stood waiting uneasily beside the children.

'Can you swim?' he asked Vicky conversationally.

'Sort of,' the little girl replied in dubious tones. 'I'm a bit heavy.'

She's not picking up her mother's anxiety, he thought. Surely that must be a good sign?

'Sarah can swim,' she added. 'Like a duck.'

Sarah was staring at him with disconcerting intensity.

'She doesn't mind getting water in her eyes or up her nose,' continued Vicky. 'She just spits it out.'

'Sometime I drink it,' Sarah added sagely.

He was deciding he ought to enter the house in search of Kathleen when she came hurrying out with a wicker bag overflowing with brightly-coloured towels and costumes. 'Sorry to keep you waiting.' She glanced uneasily at the car again, then peered cautiously up and down the street. It seemed a great effort for her to overcome her reluctance to get into the passenger seat.

'Lost my swimsuit somewhere in all our moving,' she said. 'Sandra's given me an old one left behind by her daughter.' There was a brittle shiver in her voice, and her eyes flicked about uneasily. 'Maybe I'll not bother anyway. It's always cold up on the coast.'

'I've brought a windbreak,' he said. 'And some rugs.' He grinned at her, trying to urge her to smile in response. But she pushed herself down in her seat like someone being driven unwillingly to hospital. Only a few minutes ago all his senses had been on tiptoe, exultant, but now they crouched, watchful.

'I found some old buckets and spades in a cupboard under the stairs,' he said. 'Been there unused for ten years. Can't go to the seaside without buckets and spades. And I've brought a picnic,' he added. 'Coca-Cola, orange-juice. I didn't know what you'd like to drink.'

There was a duet of approval from behind him. The clamour of her children's voices seemed to rouse Kathleen. She pushed a hand through her hair, hooked up her smile. 'You've thought of everything,' she said, stretching out her legs. 'Even the weather.'

A great weight lifted off him. The road beneath became smooth as a table, his fingertips controlled as the pinions of a bird gliding in the air as he guided their velvety cubicle on its trajectory through the suburbs and headed out into the countryside.

The sky above appeared immense after the confines of the city, a silver-blue infinity over the blond and olive land, the cornfields and oak trees, the supermarket nature of the farmers. Here and there were outbreaks of red poppies, clusters of marguerites and pink mallows along the verges, and once a streak of yellow corn marigolds along a headland, rashes of acne to the agriculturists. The second suite of Ravel's Daphnis and Chloe flowed into his mind, and he tapped a finger on the wheel.

He kept glancing sideways at Kathleen, meeting her eyes, lifting her smile up like a skirt. He wanted to tell her... it was obvious what he wanted to tell her, but the presence of small acutely-eared children inhibited such pronouncements.

Her appearance was so light and harmonious that his senses rang with music, changing now to those diapasons of melody in Debussy's Danse Sacrée. He let his left hand stray back from the gear-stick, hang in the air, so that she took it onto her thigh.

He had considered all the possible places to go to along the coast, the easiest access, not too many people, clean sand for the children; Wells, Holkham, Blakeney, Stiffkey, and chose Holme. They stopped in a small car-park hedged in by whinberries and brambles near the dunes, unloaded, handing the buckets and spades to the children, sharing the rest between themselves, rugs, basket and picnic case.

Kathleen stood breathing in the sea air, looking round, her eyes shining. 'What a feast of briny smells. Hardly a breath of wind.'

They set off along a path into the dunes through the leg-stroking marram grass, then descended onto the beach. Being midweek, there were not too many people about. Near a lagoon of trapped sea water they laid out the rugs on a ridge of dry sand. While Vicky changed into her bathing-costume, Kathleen took all Sarah's clothes off to let her run naked, first rubbing them both with sun block lotion.

'I used to bring my children up here when they were this age,' he said.

They sat on the rugs side by side while the children went off to explore, one slender, in a red costume, the other short and fleshed like a cherub, paddling along the edge of the pool. For a while they sat watching them, tempered by their own diminutiveness in so much space, seven-eighths of the world sky, the rest a dish of sand stretching for miles to either side, the slate-blue rink of sea beyond flat to a hazy horizon.

In all this emptiness most other figures were dots in the distance. There were a few families nearer, a group of children playing with a dog, a couple walking, and far out on the water a pair of motionless fishing-boats. The birds provided the movement, they were everywhere; oystercatchers, gulls, terns, small waders; swallows and swifts looping above them in the warm air.

'You look stunning,' he said, shading his eyes from the sun.

'You look pretty good yourself.' She smiled at him and they leaned close and kissed while the children's backs were turned, constrained against allowing any demonstration of their feelings to be witnessed. 'I spent all night looking forward to us being together,' she said. She shook her head and her hair fell across her face. She brushed it back, gazed at him crystal-eyed. 'Now we're here like this, it seems unbearable.'

He blinked at the rush of emotion, so long disused.

'Look what I find,' said Sarah, dangling a small dead crab in front of their faces. 'It doesn't work.' She laid it down on the edge of the rug and skipped away with cherubic solidity, changing to hopping, sometimes jumping, then squatting down to examine something. Vicky was the far side of the lagoon on her hands and knees, digging and patting; the sand all around her marked and pitted by her efforts.

Mark took off his shirt to bare his chest to the sun. Kathleen looked around. 'I should have changed in the car.'

'Nobody'll notice out here. I'll turn my back if you like.' He swung round to face away.

She leaned against his naked back. 'Don't be silly. I want you to see me.' She looked behind them, shading her eyes. 'There are people in the dunes.'

He got onto his knees and unrolled the windbreak, stuck its poles into the sand behind them. Sitting on the rug she unbuttoned her dress, pulled it over her head. 'In my parent's house there were naked marble caryatids in the mantelpieces, porcelain nymphs on the vases, an oil painting of Susanna and the Elders, another of the Decision of Paris.' She unhooked her bra and drew its straps down her arms. 'But my friend Carmel whenever she came into the house would put her fingers over her mouth and giggle at them.' She wriggled to slide her knickers down her legs.

As she sat peeled and almond-nude, feeding her feet into the shrivelled black costume lent by Sandra, he saw the narrow muscularity of her back, the spongy spread of her hips, the cream of her skin, her breasts fleshy as mangoes, the nipples like enlarged calyxes, viewed her with total appraisal as if the human form is the exile's nostalgia for the lost homeland, while a part of him felt a puritanical disturbance for the primitiveness of his arousal.

The costume caught halfway up her buttocks, ballooning them out as she tugged unsuccessfully. She knelt up. 'I don't think it's going to fit,' she exclaimed, hauling frantically.

'Here, let me help.' He could feel the blood and juices of his lust stirring as he touched her body to unravel the material, her skin against his hands cool as glass. He pulled the swimsuit over her hips, then up her waist, covering her breasts, looped the straps over her shoulders.

'It's worse than a corset.' She looked round to see if anyone might have been watching.

Vicky stood before them, eyeing him for a moment, then quizzically regarding her mother in the tight black costume. 'Why don't you come and see what I've been doing?'

Has anyone ever recorded what becomes of wise children, he wondered, watching Kathleen walk away barefoot across the sand. Women change their personalities when they shed the facade of their covering, he thought. Madeleine would become a greedy child when undressed, Nicole light-hearted. The silent Veronique, whom he did not care to remember much, had been garrulous when without clothing. Whereas Kathleen, as her hands reached behind to pluck at the hem of the skimpy swimsuit in futile modesty, seemed to return to the wariness he remembered at their first meeting.

Suddenly there was a loud engulfing splash from the far side of the pool. He had not noticed Sarah in the last few minutes, and started up in alarm. There was no sign of her, only the surface of the water rippled with disturbance. But almost immediately she emerged, hair plastered down, spitting out water and shrieking. Not with fright, as he first thought. It was laughter. She clambered out and hurried along to where the sandbank was steeper and with a yell hurled herself in again. Repeating this manoeuvre seemed to give her endless amusement. When she failed to resurface and he was about to propel himself across the sand, her head bobbed up twenty feet on, near an old wooden groin that acted as a dam. Then she swam back, dipping her head underwater as she came. He was filled with admiration at the confidence of one so young in so insecure a medium.

He slid his trousers off and pulled on his swimming trunks, then walked across to where Vicky was showing Kathleen her sandworks. Perfect weather, he thought. Fresh sea air, a great plain of empty sand, an attractive young woman, two children enjoying themselves... though he would have preferred Kathleen to himself.

'Would you like to buy something from my shop?' Vicky asked him.

This must explain, he thought, why her mother is walking up and down among multitudes of small shapes in the sand with a bucket over one arm.

'These are sweets,' Vicky explained, waving an arm. 'These are boxes of chocolates. We only have ones with soft centres. These are ice-creams. And here are the toys.'

He could recognise the bas-relief shapes of small figures, animal or human he could not tell. 'What do I pay with?'

'Shells, of course,' she replied dismissively, as if he should have known. She pointed to a hollowed-out structure filled with cockles. 'That's the till. And over here's the food and clothes.' Here her three-dimensional resources had run out and she had drawn outlines on the sand.

He glanced over towards the pool to check what Sarah was up to. The child was standing up to her navel in the water, sucking her thumb, staring at a beady-eyed seagull perched on one of the posts of the groin. He turned to find Kathleen close beside him. What began as adult concern to indulge a child in her game, grew into a mutually lascivious exchange of desire. They pressed their hot skins close under the burnishing sunshine, eating each other with their eyes, while at the same time asking Vicky the prices, and pretending to make purchases.

A bundle of small wet limbs thudded into their legs, a shrill voice squealed up at them. 'Want to go in proper sea.'

There came a howl of rage from Vicky. 'You're standing on the till. Look what you've done, you've broken it.' And she leaped across and delivered a resounding smack on Sarah's youthful amplitude.

Sarah promptly let out a wail and burst into tears. 'Vicky,' exclaimed Kathleen, scooping Sarah up into her arms. 'What did you do that for?'

Oh Lord, groaned Mark to himself, now the day will be spoiled, Kathleen will belt Vicky, then there'll be more tears, followed by sulking.

'It's all right, darling,' Kathleen was saying soothingly to Sarah. 'You didn't look where you were going. This is Vicky's shop, see, look at all the toys she's made. Here are the sweets and chocolates. She's done a lot of work, so you must be careful.' She disengaged an arm to put it round Vicky and hug her. 'We'll help mend it, darling. Sarah didn't mean to knock it down. Come on, let's go down to the sea first and have a swim.'

As they set off Sarah ceased crying, Kathleen leaning aslant as she bore the little girl on her hip, Vicky holding her other hand.

It was a deceptively long walk to the edge of the sea. When they were about fifty yards from the water's edge Vicky ran on ahead and Sarah wriggled to get down and follow her. Mark took the hand that was still warm from Vicky's. 'I admire you,' he said.

They clung together as they walked. Seagulls at the sea's edge flapped languidly away and alighted farther along as the children raced through them. 'How can that be?' she asked.

A pair of oystercatchers flew overhead with their shrill kleep-kleep.

'The way you manage the children.'

'They're hardly difficult. Not like everything else.' Her eyes gleamed. 'If you could imagine paradise, would it be like this? I know that tomorrow there could be a gale here, wild waves, dark skies, chill winds, but today it feels like eternity. And here we are, just as I would wish us to be. It's a dream. The problems of the real world seem a million miles away.' She gripped his arm tightly.

The sea was smooth as a steel-blue dance-floor, fading in the distance, impossible now to tell where it met the sky. Little waves lifted near them no bigger than rucks in a carpet. Vicky was wading out, kicking the water into showers of white beads. Sarah lay in the shallows, letting the miniature waves stroke her plump little body. There was another group of bathers about a hundred yards to their left. To their right a solitary swimmer wearing a white cap was emerging, and far beyond, a line of fir trees rose over the dunes, hazy as a distant oasis. Ten yards out and there were still only six inches of water over their feet.

'I used to come out here as a restorative,' he said. 'It has such healing powers.'

'You are the healer,' she said. 'If there's any admiration around, I have it for you. Look what you've done for me.'

But then I cheated, he thought. Broke the code and stepped over the boundary, used my trump card, the ace of hearts.

Vicky came up and kicked water at them, then ran away laughing.

'I'll get you,' he exclaimed, and rushed after her, slashing calves impeded as if he was wearing heavy boots, spray gushing outwards. This is me chasing Nicole, he thought, amazed at himself gambolling in the water, he who hated the coldness of the North Sea and hadn't ventured into its icy cling for a decade. Now it was tempting him with its cordial succulence and unusual warmth, and he flung himself downwards to pretend to be a water-monster. How little girls love to be chased, he thought, careful not to catch her.

Suddenly someone was on top of him, shoving him under. As he surfaced, spluttering, he saw Vicky jumping up and down in the water, beside herself with delight. He turned on Kathleen, the perpetrator, to pursue her. This was someone he could catch, he thought, as he threw himself after her glistening body coiling through the water, lured by the wet orbs exposed from her ever-shrinking costume. As his arms gripped her slippery form she squealed in alarm. They fell gasping in the shallows, and he laughed and hugged her to show that his intentions were entirely playful. But he could see the traces of fear in her eyes, even though she clung to him ardently. 'I love you, I love you,' he growled, kissing her saltily.

'I know, I know.' Her voice was a crushed whisper in the noise of the water, as if she was saying, 'Save me, save me.' He could not tell with the wetness of her face if she might not be crying.

Then the children were upon them. They played and romped

with them, till Kathleen took Vicky off to give her a swimming lesson, while he carried Sarah piggy-back out to where the water rose level with his chest and became cold round his legs. She swam quite fearlessly out of her depth, a little sensual merchild. As he porpoised about with her, he thought how fascinating it would be to become her stepfather and observe her develop.

He had already visualised his relationship with Kathleen progressing to his taking on that role. He would have the advantage of detachment. He had noticed how the potential of small children at this age faded the older they grew, as each buried their individuality in the need for conformity, or were squared to size by the saws of education and the chisels of their contemporaries. He had been too involved with his own daughters, over-anxious, too nagging with Angela, withdrawing from Marianne because of her tantrums till she had controlled herself to coldness, over indulgent of Nicole. Sarah in her originality could not last long, the world was only interested in standardisation. But he felt he could be a better father now, with hindsight.

When they returned to the rugs by the pool the tide was creeping back, gnawing away the edge of the endless sand. The sun was so warm they scarcely needed any drying.

Mark opened the picnic case. He had bought ready-made sandwiches in clingfilm, egg and ham, tomato and lettuce in mayonnaise, a chocolate cake, biscuits, cans of orange, Coca-Cola and a bottle of Frascati. Overcome with hunger they sat in a huddle and spilled crumbs over their legs.

Small figures passed along the shoreline, closer now as the sea surreptitiously sucked in the beach. There were more people about than before, voices carrying over the quiet rustle of the embracing tide, children running past them, figures walking through the dunes.

Mark and Kathleen lay side by side on the rugs while Vicky built walls near them, her avowed intention being to build a house. Sarah was more concerned with the imprints she could make with her body in the sugary looseness of the dug sand. 'If only this could go on for ever,' sighed Kathleen. She was lying on her back gazing upwards and Mark was on his front, propped on his elbows, close beside her. 'I dread going back to the city. It's as if we've been paroled from jail and we know the rules. Freedom ends at sunset.'

'I'll tell you what we'll do,' he said. 'We'll find a cottage up here to rent. You and the children could stay in it, and I'll come up after work. I'll get a car. You'll be safe from Mark.'

'Won't everything be booked-up at this time of year?'

'I know a few people I could ask. I'll ring round this evening.'

She swung herself round to hug him.

'What are you doing, Mummy?' Vicky asked, observing this exercise with interest.

'I'm just thanking Montjoy for bringing us here and giving us such a marvellous day,' she said, lying on her back again, stretching her legs close together, folding her arms across her stomach.

Each time she mentioned his name, he felt a pang of guilt.

'You like him, don't you?' said Vicky, suspiciously.

There was a loud splash, and they all looked round. Sarah had hurled herself into the pool again.

'I don't know where she gets it from,' said Kathleen. 'She's never been taught, it's all quite natural.' She lay with her eyes closed. 'When I was little I remember a man with a guitar who came to our house and sang at parties. Sarah's out of the song about the Keeper of the Eddystone Light and his affair with a mermaid. One of the offspring.'

Mark sat up to watch the amphibian Sarah, bemused at her antics in the water. The sun was descending, a fluorescent disc in the opalescent sky. Soon they would have to go home, he thought. Pity it all had to come to an end. But there would be plenty more such days.

Kathleen closed her eyes. 'Every summer we used to join with some cousins at Annagassan, about ten miles from Collon. There were three converted railway carriages set in a T near the shore, no electricity, just paraffin lamps, and candles to go to bed with. We wore nothing but plimsolls and shorts and our skin was dusky as peanut butter. There'd be sand everywhere, damp swimsuits and towels draped over chairs and a seaweedy-sweat smell mingled with fried bacon and burnt toast. At night our parents would drink wine out on the verandah and watch the Aurora Borealis, while we played Buccaneer under the Tilley lamp with the moths rattling round it. When the tide went out there was a fine strand like this and we could play rounders and tig till it came right in to the rocks and fill little pools that were like my mother's jewel box, anemones crimson as rubies and small crabs delicate as cameo brooches and little shells like earrings.

Sometimes we'd be left on our own there, seven or eight children with Rose, the cousins' housekeeper to look after us, a big woman we used to tease something terrible. The dare was to get her in a bate so she'd chase us threatening to give anyone she caught a tanning. We'd sit round the table at meals giggling away at her, and I don't know how she stood it, little horrors we were. One day she raged after us and we were scattering like birds across the rocks, and wasn't it me who fell and cut my knee on the barnacles, blood pouring out of it like a broken bottle and me wailing like I was dying, and she picked me up and ran back to the carriages, and bathed it and hugged me and put a bandage on it, and I was ashamed for ever afterwards that we'd been so cruel to her.

There used to be a man came to stay when I was small, a poet from Oxford, quite famous, and he kept an old rowing-boat there for he was fond of fishing, and sometimes we'd go with him with our rods, keen as cats at the pleasure of having plump silver bodies dancing on the end of our lines. When the fish lay quivering on the boards I always wanted to throw them back before they died. There'd be a great fry-up for supper and delicious smells, but I could never eat them, and this man, I wish I could remember his name, he'd say to my mother, never mind, give her some bread and butter spread with screaming raspberries and bleeding plums; and they'd all laugh their heads off.

There was a ruined house nearby with stables where we kept our ponies and went riding in the sea in our bathing-costumes. Across the strand to the north you could see the Mourne Mountains always changing colour, from purple to blue to grey. I'll see them in my mind's eye till the day I die. When I went to live with my aunt and uncle in England we only went on foreign holidays, just a couple of weeks and never the same place twice, so there was never time to get to know them.'

Sarah came and sat on her. 'You soggy little beast,' Kathleen gasped, struggling up to lift her off. 'You're icy cold, darling.' She wrapped her in a towel and hugged her.

'Listen my teeth,' said Sarah, making them chatter. Kathleen rubbed her little plump body vigorously till the chattering ceased.

'We used to stay with cousins too, when I was a child,' mused Mark. 'They had a villa near Antibes. A crowded world down there, but hot like this every day. My cousins were athletic, brown as coffee and into water-skiing and tennis, which I was useless at, being a pale and insignificant weakling.

One of the cousins was called Marie-José, a blond stunner whom the boys spent all their time trying to impress, constantly showing off their athletic prowess before her. But she preferred my company because she loved the piano, and I was her eager pupil. The boys were madly jealous so I was known as the bloody cousin Anglais.' He shook his head. 'A few years later we were all disgusted when she married a rich businessman who was fat and bald as a teapot.

I prefer the emptiness of this coast. We kept a boat at Burnham Staithe, a shallow-draught half-deck with a drop keel so that we could sail if we wanted, a pottering sort of boat for exploring the creeks in the marshes or sailing out round Scolt Head. Sometimes we'd get trapped by the falling tide in narrow channels and have to haul the boat like Humphrey Bogart and Katharine Hepburn in The African Queen, floundering through the mud till it looked as though our legs were coated in chocolate.

Angela was a keen bird-watcher. "Look, there's a godwit," she'd cry. "Wow, a phalarope." "Can't you even tell a redshank?" Whereas Marianne was the sailor, the bossy one never happier than when being skipper and ordering us about. Nicole was like Sarah, a water-sprite.

Maybe the secret of a place like this is that it's far from the organised world, right on the edge where all the elements meet in their natural state. It liberates us from conformity. Where else can you take off your clothes, lie about without fear of being run over or polluted, and dig up the ground and build pretend castles, and there's hardly a single human artefact in sight?'

Kathleen had put a t-shirt on the dried Sarah, who lay contentedly against her mother. 'You are lazy,' complained Vicky, pausing from her labours to survey them. 'You just lie there and talk. Look what I'm doing. It's very hard work. I can't really manage it on my own.'

'Time for exercise,' said Mark, getting up reluctantly.

'We haven't enough spades,' said Kathleen, rising to her knees, trying to pull her costume down over her sand-coated haunches.

'Use the buckets like this,' said Vicky, demonstrating. She soon had them organised, dredging sand for the walls.

The heat had gone out of the sun and it hung over the Hunstanton end of the beach like a circular hole into a distant furnace. Only overhead did the blue remain. A solitary tern arced down over the pool, soaring up again like a white boomerang. Its kee-yar cry sounded disappointed as it flew off towards the sea. There were several groups of children strung along the advancing tide, their laughter carrying among the mewing of gulls and shrill cries of the oystercatchers.

Sarah, tired of organised work, turned saboteur, clambering onto the walls and stamping about with stubby legs. To distract her, Mark grabbed her and tickled her, so that she ran off, shrieking with laughter. 'Let's play catch,' cried Vicky enthusiastically, throwing down her spade and joining the pursuit. So they all ran about, in and out of the half-constructed walls, along the edge of the pool, laughing, Vicky as quick as a lizard and twice as adept at the game as the rest of them, till Mark, tiring, subsided among the tumbling sandwalls. They pounced on him, all sitting on his prone body, Kathleen astride his hips, her hair dried out and falling in dense fluffy ringlets over her laughing face. Never had she looked so beautiful, he thought.

'You have the body of a young man,' she said.

Her words filled him with guilt. His groin ached as he put his hands around her onion hips, aware of the irony that they were in a position of coition, genitals separated by thin layers of fabric.

'But he's much older than...' began Vicky, stopping as if she had no wish to mention her father.

They sat on the rugs and drank the rest of the wine and Coca-Cola, finished off the chocolate cake.

While Sarah chewed at a biscuit and Vicky wandered about collecting shells in a bucket, they packed up the picnic and dressed themselves. The sun had dimmed to a disc of pink, enlarging as it hung over the gunmetal sea, casting rose-petals of reflection towards them across the water. Kathleen put her head on Mark's shoulder, their hands clasped. 'Thank you for bringing us.'

THE JOURNEY back in the darkening twilight was smooth and silent. They were all scorched and satiated from sunshine and sea air. Sarah had fallen asleep. Even Kathleen began to doze.

She roused herself under the street lights, looked round her uneasily. 'I dread coming back to this city.'

'I'm involved now,' he said. 'If anything goes wrong, ring me. I'll come round, or you come to my house.' He was already visualising tidying up to accommodate them all, clearing out rooms for them.

As they swung through a roundabout a piece of paper fell off the dashboard. She leaned down to pick it up. It was the car-hire docket. Something on it caught her eye. 'Mark...' she muttered, then began to read aloud. *'Cambridge Motors, a Vauxhall Cavalier 2.0 litres... hired to Mark... Clement.* Mark?' Her voice suddenly shot up, breathless and sharp. 'This says Mark?'

'Montjoy's my second name,' he explained quickly, cursing him-self that he hadn't put the hire-note into his wallet. He tried to keep his voice casual. 'I didn't tell you my first name was Mark because I knew it would have bad associations for you.'

'I thought it strange this morning.' She put a hand up to her head, leaning away from him, wide-eyed. 'The car the same colour as his. And now you've the same name?'

'It was pure coincidence...' he began.

'It can't be,' she cried agitatedly. 'I don't understand what's going on.'

'Nothing's going on,' he exclaimed.

'It's beginning all over again,' she cried, looking round her wildly. 'Stop the car.' She was already unbuckling her seat-belt, hoisting her handbag strap over her shoulder, fumbling to open the door. 'Please,' she screamed frenziedly. 'Let me out.' The children were staring at her in alarm, open-mouthed.

'I promise you there's nothing wrong,' Mark said, gritting his teeth, pulling into the kerb quickly, afraid she might leap out and hurt herself. 'It was just coincidence we had the same name.'

'How could you lie to me?' she cried, throwing open the door. 'I don't know what you're up to.' She jumped out and snapped open the back door, pulling the children out. 'Come on Sarah, quickly Vicky.' She left the car doors stuck out like wings over the pavement, and with a child in each hand hurried away under the tree-shrouded street lamps.

He had to reach across to shut the doors. Despite the traffic building up impatiently behind him, he drove slowly alongside her, wound the window down. 'Please get back in, Kathleen,' he called. 'I couldn't help having the same name, could I? It means nothing.'

She broke into a run, ignoring him, dragging the children. Sarah was crying. People passing paused to stare curiously.

'Don't you understand?' he shouted. 'I'm on your side. I love you.'

'That's what he would say,' she cried.

Among the traffic passing out round him was a small city-bus that then slowed down to pull in at the stop ahead. She picked up Sarah and ran to catch it, Vicky running beside her.

Damn, he thought, watching them climb inside. He was trembling with shock; stung that she should identify him with her husband. He could see that each time he opened his mouth he would sink himself deeper. The bus started off.

Instead of following it he turned off and took a short-cut, drove quickly through innumerable side-streets to arrive at Sandra's house ahead of them. He hoped Sandra would be there so that he might enlist her help. But when he drew up outside the house it was in darkness. He ran up the red-and-cream tiled path. No response to the bell. I'll wait, he thought. Confront Kathleen when she gets back. She can't be long. Perhaps she'll have calmed down.

He was careful to hide the car down a side-turning. It was easy to see in retrospect how its whiteness must have blazed with significance for her. In a garage full of white cars his mind had been on the pleasure in store. How insensitive he had been. If only he had put that receipt with his name on into his wallet. A little piece of paper had ruined everything. He would have had to reveal his name eventually; but when their relationship had become cemented with trust. It was one more aspect of his failure over this case. He should have known that rational measurements of people's anxieties were always under-estimates. But he had never had to take his own feelings into account before.

He hovered on the doorstep while the minutes ticked by, staring down the lamplit street, listening impatiently for sounds of them coming. Then he started to prowl up and down the pavement. In his head he relived the afternoon like an obsessed cinéaste. Its pleasure burned with irony against his present agony. Every moment had seemed to bind their relationship closer. No threat in sight with the sun blazing down on the empty sands. But once back in the city unease had returned. The name Mark had leaped out at her with the same connotation as Lucifer. Poor girl, he kept thinking. What have I done to her, how can I make her understand?

People passed by with soft chirrup of voices and sharp click of heels, front doors slammed on their Yales, cars parked, others drove away. He began to realise she wasn't coming. Sandra was probably on night duty, so Kathleen had gone to her friend Paula's, knowing he had no idea of Paula's surname or address. He should have followed the bus; hurrying ahead to Sandra's house was another miscalculation to add to the list.

After about an hour had passed he thought he noticed the curtains in several houses being twitched aside suspiciously. The night air became prescient with the imaginary muttering of comments, whispers considering phoning the police, there's a prowler on the pavement, someone up to no good.

He drove back to his house, climbed the stairs with feet of lead. He left the lights off, scattered papers and a complaining Mo off the sofa, lay slumped. The night glow from the illuminated city crept through the window, half-lit the chaos as if the room was full of autumn leaves.

Inversely, the inside of his head still glowed with the sunbathed beach. He thought of them romping in the sea when he had pulled her down in the shallows. He saw again the fear rolling in her eyes, felt the stiffening of apprehension in her body.

Perhaps he had assumed a normality in her that didn't exist. Could it be that he had mis-interpreted the whole story? That it was she all along who was ill? She had been in an acute state of depression when she first came to see him, shrunken as an old woman. The tale she had woven of a monstrous husband could well be paranoia; was any man as vicious and smooth-tongued as she described? Shouldn't he have been suspicious at the speed of her recovery? Had he forgotten how soon she began casting overt glances at him, his own disquietude... and his failure to take control?

Now he was falling into the same doubting mode as the rest of officialdom, he thought, ashamed of himself.

Prokofiev's Romeo and Juliet was already jarring its drama through his head when eventually his hands came to spread across the piano keyboard in the still night-lit house. He could be said to be extemporising the precise musical intention with the brash fashion of his fingers over Tybalt's Death, back to the Montagu and Capulet theme, and then on to the Tomb. It was to invoke his pain rather than blot it out, rending himself with the tearing emotion of the music.

After half an hour a persistent ringing on the doorbell penetrated his playing. He was soaked with sweat. Just for a moment he thought it might be Kathleen. But she didn't know his address. It was a neighbour, a woman in her early thirties. Her mouth was already open to harangue him.

'You've woken both my children...' Then she saw his distraught face, red-eyed, soaked with tears.

'I'm sorry.' It was all he could say.

Soon afterwards, at around eleven, he went downstairs and got into the car. He drove through the still-active city and out to the quiet streets around Sandra's house. He drew up outside. Each window was black as coal, no curtains drawn. It had been pure optimism that there might be any indication of life.

Back home he drank a tumbler of whisky and played Debussy's La Mer to try and recall the spell of the afternoon. Then he sat on the sofa drinking the rest of the bottle till he lost consciousness.

His first act in the morning was to ring the clinic to cancel his appointments. He told them he was ill, which was true enough. He felt terrible, his body riven with trembling, his stomach sour and his mental state like a battlefield crawling with the grievously wounded.

Later he took the Cavalier back to the garage. He asked if they had anything that wasn't white, knowing it must sound peculiar explaining that he didn't like white cars, especially since he had never complained before. But it turned out that they had a few black limousines for funerals. He drove away in a stretched Carlton.

He went at once to Sandra's house. His chest was tight as a steel keg. Would Kathleen be there? Could he restore all that seemed lost?

Eventually the door was opened by a tall woman with red hair, wearing a dressing-gown.

'Is Kathleen here?' he asked.

The woman regarded him hostilely. 'Who?'

'I know she was staying here.'

'She's gone.' She began to close the door.

'Please,' he pleaded. 'It's important that I contact her.'

'A friend came and collected her things an hour ago.'

'There's been a terrible misunderstanding.'

The woman scowled at him. 'You're the last person I'd tell where she is. Pretending to be her friend while working for her husband, trying to break her down with your dirty tricks. You should be ashamed. I'm going to report you to your professional body.' And she slammed the door shut.

'Damn,' he exclaimed aloud, mentally reeling. Now what was he to do?

He drove to where he thought Paula might live, went up and down the streets. Rows of tightly packed terraced houses stared back blankly at him. He knew it was futile. He considered ringing Greg Fulcher, trying to extract Paula's address from him under some pretext of wanting to clear up a few points. But he could see that he would be behaving like the other Mark, hounding her.

He sat miserably in his kitchen, thinking that he ought to eat something. But he could only think of Kathleen

When he looked at his existence, it had been sliding over the years with a grey uneventfulness. He was fond of Madeleine, but their relationship had resorted to companionship and mutual servicing. He no longer viewed it as having any prospects of development. Almost without being aware of it, he had been presented with a dossier of evidence to show that love of the kind he so cynically dismissed really existed. All he had to do was follow a few simple provisions. Any fool could have done it. But he had cocked it up as if he'd lost his mental faculties, and thrown away his chances.

The telephone rang. He scrambled to pick it up, burning with excitement, convinced he was about to hear Kathleen's voice.

'DAD, I'm at Liverpool Street,' came Nicole's voice. 'I'll be with you in time for supper.'

His mind reeled with guilty disappointment. 'Look forward to seeing you, darling,' he got out.

I'd better go shopping, he thought, sitting at the piano. He drifted into the abstractions of the baroque Scarlatti. Like Bach he imagined it representing a methodical rendering of the emotions, placing them in symmetrical progressions to eliminate disharmony, and however the senses might strive to introduce overwhelming passion or sorrow, the structure would retain control. If he could but order life like that, his rending of the music carelessly illustrating the rift between his imagination and reality, his near-perfect mimicry of the style and content vying with the collisions of his fingers with the keys.

How was he going put Kathleen out of his mind and concentrate on Nicole's problem?

He forgot that he had a hired car and could have fetched her.

She arrived at seven-thirty, a wide grin on her face, the feminine archetype of his own youth. The same long flat eyes, marsala irises that almost occluded the whites, big cheekbones and cat-like chin. He enjoyed the taste of his daughter's lips. Their mutual pleasure to see each other was reassuring to him. He wondered how long it would take before she noticed how ravaged he felt.

'The train was packed, didn't get a seat till Ipswich,' she said. She looked round and shook her head at him, grinning again. 'You and your chaos, Dad.'

He'd spent an hour frantically tidying up, he thought, chagrined. In his eyes he'd made it all look dreadfully sterile. He mixed her a gin and tonic. As he carried the thick glass across to her, it seemed to him the ice tinkled the first bar of Furry Lisa, as she called the piece when learning to play the piano at the age of six. Her smile is full of warmth, he thought, perhaps the same one she gives her lover, Terence, or whatever his name is. He felt oppressed by his anxiety, as if he was looking out at her from tiny holes in his head. 'Tell us your news,' he said, sitting beside her on the sofa.

She was silent for a while, as was her wont. 'Just tell me again what you said on the phone the other day?'

He felt his concentration dissolve and effervesce like balsam crystals dropped on boiling water. He fumbled to grope in his memory. 'That I'd be happy if you had the baby?'

'You haven't changed your mind?'

He blinked to stall the tears brimming in his eyes.

'I know you're soft on kids, dad.'

He shrugged. 'I'm stuck with my prejudices like the size of my feet.'

She sipped her gin, silent again. She glanced at him. 'It's funny, isn't it? It doesn't seem so important any more, now that I'm here with you.'

He had learned to cook while looking after his three children. He took a bacon and mushroom quiche from the oven, poured vinaigrette over a tomato salad, opened a bottle of Rioja. They sat opposite each other in the dining alcove. A fiery sunset pinkened the walls around them. The reminder made tears well again. He looked down at his plate so that she wouldn't see.

'Terence and I were nearly busting up,' she was saying. 'Shouting and yelling at each other like a couple in the throes of divorce. He's gone down to stay with his parents, too. They live in Oxford. His mother's the head of some sixth-form crammer for well-heeled young ladies. His father's a stockbroker. They're a real pair of backwooders; bring back hanging and darkies should stick to grass huts. They can't understand Terence going egalitarian, and suspect he's gone soft in the head from overwork. He's a real stayer, I'll say that for him. If I'd been him, the hard time I've been giving him the last few weeks would have sent me packing ages ago. Anyway, things are better now.' She waved her fork. 'This is scrummy, dad.'

For a while they ate in silence. 'You're not coming down with something are you?' she asked, peering at him.

He shook his head.

'I know you. Is one of your clients suing you for erroneous analysis?'

The unwitting barb of her question stuck in his throat, tears pricked his eyes again. 'I've got to tell someone,' he said, getting up to go into the kitchen.

He served up meringues coated with chocolate sauce and roast almonds. He had been glad of the opportunity to prepare a meal, to have a distraction to concentrate on.

The inclination to weep disappeared as soon as he started to tell her the story of Kathleen and the consequences. He was aware as the words poured effortlessly from him, of the irony that it was Nicole who was now listening to his woes, that it was his daughter he was using for the off-loading. He had always found himself avoiding the routine set up by the clinic for that contingency.

Later, he made coffee. 'I can't understand it. Why our feelings for each other couldn't have survived such a ridiculous misunderstanding. I mean, what's in a name?'

'Ridiculous?' echoed Nicole. 'But we identify strongly with names, especially if we've invested a load of emotion in someone. Ten times more so after suffering terrifying traumas through that name. The shock when you, her knight in shining armour, suddenly turned out to be another Mark, must have been like a nightmare returning in broad daylight. No wonder she flipped.'

'D'you think so?' he exclaimed in anguish. 'I keep reliving that stupid mistake a thousand times.'

'It wasn't very professional of you falling for a client,' muttered Nicole, getting up from the table. 'So maybe it's all to the good.'

'Jung did, Freud did, they all did. Anyway the case was completed.'

They went into the sitting-room and sat on the sofa. He brought in a bottle of whisky and two tumblers.

'Have you considered she mightn't have been as normal as you thought? Perhaps she was the real psychopath, weaving a plausible fantasy?'

He nodded. 'I've been a doubting Thomas, too. But there's a strong clue in her favour.'

'What's that?'

'The two girls, Vicky and Sarah. They're too stable. They are not the product of a neurotic, devious mother.'

'But equally, surely if all the appalling events she described had really happened, those kids should be as hysterical as chickens locked in a shed with a starving fox?'

'Except that Kathleen is a good mother. She impressed me. She never raises her voice with them, is always relaxed with them, however much she gets fazed by everything else.'

'If that's the case, perhaps they're what kept her sane?'

He nodded. The tears had come back, moistening the edges.

Nicole rested a hand on his thigh. 'Since I'm here, Dad, why don't I take a hand? I could try and see Sandra for a start. She might be more sympathetic to a woman.'

'Would you?' He put a hand on top of hers, squeezed it. 'Would you really?'

'First thing tomorrow.' She sipped her scotch. 'What about Madeleine in all this?'

'She's at a symposium in Budapest.' He looked at her. 'I'm not in love with Madeleine, you know. It's been a relationship of mutual support, not going anywhere in particular. I know she'd be hurt if she knew. But I can't help it.'

Nicole frowned into her glass. He was not sure whether this meant disapproval.

'D'you think I'm an old fool?' he asked.

She shook her head. 'You're not old. And is one a fool to love someone?' She put her glass down so that she could slip her arms round him to hug him tightly and comfort him. 'This is a reversal of roles, isn't it?'

But he, inside their embrace, clinging to her body, thought they were more like old lovers from a long time ago.

'Play me something,' she said.

'I'm just a record-player to you,' he complained.

He knew she and Madeleine were his most ardent admirers. Though he had never considered that through his closeness with them, they were the only people whose indulgence of his playing had allowed him to remain innocent, which in turn fed the attribute they recognised and enjoyed; that when an artist becomes confident his art acquires its own currency.

He felt a faint sense of optimism as he went into the darkened room, switched on the brass lamp over the keyboard. A Bach Invention went scattering from his fingers like beads over a polished floor.

NICOLE had taken the hired black limousine. He had arranged to meet her for lunch at The Anchor pub across the river.

She was already at the bar when he pushed open the frosted glass door. Instantly he feared her earliness indicated failure, and was numbed with disappointment, reading her smile as mere establishing contact with a familiar among a crowd of strangers, pity for his woes, tenderness for her parent.

'I saw both Sandra and Paula,' she said as the barman drew him a pint.

His spirits rose. 'And Kathleen?'

Seeing the lines of strain etched across his face, she put a hand on his arm. 'Let's go and sit down.'

The pub was busy but they found a table downstairs. 'I had to work hard on Sandra. Eventually she agreed that before this happened you'd done Kathleen a lot of good.' Nicole shook her head. 'But she thought the business of the same name and car had to be deliberate, and what else could anyone think but that you were working for Mark, all part of his diabolical scheme to send her round the bend. It took a lot of explaining.'

'So you did see her?' exclaimed Mark, as if nothing else mattered.

'Sandra assumed she was staying with Paula. She said she'd go round and find out, and that I was to wait for her there in her house. After about half an hour she came back with...'

'Yes?' he exclaimed excitedly.

She shook her head. 'Gently, Dad. This isn't going to be easy for you. It was Paula she brought back. Sandra felt I mightn't believe it if Paula didn't tell me herself. Kathleen has been admitted as a voluntary patient to a mental hospital, suffering from a nervous breakdown.'

'Oh no,' he cried, putting a hand across his eyes. 'That's terrible.'

Nicole put an arm round his shoulders. 'At least I think I persuaded them that it wasn't Mark who'd finally achieved his aim, but an accidental twist to the whole dreadful saga.'

He looked up wearily. 'Which hospital?'

'She didn't know, or wouldn't say.'

'It doesn't matter. I can find out. What about the children?'

'Paula said she'd offered to look after them, but Kathleen wanted them taken into care. Apparently she'd gone very strange and wouldn't listen to anything. She was convinced she was going mad.'

He groaned and sank his head into his hands. 'I am supposed to be the healer. And I tipped her over the edge.'

Nicole shook him gently. 'She must have been much closer to the brink than you realised.'

'How could I have failed to notice?'

'Perhaps falling in love with her, you didn't want to.'

A young woman with red-painted lips brought them the paté, salad and French bread they had ordered.

'Poor Dad,' murmured Nicole. 'And I thought it was going to be me pouring out my troubles this weekend.'

'It looks like we're both in the same boat,' he said darkly. 'Looking back and regretting we didn't act differently.'

Nicole went upstairs to the bar to refill their glasses. 'I wish it wasn't the weekend,' he said when she returned. 'It'll be impossible to contact anyone. I suppose I could ring round the hospitals, pretend to be a relative.'

'What good would that do? Think of the state she's in. If you find her and go to see her, the sight of you could make her worse. Paula said she was confusing you with her husband.'

Mark groaned again. 'There must be something I can do.'

'You'll have to give it time,' Nicole said gently. 'All men must be anathema to her just now.'

'But her dreadful husband will get her children.'

'Will he really want them? Once he knows Kathleen's in hospital? I doubt his sister'll want three extra.'

He felt a sense of loss after Nicole went back to Cambridge. Yet it was a relief not having to make the effort to respond all the time. The world is a deceptive place, he thought. Each person shares the same paving-stones with everyone else, but not one is on the same level as another. Each is on their own plane, none of which converges with or fits any of the others. Each person walks alone.

He was glad he had told Nicole. Had he considered doing so before the bungle, he would have dismissed it at once, like slamming a book shut at a point where the emotion exposed is too unbearable to endure. Now he felt her involvement a comfort.

He had driven her to the station in the limousine. 'What are you going to do?' he asked, as they stood on the platform beside a door open like a waiting scoop into the hollow body of the train.

She patted her unobtrusive belly. 'My decision is growing of its own accord. I'm glad I came down, Dad. It helped me, too. I'll keep in touch.' She kissed him on the lips.

Like a lover, he thought, the sensation still pungent as he waved at the knob of her head still protruding from the shiny flank of the train snaking past the distant signal-box.

He played Chopin the rest of the afternoon. All four Ballades. He thought Chopin easy because his whole body could play the music. On his terms he could have banged it out with his head. At about six o'clock the sky went black, thunder rumbled and rain began to rattle at the windows. He changed to Mussorgsky's Night on the Bare Mountain. He was acting out the whole nightmare in his head, the full orchestral version. His despairing fingers stabbed into darkness, satisfied with whatever keys they found, like any lover in the dark would do.

At eight the phone rang. Once more hope grated through him that it might be Kathleen.

'I can tell you've been playing,' said Madeleine. 'It's like interrupting someone in mid-orgasm.'

'Where are you?'

'At Heathrow, darling. I just wanted to hear your voice. To know I'm back in reality. It's been like somewhere in Gothic outer space these last few days, marvellous, baffling, unique, but ever so frustrating. Even when you agree with everything they say, they still behave as if you couldn't possibly have understood...'

He only half-listened, in anguish at her confidence in him, at her ignorance of all that had been happening, half-afraid she might notice his voice straining to sound normal. But she chatted on, quite unaware. Tomorrow, he thought, would be the real ordeal. However would he manage? Perhaps he ought to tell her everything...

But Monday morning had other priorities. Luckily he had only one client, a young woman with a face like a watercolour that had been crumpled up and never quite restraightened. She heard voices. She was convinced they were angels. As they discussed a number of other possible sources and associations with these voices, particularly the way they used the didactic mannerisms of her parents, all he was thinking of was Kathleen.

After the young woman had made another appointment and gone, he put through a number of phonecalls from his office.

He knew staff in all the mental hospitals. Nobody by the name of Kathleen September had been admitted at any of them, let alone a young woman of her description. Social Services had not taken any young girls into care in the last week. Greg Fulcher had heard nothing.

At first he was puzzled. Then relief swept through him. My God, he thought, I've underestimated her. She hadn't had a breakdown. Paula's story had been to throw him off the scent. He tried a number of regional hospitals to make sure.

She was still out there somewhere, he thought, stunned with admiration for her. She was still eluding the hunters, seeking safety. The three of them still together. He was glad of that but disturbed by the thought of all the fear and stress she had undergone, and must still be suffering. Papers beneath his hand had become clawed and crumpled in his fingers before he realised what he was doing. It was hopeless, he thought. How could he ever find her? And even if he did, she would reject him as another deceitful, persecuting Mark. Then he thought how she had told of Mark talking his way back into her trust on so many occasions, as if she always wanted to believe the best. He shook his head angrily at the thought. It wasn't in his nature to connive. Yet were the end results of his actions any different to the other Mark's? But how was he going to find her?

THE MONTHS had passed into autumn. The streets were littered with loose leaves, the ash-trees were bare, the beeches turned to beaten copper, mists coiled damply in the early afternoons. But that was in England.

'I'm taking you away,' Madeleine had said. 'You look like someone who's been on meths for months. I don't want you cracking up. I need you. Your sort of work must be a terrible strain, endlessly listening to misery and disaster, living in the minds of the disturbed week after week. You need a holiday to recharge.'

He had been too abstracted to summon up a cogent refusal.

Now he was lying semi-naked on a beach far removed from the great strands of the north Norfolk coast. This was a cove among volcanic cliffs dominated by a concrete pyramid sheeted with gentian-blue windows. There were ranks of parasols stuck in the sand like rainbow mushrooms. The beach was short and shelved steeply into water whose clarity was close to crème de menthe and whose temperature was near blood-heat. It was not overcrowded, but there were plenty of other roasting bodies around them, some with nothing but eyepatches of decorum over their genitals, while others, burned darker than roast beef, pranced about with drunken or sunstruck athleticism. The consonants were American and the vowels Teutonic. It had not been his choice to come here, but the food was good Creole and the drink flowed incontinently. Beside him reclined the Rubenesque amplitude of Madeleine, glossy as she roasted beneath her coat of suntan oil, sunglasses astride her face like a welder's mask.

He had brought a pile of books and newspapers, determined to catch up on his reading. On the third day he was in the depths of the previous Sunday's Observer when he found something that made his senses darken so that he could barely see to continue reading. He rolled over to face Madeleine.

'D'you remember me telling you about the September case?' he asked, folding the paper round the paragraph he had found. 'About the woman with young children being hounded by a psychopathic husband?'

Madeleine grunted. 'We make a fine pair, you and I, me discussing confidential council matters with you, and you divulging the confidences of your patients to me. Was that the young woman nobody would believe?'

'There's a report here of a court case against her husband, Mark September. He was accused of swindling a large number of people out of deposits and money they had paid for fitted kitchens that were never delivered.'

He quoted from the paper.

'The defendant complained that he had hundreds of satisfied customers, but that because of the reasonableness of his offer, he had far too many clients, and had simply got behind, and that he had every intention of fulfilling his obligations. The judge remarked that the country was crawling with vicious criminals, mugging and robbing at gunpoint, raping women and abusing children, and here was a decent man trying to make an honest living, who had simply been swamped with orders, and if anybody was to blame, it was the public's greed for a bargain. It was especially unfair when considering how distraught the unfortunate man must be over the disappearance of his wife and children. Case dismissed.'

He threw the paper down. 'It's incredible.'

Madeleine laughed outright. 'You can't beat British justice.'

So they're still out there somewhere, he thought, his hope reviving like a guttering candle.

He had exhausted people's patiences trying to trace Kathleen. He had talked to Sandra, located Paula. He was convinced both had begun to believe his sincerity, but neither had apparently heard a word from her. He tracked down Clare, talked to Kathleen's aunt on the phone, even visited Aileen in London as a remote chance. It began to look as though he was up against a deliberate wall of silence, a conspiracy of protection. He even wondered if Nicole hadn't become part of it, perhaps concerned that he should not hurt Madeleine. The possibility had occurred to him recently that Kathleen might have gone farther afield. Perhaps even back to Ireland. What was that village called? Collon?

Madeleine sighed, rolled over onto her stomach, spreading herself out to present the maximum surface for the sun to burn.

'Dear man, put your cases behind you. We're supposed to be on holiday.'

Sometimes he wondered if perhaps she knew, and had instigated herself as gaoler.

As he watched a bronzed young Amazon emerge dripping from the emerald ocean with a small and equally sun-browned offspring holding onto one hand, his vision became occluded with memory of a paler young woman taking her children down to a slate-blue sea, till it mingled with the sweat around his eyes.

'Come on,' said Madeleine, her shadow falling over him. 'We've got an hour before supper. It's the only exercise we get.'

'We could take a swim?'

But her lust, he thought, was part of his retribution. As they stood together in the lift he could already hear their panting echoing round the bedroom walls, feel the sweat drenching their bodies, his hips pounding with pestle motion, endlessly grinding out the futile flour and water of human seed.

Sometimes he imagined himself crying, STOP, and all traffic and sound would cease upon the expectation of his pronouncement. But since Kathleen had veered from fugitive reality now to hope beyond the horizon, the least he owed Madeleine was to say nothing.